DRAGON UNVEILING

DRAGON UNVEILING
DRAGON APPARENT™ BOOK EIGHT

TALIA BECKETT

DON'T MISS OUR NEW RELEASES

Join the LMBPN email list to be notified of new releases and special promotions (which happen often) by following this link:

http://lmbpn.com/email/

This book is a work of fiction. All of the characters, organizations, and events portrayed in this novel are either products of the author's imagination or are used fictitiously. Sometimes both.

Copyright © 2023 Talia Beckett
Cover by Bandrei
Cover copyright © LMBPN Publishing

LMBPN Publishing supports the right to free expression and the value of copyright. The purpose of copyright is to encourage writers and artists to produce the creative works that enrich our culture.

The distribution of this book without permission is a theft of the author's intellectual property. If you would like permission to use material from the book (other than for review purposes), please contact support@lmbpn.com. Thank you for your support of the author's rights.

LMBPN Publishing
PMB 196, 2540 South Maryland Pkwy
Las Vegas, NV 89109

Version 1.00 June, 2023
eBook ISBN: 979-8-88541-783-9
Print ISBN: 979-8-88878-466-2

THE DRAGON UNVEILING TEAM

Thanks to my JIT Team:

Jeff Goode
Christopher Gilliard
Dorothy Lloyd
Diane L. Smith
Jan Hunnicutt
Paul Westman

DEDICATION

To Bear. You've been a good friend for a very long time now and we've gone on quite a few adventures together. Thank you for being there when sometimes I think you get overlooked.

— Talia

CHAPTER ONE

Looking out over the dragons around me, I couldn't help but beam with pride. Now that we were training all dragons to use abilities long thought available only to those with red scales, they had made strides.

Many still struggled to learn, but Jace, Alitas, Neritas, and Flick continued to work at it tirelessly.

While I watched, they were slowly moving magical energy around, their connections stronger than ever and the magic flowing through them more than any other four dragons on the planet. Here and there I made suggestions and corrections, but they were few and far between now.

Around the city, they were guiding the magic of all the dragons where it needed to go, including out to the equipment that sat in the soldier camp to our east. It was one of the basic agreements I had with the general out there. He was growing a base of soldiers and weaponry to help me when the demon came out of hiding again, and in return I'd agreed to charge all their weapons, armor, and equipment so that he could become a worthy ally to the dragon race. I would message the general when it was done, and he could send the ammunition and arms somewhere else and bring in a fresh load.

The demon himself hadn't been seen since he had flown away from the last battle. Since then, I had taught many more dragons how to harness our power, and held a funeral and ceremony of life for the captain of our city guard, Capricia, after the demon had killed her. I'd also appointed a new captain of the city guard, Kryos, from one of my honor guards.

It was a bold move that not everyone in Detaris liked, but it ensured that the city wouldn't ever rise against me again, and not a single elder had been against the decision. Not even Brenta. We were at war, and I'd given the city a soldier to lead them who knew the enemy and how to best fight them and survive.

I wasn't the only one training other dragons to use the magic all around them. The dragons before me all taught lessons of their own, but this was the masterclass, so to speak.

But my heart wasn't in it today. I was only half paying attention as I considered what was happening. I was waiting, biding my time while others worked busily away. Even I couldn't train all the time, and there was only so much I could learn at this point. I flew as often as I could with Jared, practiced sword fighting with Alitas, and sat with my mother, controlling magic and reaching as far out with my mind as I could.

None of it felt like enough when I knew there was a demon corrupting the world somewhere and racing me to the next hidden piece of artifact. On top of that, the entire world was looking to me. The news and social media was mostly supportive, but the longer I hid in Detaris and appeared to do nothing, the more likely it would turn sour swiftly.

"You're not really here, are you?" Flick asked a short while later, stirring me from my thoughts. His words made me jump, only confirming the answer.

"We've finished powering everything we can reach," Neritas added, smiling at me in his usual cheeky manner. These two were the first two friends I had made in the city when I'd arrived. I'd barely discovered that I was a dragon after living my entire life as a human and then I'd run into Flick and a few minutes later Neritas.

At first I hadn't been sure about them, but they'd decided that they would have my back and they had been there for me ever since. Over the last month or two, things with Neritas had grown even deeper. Before we'd discovered he could use the magical ability we thought was exclusive to red dragons, I had been worried that being with him romantically would be frowned upon. That I would be forced to choose Grigick or another red dragon—if there were any—as my long-term life partner. But now that I didn't have to worry about that, I felt at liberty to show my enthusiasm toward Neritas a little more.

I tried to push those thoughts away as well. They were not the only ones in hearing range.

"You look like you need a break and I think the rest of us need a drink. Let's get you safe to the tower and call it a day." Jace got up as well, and Alitas came close to me for the flight over.

"I'd like to check in with Ben first," I replied. "See what he's found."

Alitas gave me a nod as I heard Flick sigh. It was relatively normal for me to do so, but I'd been going to see Ben in the library sooner each evening and staying later each time. And I preferred to go alone.

With Alitas being the head of my honor guard, I knew I was making him worried and making his job harder to do. I was almost certainly safe in the city right now, but I hadn't always been, and he didn't like me being somewhere alone when it could make it harder for him to protect me.

Flick felt similarly, and Jace didn't appear to care either way. Her focus was often on other things.

Only Neritas understood. He almost seemed to encourage it. Ben was the closest thing I had to a father figure, and as far as some magic rite of passage with the dragon ancestors was concerned, he was my stand-in father. After Anthony had been killed by shadow catchers, Ben had become my mentor.

Before anyone could say anything else or give me any more concerned looks, I jumped out of the doorway of the tower and transformed into my dragon form. The cool night air immediately provided lift to my wings as the waves crashed around the base of the tower below.

I soared for a moment before flapping and banking so I wouldn't hit the tower ahead. Detaris, the dragon capital of the world, was a city almost entirely on the water. It was made up of hundreds of tall, large towers with bridges between them at various levels.

At any given time there were always some dragons in the air, but once the sun set it was always less busy and the whole city twinkled merrily with the evening lights. There were several very tall towers near the back of the city. The tallest of those held the royal chambers, where most of my companions were now aiming for.

I was the dragon queen, although I tried not to make too big a deal about it, but it was why I had the honor guards and was in charge of a lot of things. Of course, it had been the color of my scales that really gained me the throne. When I'd been crowned, every dragon had believed that only red dragons could combine the magic of the different dragons and channel it to defend against the demon and his minions.

It turned out that my ancestors had been lying about that, or maybe hadn't known the truth—that all dragons could use magic like that. It was just hard to learn and required a teacher. And all red dragons in the past had only taught other red dragons. It was possible that none of them had thought it was a skill that could be learned.

Neritas had figured it out by himself, when his mind merged with mine and followed what I did as he tried to understand what was so special about me. He had needed me to guide him for it to work.

No one had shown me how to do it.

The thought hit me like a lightning bolt. How had I learned if no one had taught me as such?

I tried to remember as I swerved at the last minute past a bridge and then climbed to get to the top entrance to the library tower. I turned back into a human as my momentum carried me through the door. All dragons in Detaris knew how to transform in the exact instant to travel through doorways in the only form that could fit.

Alone in the room full of books, with a small lamp in the center as the only source of light, I paused.

I had somehow worked it out after finding Anthony dead. I'd been with two city guards and Ben as we tried to get away from two shadow catchers. The magic had just pulled through me as if the connection had always been there. As if I'd always known how to do it. It made me wonder what had happened before I'd been given up for adoption.

I'd had no memory of being a dragon before I was put into the human world. It wasn't until Anthony, the handyman for the block of apartments I'd lived in, had disappeared that anything out of the ordinary had happened in my life, and even then it had only been when a shadow catcher had attacked me that I had changed into dragon form to get away.

Ben had commented on how fear had brought out my natural instincts and abilities. When it had mattered, I had always known what to do. I felt out of my depth now though.

I had become a magic- and sword-wielding fighting machine, and I didn't know where my enemy was, or where he would be next. Hoping that Ben might have a direction to point me in now, I headed toward a small door near the back of the tower room. This tower was unlike many of the others.

There was only one way to access the top section of the library—through a door that was usually locked and guarded by a fierce librarian. More than once she had gotten between me and Ben when he was on the other side, but these days she was used to my passing. At this time of the evening, she was nowhere to be seen.

Although I'd never have admitted it, one of the reasons I came to visit Ben so late in the day was because I could get to him without having to fight my way past her. Even now, she intimidated me.

On the other side of the door was a dimly lit staircase that wound around. It came through the floor of the room above. The library floor was so large I was never sure how it fit inside what looked like a tiny space from the outside. Normally Ben was sitting at a round table, not too far away from the opening I climbed out of, but today I couldn't see him.

Hmm. Since I'd become a magic- and sword-wielding machine, Ben was helping me find my enemy or guess where he might be heading next. As it was crucial that we kept a step ahead of the demon, and time was of the essence, it was unusual for Ben to abandon his post. Not without a good reason, at least.

After peering around to see if he had fallen asleep somewhere among the books, I walked closer to the table. Books and notes on pieces of parchment paper were scattered everywhere. Most of them had nonsense scribblings on them, the failed attempts at cracking the code for Anthony's journal.

Anthony, in addition to being the handyman for my human apartments, had been my protector for the whole of my adolescence, although I hadn't known it at the time. He had left his journal for me and it had led me to Ben. Ben had begun helping me decode it, but we still hadn't managed to read all the pages.

The journal notes we did have were stacked in two piles, only one of them visible. It contained a rhyme that we had decoded more by luck than judgment, along with a little nudging from the ancestors when I went to commune with them at the island of Kilnar.

I looked at it now, knowing it was what Ben was puzzling over.

> *A dragon king's decision made*
>   *To ever use again, he forbade*
>   *The weapon, crown, and defense combined*
>   *Of precious ether, metal, and gems refined*
>   *One goal they had on Earth to protect*
>   *One foe designed, his attacks to reflect*
>   *Too powerful when their task was done*
>   *Broken up and scattered, all undone*
>   *Placed in ten, their pieces protected*
>   *Information on all never to be collected*
>   *Ten great dragon lords tasked to take*
>   *Across the world over mountain and lake*
>   *Five nearby, half within reach*
>   *Another two upon the distant beach*
>   *One given to safety in the tallest peak*
>   *With its twin buried where the earth does leak*
>   *The final part the key of all*
>   *Kept safe with the strongest one standing tall*
>   *Where each may be guarded, no purpose known*
>   *The existence hidden and secret by him on the throne.*

The demon and I had found four of the artifact pieces so far, but I only had one of them: the leather arm bracer that looked as if a shield had once been attached to it. The other six were proving more tricky. We'd found the four nearby. The rest sounded as if they might be in different countries. Perhaps even half the world away.

The elders were trying to help. Many of them had been messaging from around the world, and I had tried to gather all the information I could on where artifacts might be, but the truth was that the dragon world had been dying out for a long time. Hiding from humanity as they spread had made us spend more and more time in our cities and away from each other, and not all the cities had survived the isolation.

To some degree, it made me feel guilty. These were my people, and I was responsible for them. But it was not me who had made the decisions to hide so much about our role, what we could do and what we were up against from the dragons of the world, nor to hide from humanity for so long.

The cities didn't know where the artifacts were, not without a dragon like me turning up and seeing what magic they could feel buried somewhere. I only knew of six dragons, including myself, who had the skill level to pick up on the power at a distance, and only three of us were confident of our skill. With hundreds of cities across the world still active and some of the locations possibly empty now, it was like looking for a needle in a haystack. But I was running out of other options.

I read the poem a couple more times, not sure it would help. If nothing else, it would refresh my memory. After that, I went to look for Ben. It took me several minutes to find him, and I finally discovered him sitting on the floor, hidden among a stack of books that shielded the light he carried.

Not trying to be quiet, I wandered closer. He jumped when a floorboard creaked. He looked up from the open book on his lap and for half a second I saw the weariness and stress this had all caused him clear on his face. It passed as he smiled at me.

"Scarlet. Are you early today or did I lose track of time?"

"You lost track of time *and* I'm a little earlier." I sat next to him and immediately felt relief from being surrounded by books and large shelves that ran up to the ceiling. It was like being cocooned in the wisdom of the ages.

"Struggling? I thought you were teaching the all-stars how to be badass like you red dragons." Ben smiled again, but the humor was almost forced.

"I did, for a while. They're already badass. I can't stop thinking about where the demon might be and needing to find him or the next artifact."

He nodded. "And I'm not delivering results."

"I'm not here to pressure you." I sighed. "Wait. That came out wrong. What I mean is I'm not very good at sitting idle with no enemy to stab. I want something to stab."

Ben let out a laugh and any awkwardness vanished. He took my hand and gave it a squeeze. "You've been a fighter since the day I met you. Sometimes, especially while translating these journals, I wonder how Anthony could have left me in Detaris and stayed in the human world with you for so long, but every day you remind me what mattered most. He knew the potential you had and that he had to make sure you were okay."

I glanced at Ben, too big a lump in my throat to respond. His eyes glistened in the dim light, tears threatening to fall from them.

Instead of either of us saying anything, I hugged him. If nothing else, Ben understood without me really having to say anything.

CHAPTER TWO

As Neritas slipped from bed beside me, I groaned, not wanting to be awake. I opened my eyes rapidly a few times before closing them again. The morning sun was streaming in through the far window.

"You should get up," Neritas said as he pulled a shirt on. "If I remember right, you've got politicians to talk to this morning and then General Miller asked to talk to you about the plans for the base nearby."

I let out another groan and reached out a hand toward the sound of his voice. "Can't we stay in bed like normal people on a Sunday morning?"

"You're a queen. That's about as far from normal as it gets."

"Don't forget that I'm also a dragon."

"For some of us, that is normal." Neritas leaned back on the bed and gave me a quick kiss. Finally, I properly opened my eyes and looked up at him. The light was shining from behind him, and it made his dark hair glint and shine. In that moment I didn't want to go anywhere or do anything.

"How about we take a vacation when the world is safe again?" I asked.

Neritas chuckled. "Sounds perfect. Assuming we're not going to see half the world traipsing all over for these artifacts anyway."

He had a point. I was possibly about to travel to some very far-flung places. Whether Ben found out exactly where to go or not, I was going to have to just start trying likely places for sure.

I got up and quickly got dressed, adding some of the armor I might need and slinging my sword about my waist. After so many weeks of having it on me at all times, I felt strange without it.

Finally, I checked my ready pack again. It was everything I needed to go into battle. For a while, it had also contained everything that mattered to me, but now I was queen and Detaris was a home no one could take from me, and I had stopped. Not everything was out on display. My copy of Anthony's journal was hidden, along with several other key possessions and a few things of my father's. Neritas and Flick knew where they were and knew if the worst happened I would want to get them safe.

But no matter how settled I felt here, I was always prepared for battle. I had to be.

Even though I wasn't leaving yet, I took the pack through to the dining area and dropped it by the exit. I was going to take it with me when I visited the base, even if I didn't expect to need it there either. I just never went anywhere without it. It was just in case, and in some ways, a hope that the demon would show up again somewhere and I could immediately fly off into battle.

While I ate, everyone slowly joined us, including Griffin, who had my itinerary for the morning. It wasn't as bad as I'd feared. The politics were condensed into one meeting at the human base. That gave me one destination and one destination only. I could live with that.

The usual dragons were coming with me. Neritas and Flick, who were always included in whatever I was doing, Alitas, who never seemed to even sleep, and Reijo, Jace, and Jared. With Capricia gone, I felt as if my team was missing something, but Jared was doing everything he could to step into her shoes as the next most powerful white dragon.

I'd expected Griffin to come with me to the meeting, as he had many others, but he excused himself, offering instead to help Ben and get me the next target.

Knowing that meant I would have to make small talk, I opted to get it over and done with and headed out. As we flew toward the land, I marveled once again at how quickly a base had formed beside Detaris.

A perimeter had been partially formed around the front, with fences, razor wire, and soldiers guarding the area. The fence to the sides and around the back was more temporary, as the base was still expanding, and that was part of why I was heading there today.

I flew down to the other side of the road. The layout had been changed now that the base was to be permanent. As I landed and turned back into a human again, no one flinched at the shift. Everyone here was used to dragons coming and going. They'd even left a clear area for us to land that gave us enough wing space and clear room to gather around.

There was also a small hut that contained some prototypes for harnesses and saddle-like contraptions so the soldiers could come with us into battle and keep their seats no matter what we did. Thankfully, I hadn't been involved in the testing so far.

As soon as my party was assembled, I walked over to the soldiers at the gate. Lieutenant Douglas, one of my favorites of the regulars stationed here, was already hurrying over to us. He saluted and bowed, one after the other in a swift move that somehow seemed graceful and appropriate.

"Good morning, Your Highness. We've had the meeting room set up for you in the main block and I got those mini croissants you like."

I grinned at his enthusiasm and went in for a hug. He didn't resist but he still felt a little stiff.

"I've fought beside you in battle and you've protected my folks as we've protected yours. You don't have to bow to me," I said quietly in his ear. The words helped him relax a little and hug me back.

"Thank you," he whispered back before letting me go and leading me in as if I didn't know the way. The main meeting room was large enough to hold about fifty chairs if everything but the screen at the far end was cleared away, but for today a decent-sized table sat near one side, laden with food, and only a dozen or so chairs were dotted around.

No one else was in the room yet, but Lieutenant Douglas stayed with us. Although I hadn't said anything, I'd noticed that no dragon was ever left alone on the base, and it made me wonder if this was normal for visitors or if it was a sign that despite working together, we still weren't fully trusted.

I had no idea and no way of working it out, but I didn't get to think about it for long. No sooner had I taken a bite of my first mini croissant from the plate of them someone had shoved into my hand, than the door opened again.

The soldiers showed in the political delegation we were there to meet. It involved ambassadors for the G7 and was the first step to officially negotiating our claim to the land our cities had been built on. It had become clear that almost no country in the world was happy to learn they had dragons living among them and that our race was laying claim to land everywhere.

I chewed and swallowed as hurriedly as I could, putting the remaining food back down on the plate. After giving my hand a quick, surreptitious wipe on my pants, I walked toward them and offered to shake their hands. They were all very polite, offering me their names in a whirlwind of speed as they came past me further into the room.

Alitas and Reijo were next to shake hands and make introductions, and made sure to get every name, something I knew I would find invaluable later in the conversations. This wasn't easy for me, or part of my skill set, but I was learning.

After a few minutes of small talk, Reijo decided to take the bull by the horns and get on with the meeting.

"Thank you all for coming to this meeting and agreeing to talk to us about the cities within your nations. I trust that every one of you got the list of cities we have in each of your respective countries and the land we claim?"

"Yes, we did, but it is most irregular to present it in this manner. Up until now, this land was owned by our nation and protected and governed by our nation," a petite woman said. Her French accent made it obvious what country she represented without anyone needing to state it.

"You mean, you *thought* you owned," I said. "Our people have been there since before Normandy existed, let alone France. Before there were humans there at all. We just never revealed this to you—that you weren't the owner of the lands beneath our cities—until a few weeks ago."

This made more than a few of them purse their lips and glance at each other. I wondered if they had thought this was going to be a negotiation of sorts. Reijo met my eyes, his face expressionless. I couldn't tell if he thought I'd made it worse or not, so I shrugged and stepped back a little.

"I understand that this is difficult for all of you and an unprecedented situation. We're not sure how best to work this out either. That's why we're all here." Reijo made a very deliberate show of looking at all of them and waiting for them to respond in some way, and I paid attention, eager to learn how to get better at this.

The UK ambassador waved a piece of paper around with a map of his country on it and what appeared to be location markers of our cities. "When you add the acreage of all these cities up, your reach across the globe, power levels, and ability to wage war must be immense. You must understand that many of these locations would be far better scrapped and your population moved into one place rather than scattered like this."

"We have no ability to wage war at all," I replied. "That will not, is not, and never has been our purpose in this world. We are here to protect humanity from the demons. We have no guns, no drones, no nukes, and our fighters are trained to fight demons. All we have are our swords and magic and the ability to fly. Our cities are scattered because once upon a time this was needed to protect all of you from the spreading darkness. And it may be needed again in the future. If we are all brought together in one place, who will protect the humans halfway around the globe when the demon and his army show up?"

This finally had some effect, and the room of politicians went from hostile to contemplative.

"You truly have none of that? Can you prove it?" The French ambassador looked as if she couldn't believe it, but I nodded.

"I'm not completely sure how we'd prove it, but I can certainly try to do so to everyone's satisfaction. Either way, the cities need to stay where they are."

"You act as if we need protection," the German ambassador, one of the larger, more bulked-out men in the room, decided to chip in. "But Germany has been able to protect her own interests for centuries. We have soldiers and weapons."

"Do you have anything that will kill a shadow catcher or the demon and his handlers that command them?" I asked. "Have you watched the videos of what they do if they touch anything not protected by the magic we wield?" As I spoke, I noticed Reijo going to the screen at the end of the room. He quickly connected his tablet to it and pulled up a video of one of our fights in the early days outside a restaurant.

My heart started to race as I watched a video of myself fighting the creatures and then retreating inside the building. The magic quickly ran out on the blockaded door and the demons attacked it with even more ferocity. It was a section of the video I'd never seen, and even I was stunned by how quickly the building and material decayed, rusting and rotting away before our eyes.

"This has got to be some kind of chemical warfare. I'm sure our scientists can counteract it…"

"What if the demon turns up tomorrow?" I asked.

"Germany does not agree to allowing the dragons to stay on *our* land." The German ambassador ignored my question, getting more irate. "We do not need your protection and we—"

"With all due respect, sir." Lieutenant Douglas got up from the seat he'd taken by the door, merely there as a show of safety than anything else. "Her Highness is telling you the truth and you might want to listen to her. She's just trying to stop this demon from killing people."

The room turned to look at the soldiers and for half a second I wondered if he would balk under the attention, but he lifted his chin.

"And what do you know of the dragons and what they want or intend?"

"A lot. I've seen her risk her life again and again and give all the energy and magic she possesses to save humans she doesn't know. I've seen her exhaust herself beyond anything most soldiers are capable of to get to a fight in the first place, and *then* put her all into defending the innocent. And every dragon beside her, in this room or not, does the same. They are a nation of people who believe it is their calling to protect and serve the planet."

"That's high praise." The US spokesperson was the only one of the people I recognized from before today. He'd been at my first-ever meeting with people and was generally relatively positive. I wasn't sure exactly what he thought of me, but he looked at the others and stood as well.

"My involvement here is fairly simple. The US has already agreed to keep the dragon cities exactly where they are and to even increase the spread of the trained dragons among us. Our cities are the ones that have been targeted so far, but it is everyone's understanding that these...*monsters* won't stop with us. Our forces will be working *with* the dragons to ensure the safety of our citizens."

The spokesperson nodded at me and went over to Lieutenant Douglas. "I'm done here, Lieutenant. I'll see myself out."

I fought not to show the grin I felt as the spokesperson gave a smile and left the room. The rest of the ambassadors looked between me, Reijo, and Douglas as if they weren't sure what to expect next.

"I know that many of you have to go back to your country officials to talk about this and put it to your governments. We will be open to answering any questions they may have, but we're going to strongly resist any efforts to have us removed from our homes—which we've inhabited for longer than your own nations have existed, may I remind you—and we will continue to focus our efforts on fighting the demons in the meantime." Reijo went to shake the nearest hand and officially ended the meeting.

I wasn't sure what it had really achieved other than political posturing, but I was going to trust that Reijo knew what he was doing. He was one of the few dragons who had spent a lot of time in the human world and in social circles far different from mine.

The ambassadors all left, leaving me to deflate in a room full of dragons and Douglas. I barely got a chance to eat some more before the general came in.

"Keep eating," he said as he saw me exhale and go to put the plate back down again. "The food is about the only good thing about meetings like these."

Everyone smiled and the atmosphere shifted to a more relaxed mood as he went to the table and grabbed a plate to fill with pastries.

"What brings you in here, General?" I asked after I'd allowed myself time to enjoy my own mini croissants.

"I'd be a liar if it wasn't also business, sadly. But both the higher-ups and I agree that if this demon is hiding up somewhere with his army and licking his wounds, it would be a good time to find him and attack. We're stronger than ever. We don't want to wait for him to get even stronger if we can find him." He gave me his full attention as he spoke and made it clear he was concerned.

"You have my full agreement, but finding him isn't easy." I frowned, not sure how to explain that I had no idea where to begin.

"The soldiers have talked of you being able to sense the

enemies coming. That several times now you warned them of approaching danger and even roughly how many attackers to expect." There was no suspicion or accusation in the general's eyes as he mentioned the rumors. He was trying to help and wanted to understand.

"I can. Sort of how I know how to move magic around and charge up things. I feel it with my mind. And I have trained to feel the opposite feeling from the demons. There's a sort of absence of magic and energy, for want of a better phrase. This is something I can feel." It was only as I finished speaking and explaining that I realized what the general had been thinking and as he opened his mouth to respond, I was fairly sure of what I would be asked next.

"Can't you use this ability to track the demon down?"

I was shaking my head before he finished speaking. "Not easily enough. My range is limited, and I am not the only one who can sense my adversaries. The demon can sense me coming as easily as I can find him. I would need to fly within, say, a mile of him, and even then, I couldn't be sure it was him and not just another more minor demon, or a handler, or a trap."

The general didn't look happy about my answer, but he accepted it. "It was worth a consideration."

"If it comes to it, I may start trying something like that anyway. Or at least try and pair combing an area with any public sightings," I voiced a thought I'd already had, though I didn't have much faith in the sightings humans had reported so far. They were in strange places that rarely made sense, and some had proved to be hoaxes or people seeing things that weren't there.

"I appreciate your willingness. Let us hope we can

figure out another way to find the bastard." The general squeezed my shoulder before he shuffled away again, taking his plate of food with him.

    I stayed a little longer, discussing the supplies we were charging and when we would visit next with Douglas before heading back to Detaris and the training I would both conduct and receive.

    Something had to change soon.

    We needed to stop this demon.

CHAPTER THREE

The sun had long since set and wasn't due to rise for many hours yet, but I couldn't sleep. I'd once again left Ben poring over books and gone back to my royal tower. Despite Neritas' normally soothing presence in bed beside me, Flick in the room next door, and the constant watchful presence of all the honor guards on duty through the night, I felt alone.

Everyone appeared to be coping with the wait, and I just couldn't. I needed to be doing something, and I couldn't sleep until I'd made some progress somehow. Not wanting to wake Neritas by staying in the room making noise, I had gone through to the dining area and left him sleeping. There were a few snacks laid out and a fruit bowl was so laden that I wouldn't have gone hungry no matter how long I'd sat there. I ignored all of it and paced instead.

Although the general hadn't taken me up on my offer to look into the claimed sightings of the demon or his minions, I had asked Douglas to get me a list of them all anyway, and as much information as possible to work out if they were legitimate sightings or not. He had gone one better and given me a list that someone else had already sorted by how likely they were to be true.

I'd looked it over, but no patterns emerged. No one area or place had shown more activity as far as I could tell. The demon could have been anywhere in the US. Beyond the US I didn't have data and I wasn't going to get it. He'd never officially been seen out of the US so far, despite my warnings to the ambassadors. I had no idea if the citizens of other countries were in danger or not. Maybe I should bring my foreign forces back to the US?

No sooner had I thought this than I shook my head. Some of the artifact pieces were almost certainly elsewhere. Did I go after those, or the demon first?

I sighed, wishing I could wave a magic wand and have both brought to my attention. Being stuck in my tower, doing nothing, was making me want to scream. Instead, I paced and tried not to wake anyone.

"You can't sleep either?" Jace asked, her voice quiet as she came into the room. So much for not waking anyone.

"Not really. I need to make some progress and there's not a lot for me to do until I have a demon to stick a blade in or a plan to catch one." I sighed and sat as she came over to the dining table. She grabbed one of the other dining chairs and turned it so she could straddle it and lean forward onto the backrest.

She reached for an apple and took a bite before giving me her attention again.

"I feel similar. Training here is all well and good, but it's not stabbing something, getting information, or making something happen. I want to put all this learning to some use or go find some missing pieces."

"Got anything in mind that we could be working on?" I kept my voice down. I already felt better for having company. Even if she didn't have a solution, knowing I wasn't alone in feeling the way I did helped.

"Not for both of us. But I've been speaking to Elias. They're trying to recreate the gate. At some point, we've got to try and trap the bastard in a pit again and I want to make sure we're not going to fail. Elias says he could do with someone who could contain a shadow catcher long enough to get it in a smaller version."

I lifted my eyebrows, considering the experiment. It was an interesting idea, but it would mean her leaving the city. They needed a dragon who could move magic around to power it.

"It'll be harder without having some of my magic in the mix. Fewer different colors is also less potent," I pointed out, knowing I sounded as if I was begging to go with her.

"I know, but I've got some of your magic in my kit. I can draw from that as well as the dragons at the farmhouse." Jace took another couple of bites while I thought about it.

We needed a new gate, but I'd always thought I would be involved in getting it tested and ready for the demon. There was so little time I could be away from the city, however, that I didn't feel as if I could leave and help her. And everyone in Detaris was helpless. Well, almost everyone.

The dragons who had already rallied around me knew how to help and function. But the majority of the dragons in Detaris had been raised on the idea that their mere existence in the world was enough to keep the demon trapped behind the gate and they just had to go about their lives and watch over the planet.

They were more used to worrying about logistics, scheduling classes, visits between cities, and things like that than how to fight, trap a demon, and make weapons. Some of the political elements were being handled well by the elders and Reijo, but even that still needed my involvement now and then.

It was just too much for one person to be in charge of and worry about.

"You want to be there and help, don't you?" Jace asked when I still didn't say anything.

"Is it that obvious?"

"You get this look in your eyes when you are torn between two or more courses of action. Like you want to do all of them."

"I feel like I'm needed here to sort out the issues in the city and keep the soldiers and everyone looking for the demon and preparing to fight him, but I want to help make sure we can put him back in the ground again when the time comes."

Jace nodded and patted me on the shoulder. "You'll get as much info from me as I can give you, and I'll still bring my group any time there's a fight. We'll help you feel like you're still in both worlds, just like I don't ever want to miss a chance to stick a sharp pointy object into that demon."

I grinned. Jace had a way with words and a perspective that never failed to make me feel better about life. She got up and grabbed her pack sitting next to mine by the door, but before she could get it on her back and fly off to the farmhouse with it, Ben appeared.

He landed almost silently, in his human form before we even noticed he was there.

"Didn't expect to find anyone awake, but I'm glad I did. I think I've found another location. On the East Coast. I think it's what it means by two on the distant shore." Ben looked exhausted, his hair stuck up at odd angles, but his eyes were bright and he was breathless with excitement.

I didn't know what to say, but Jace put her pack back down again. "I guess I'm not going anywhere just yet. We've got another artifact to go find. And if it packs a punch like the last one, this should be fun."

Although I couldn't disagree with her, I felt some apprehension. It had never been easy to go after these items, and the last time we had tried, Capricia had died. I didn't want to lose anyone else.

"There's a good chance I've found this one way before the demon will," Ben added. "If he's even ready to head out again."

"All right," I replied. "Let's let the soldiers know. I'd like to go with the right team, just in case. If we're going that far, we're going to need to plan this properly, and make sure we have everyone we might need and all the kit."

"Probably going to need a city to stay in nearby. Any dragon cities close to it, or is it in one?" Jace asked.

"This doesn't sound as if it's in a city. Or even near one. Deliberately. It might even be underwater." Ben looked apologetic, though it wasn't his fault.

"We'll have to get a hotel or something, then."

"I can sort that part out if you let me know where." Reijo had appeared from the doorway to my mother's room. I'd suspected they had been sharing it for some time, but never seen proof of it until now. Our eyes met briefly, almost as if he was checking I was okay with what I'd seen.

"Thank you," I replied. "You've handled a lot for us and been there in one way or another in the human world for a long time. I won't deny that it is likely to make our task a lot simpler."

"Just let me know who is coming with us and where and consider it done."

Ben grinned and all four of us sat again to begin planning. At the sound of our voices, more and more of the tower inhabitants woke. Our combined tones were too much to be quiet and grew louder with each new person who woke.

I messaged the soldiers to let them know what we were planning and request aid in getting there. We could fly some of the way, but we'd never tested ourselves to fly across the entire country, and with earth curvature and all sorts of other things to take into account, I wasn't even sure what route would be best for something like this.

To my surprise, the general replied within fifteen minutes that he would find out what carrier planes could be at our disposal and put together a roster of soldiers to accompany us.

After feeding the information to Reijo and putting him on the task of keeping the general informed on where we would be going, staying, and how many would be with us, I went back to figuring out whom I wanted, what equipment, and if I needed to charge anything.

Since our last battle, Neritas and Flick both had partial sets of armor, and I'd begun activating metals but not charging them myself, as the rest of the dragons using my abilities were now able to do everything but the activation.

It meant that I was frequently drained and drawing on the connection to the ancestors to restore me. It was stronger than ever. Whatever boost they had given me had returned to full strength, and then, as far as I could tell, it grew a little here and there, possibly as I did things, possibly as something they did added to it too. I had no way of knowing for sure.

Finally, we all opted to get a few hours' sleep and make sure we left a little refreshed. The sun was not yet up when we had a final team and a list of everything I wanted to take with us or have sent to our destination.

Not once did Reijo flinch, complain, or state that the money side of things would be an issue. No matter what I wanted and how soon, or how many dragons would be needed. If money was going to be a problem, he didn't let on.

I finally got back into bed beside Neritas, letting him wrap an arm around me as I tried to rest again.

"It will be okay," Neritas said, when I remained tense a few minutes later, trying to think through our plans and make sure I hadn't forgotten anything important. "You have everyone far more prepared than the last time and the demon hasn't been seen in ages. He's not going to show up."

"You can't know that," I replied.

"No. But if he did..." Neritas didn't finish but I knew what he had been thinking. If the demon showed up this time, it would start to look suspicious. There were already times that I suspected someone. So many times the shadow catchers had turned up when we were resting, camping, or at the restaurant the very first time humans had caught us fighting on camera. Too many times to mention them all.

"You need rest to be able to handle whatever tomorrow brings. Your magic and your focus are what you need most. Sleep so you can regain them."

Although I didn't want to admit that he was right and I wasn't sure I would find it very easy, I closed my eyes again and tried to push all the planning thoughts from my head. Gently Neritas stroked my back and gave me something rhythmic and slow to focus on.

It was almost like counting sheep, gentle and easy to lose myself in. And it worked as it soothed me enough to fall asleep.

No time seemed to pass before he woke me back up by moving away.

"Time to go." I wondered if he had slept. He was always there for me, pushing me and comforting me, protecting me and doing whatever was needed around me. Did I do enough for him? Could I, when I had a world to protect and a nation to run? Or would I always feel so divided that I could never perform any element of my life well enough?

One thing I did know for sure: it was an unforgiving task to be a leader and not much better to be one of the people around one. Especially as all of us were so eager to get on with our plans that my entire task force was gathered in the courtyard of the soldier camp or between Detaris and the base within a half hour of opening my eyes.

Many of them were snacking, but more were standing

and checking last-minute supplies, possessions, and parts of our overall plan to make sure we were ready. I felt as if I was spinning in circles for a while. So many people came up to me and asked me questions that I stood and swiveled between them all.

Eventually, we were ready to get in the air. We were flying under our own steam, dragons carrying humans where necessary until we could get to an air base with enough carriers for the entire force to take us closer. We were heading for a section of relatively uninhabited eastern US coastline just below Bangor in Maine, or some island around there.

Ben, Alitas, Reijo, and Lieutenant Douglas had worked together to sort out the details, and that left me with little to worry about beyond making sure we all were together and taken care of. I was mostly going to be in charge of sensing the demons and any possible artifacts or powerful magic centers along the way.

For a lot of the journey, we would be in the care of the US Army, but we were also stopping for a hearty dinner at another dragon city, one near the Canadian border that was very eager to be receiving a royal visit of sorts. It gave me more nerves about the day than any of the rest of it did, but it was yet another necessary part of my job.

A queen's work was never done.

CHAPTER FOUR

It felt strange to be riding in a plane after being used to flying myself, but it was also a relief. Everyone had taken the opportunity to get a few hours' sleep on the private plane. It was one Reijo had found with the army's help. He'd gotten it to pick us up from one army base and take us to another near the dragon city we were visiting for dinner and a brief rest.

We'd had lunch at the army base, a very stark military fare but more than enough to keep my troops going. It was only when we had filled this large plane that I really got my head around how sizable and powerful my army was. More dragons had flown in from various places, and the dragons Jace commanded were also meeting us in the air on the way.

More still were going to meet us when we landed. Another mix of soldiers and dragons, giving Reijo even more of a headache for planning how to get us all to the dragon city of Maringtel. I knew there was a chance it would be overkill, especially if the demon never turned up.

But I was going so far from my home base and there were going to be so few dragons nearby equipped to handle fighting that I had wanted to be prepared.

The hardest part had been leaving dragons and soldiers behind to defend Detaris and other places along the way if the demon took the opportunity to strike elsewhere. I didn't know if he would, but there were still five other artifacts to find and I wasn't about to assume he'd go after the same one as me every time. Somehow, he was finding them as well.

As we got closer to our first destination, my body grew more agitated. The tension in my shoulders and neck made it hard to be comfortable. I wasn't sure what to expect from this visit. Although some of the other cities had greeted me with gifts and kindness, others had been more standoffish, as if they didn't want another leader. Some had tried to get me to agree to all sorts of schemes and ideas, creating a political minefield, and yet others wanted to be reassured that everything would be okay again.

I was particularly worried about Maringtel, because it seemed we had gotten off on the wrong foot. The elders hadn't been happy about allowing in so many human soldiers. Although they had been asked if there was anything that could be done to reduce their concerns, we had needed to insist upon them allowing all of us or none of us.

Reijo had let me know before the elders had replied and I'd got the impression that it had been touch and go whether they would let us in at all. If they had informed him of any concerns and allowed Reijo to work around some of them, I hadn't been told about it.

With no idea what to expect, I feared I would be walking into an awkward meeting, with the hosts eager to see us leave instead of being pleased we were there and welcoming us with open arms. It even made me consider the possibility that I might need to be careful what I ate and drank. We all might.

Despite my worries, I had little choice but to follow the plan and get the soldiers and dragons to Maine the only way I could. I made the mental note to ask Alitas to check or have others check before any of the soldiers or I ate or drank anything. Of course, I was sure that he'd already thought of something like this. I'd seen him talking to Reijo and Douglas about all the plans to get here and I trusted my honor guard.

As the plane started to descend, I looked out to the ground below. It was already getting dark. The time zones had stolen some of the day from us. I wondered how easy it was going to be to find the artifact piece or the right location in the dark later in the night. There might be a lot of wandering around while I tried to sense it.

It was a good thing I had been practicing just that sort of thing with my mother. I was highly likely to need it.

By the time we landed, everyone was awake and very ready to get off the plane. It hadn't been a long flight, but it had been long enough.

I was soon surrounded by all the people officially protecting me and everyone who just did it anyway as we made our way to the waiting delegation. Colonel Flint was the first to greet me. He had a grin on his face as he shook my hand.

"You get around, Colonel." I hadn't seen him since I'd

shown up in Chicago to defend the people there. I had been too late, but that hadn't stopped us from doing what we could to heal everyone anyway.

"I could say the same to you. But given how many lives you save when you do, you'll hear nothing but gratitude from me and my team, Your Highness."

"Well, hopefully there will be no one in need of saving this time and we can all relax a little bit finally." I gave him a genuine smile, grateful to find a familiar face and an enthusiastic welcome.

Behind him were more soldiers and the dragons who had come to meet us here. I recognized some of them, including several green dragons from a family farm that had been over halfway in this direction. To my surprise, Grigick also stood with the dragon delegation, and another dozen or so dragons behind him.

He bowed low to me as I approached, standing at the front of the group as if he led them. "It is good to see you, Your Highness. I have been doing my best to emulate your strength and help form a militia of sorts for you in the east. I have brought my best fighters with me, one of whom Capricia also helped to train."

I nodded, feeling a lump form in my throat at hearing the captain of the city guard's name. She might have once tried to supplant me with Grigick, but after facing the demon himself in his own way, Grigick and then Capricia had given me their support to take the throne.

This was yet another way he was showing his support for me, and I was going to accept it with enough warmth that he felt as if he had made the right decision. As soon as I was close enough I pulled him into a hug and thanked him. Having so much more support than I was expecting helped to calm me.

The last part of our journey to the dragon city was under dragon power again. At least until we got to the edge of the nearest lake. Boats were going to take us the last part of the way—the city elders had asked us not to fly into the city.

I wasn't sure why that had been arranged, but given it was dark, the wind was cold, and it appeared as if it might threaten to rain, I wasn't going to argue. Flying a short distance wouldn't be wise, especially with humans riding on our backs.

My general preference soon proved to have been the correct decision as it started raining when we were still a couple of minutes from the edge of the lake. I slowed, not wanting to have my charge pelted to shreds by the sheets of cold rain, but it was a difficult call because slower flying meant it took us longer to get there.

I felt Lieutenant Douglas shift on my back as if he was hunkering down behind me. I tried to fly a little more upright, tilting my wings forward in the hopes of protecting the lieutenant a little, and I continued.

By the time we landed by the lake, we were soaked and cold, but boats were waiting for us and they had covered sections where we could huddle.

Each one took about twenty people, but there were far too many of us for the three boats waiting. After seeing all the soldiers out of the rain, I did the only thing I could think of and made the decision that instead of us traveling over in two trips and leaving over half the group waiting in the rain, we would have to fly.

Every dragon stay in dragon form and fly over the top, I commanded, using my most forceful no-nonsense tone. I wanted to get us all somewhere dry as soon as possible.

That's not what the elders are expecting or requested, Reijo replied.

Tough. I'm not leaving a bunch of soldiers and dragons out in the cold and rain so we can make two trips when it takes almost twenty minutes to get there by boat. When you include loading and unloading, it leaves almost an hour for the second group to stand out in the cold rain. I won't do it, no matter how angry they get.

I wouldn't either. I just want you to know what you're flying into. Reijo's voice was full of reassurance and respect, and it helped calm me a little. At least the dragons behind me had my back.

Although the boats were moving as fast as they could, for a dragon it was a slow pace. Our bodies were built for flying long distances in short spaces of time. It helped me feel as if I was doing my job and protecting those with me. In the heat of a battle, or when I was being put on the spot, it was hard to think of the needs of those around me and be fully responsible, but in these moments, even in the pouring rain, I had time to consider how best to handle things and look out for them.

I also needed to remember that the city full of dragons ahead of me were my citizens too, and also under my protection. I needed to reassure them and care for them so they felt safe and heard. It was going to be easier thought than achieved, however.

The city came into view in the same way all of ours did, as we passed through the barrier that kept them invisible to human eyes. I noticed that as we got closer, the soldiers grew slightly restless, but as soon as we made it through the barrier, they calmed and stared in wonder at the city ahead.

Despite now having seen many dragon cities, I was also in awe of yet another beautiful city before me. This one was very like the city I'd seen in Utah and was entirely free-floating on the water, but I could already see that it was a different shape. There were tall huddles of buildings in the middle, but they were interspersed. Flora ran between everything, the outlines of plants just about visible in the many city lights.

As I got even closer, I was also fairly sure I heard the sound of some sheep bleating. Before I could swoop down to check and let my curiosity take over, the dragons in the city responded to our presence. They flew out to us, moving fast as more and more of them rose off the city buildings.

Good evening, I sent out to all their heads, noticing that one of them seemed to be taking up a leader position, a fraction ahead of the dragons around. None of them spoke to me yet. *Please forgive our arrival not being as intended. I could not bring myself to leave any of my party out in the rain and therefore escorted them all over to Maringtel myself.*

We didn't want anyone in dragon form, a brusque voice returned. There was no clear indication of who had spoken for me to know whom to reply to.

I understand that, but it is my responsibility and duty to protect the humans with me, as well as the dragons. I could not do this any other way than by asking my dragons to use their dragon forms.

We do not have any space in the city large enough for you. Not with so many in dragon form. You will have to turn back to the shore and land and then return by boat.

I pulled up, hovering where I was as I thought I heard panic in the voice. Something bothered them beyond being heard and listened to. They'd asked us to do as instructed out of fear, but other than being worried we would fight in dragon form, I could see no reason why it would make them this scared. Even if I was in the city in human form, there would be nothing to stop me from leaping into the sky as I transformed.

You really do not need to fear, I replied, hoping that some reassurance would go a long way and I had picked up on the tone correctly. *We will not overwhelm your city and can return to human form as soon as we have somewhere to land.*

As if to illustrate my point, I swooped down toward the platform where the first boat was already tethering to allow the soldiers inside to unload.

Several dragons screeched in protest as I moved, but I was too close and too committed to slow or stop. I landed, transforming as I usually did.

There were gasps from the dragons around me, also all projected into my head. Alitas, Flick, and Neritas followed. Not a single one of them was going to let any reason, dragon, or enemy stop them from being by my side.

All of them took human form at exactly the right moment to step onto the platform gracefully. The added weight made it wobble slightly, but it was almost imperceptible. The city was connected so well that the platforms seemed to be held in place by everything around them.

The host dragons came back to the city as well, landing

in dragon form on what looked like perches. None of them changed into human form at first, almost as if they didn't know how. They were situated in places where changing would have meant they couldn't remain where they were.

I looked around for a host in human form, but there was only the driver of each boat, and the first one was only now hurrying off his vessel and coming over to me.

"How did you do that so fast and so cleanly?" he asked.

It was only then that understanding dawned on me.

I frowned, processing what must have been making them scared in a heartbeat. They had asked us to come across in human form because, for some reason, they didn't believe it would be possible for us to take human form once in the city.

"It is something all dragons in Detaris learn," I explained, trying to sound as genuinely surprised that they didn't know as I was. "We learn how to transform between human and dragon form at will and to land in our smaller form. This way the dwellings in the city can fit many more of us."

More and more of my dragons landed and did the same until my entire party was back in human form and standing on the platforms on the edge of the city. We had made some progress, but we were still getting wet.

After another minute, the figure of a slight young woman came toward me. She hurried and was panting slightly as if she had been running.

"Forgive my tardiness, Your Highness." She curtsied and bobbed her head. She was dressed in a thin, free-flowing material that made her look far more graceful than I had ever managed to, and she beamed at me as she straightened. "It takes me the best part of a minute to concentrate fully and take this form, and I am the fastest in the city. I've been practicing since we have known of your intended visit to our city and have managed to shave three seconds off my personal best."

I nodded along as she spoke, digesting the information and interpreting their past action through this new context. We weren't unwelcome at all. They had thought such a large delegation flying into the city in dragon form would be difficult to host. And from what I saw so far, they also transformed in private.

This was going to be one of the more interesting visits to a city during my reign.

CHAPTER FIVE

When the time came, I was loath to leave Maringtel. Our meal had been delicious, and I had learned a phenomenal amount about the city, its inhabitants, and what they could and couldn't do.

Unlike the dragons living in Leneoth on Salt Lake, they were entirely self-sufficient in Maringtel. They had worked out how to create floating gardens and had livestock. They were a smaller city, but it was ingenious how they had made themselves so well taken care of in so many ways. But maybe because of that, they had been stunted in a lot of magics.

We spent most of dinner trying to teach them how to do magic that others in Detaris found simple. In the end, I left with the promise to send one of our dragon teachers, or maybe even several, to help them learn how to do magic that everyone in Detaris had gotten licked.

Talking to our hosts about how they struggled to take human form, the reason soon became apparent. Because they could rely on themselves for almost everything, they barely ever interacted with humans. As such, they weren't as comfortable with them or around them, and because no one could transform well or fast, or spent much time as a human, the problem had been perpetuating.

It was fascinating in some ways, but it didn't take many glances from Ben to encourage me to get moving anyway. We had an artifact to find before a certain demon learned of its existence and made it even harder to acquire.

By the time we were ready to leave again, the rain had eased off, but not stopped entirely. Thankfully, Reijo had anticipated us being tired from here on out and arranged with the military some large, armored trucks to take us the rest of the way.

It meant that we could fly back to the mainland while the boats brought the soldiers back and then take it easy again. Although I was mentally tired, after being on the plane I could have flown the rest of the way, but I wasn't going to tax myself unnecessarily and fly when I didn't have to. Especially when I could sit among the soldiers instead and do my best to encourage them to like us more.

Alitas insisted on having a few dragons flying above our convoy and I only made one stipulation—that they be allowed to switch out regularly, especially while the weather was taxing. The captain of my honor guard smiled at my request, seemingly touched.

With all the goodwill I had managed to muster, I felt good about our trip so far. Perhaps something was finally going right for us.

It took several more hours to drive where we needed to go and a lot of us tried to sleep some more, but the vehicles weren't the smoothest and we were packed in pretty tight.

To pass the time, some of the soldiers told stories in low voices about places they had served and things they had seen. It soon got around to how many demons they had faced. Many of them had fought with me at least once in the past, although not all in the same battle.

A few had scars to prove it, and their attention soon came my way when one of the soldiers near me noticed a scar down one arm.

"You must have fought a fair few of those creatures. Do you remember the first one you killed?" he asked me.

"The first one I killed was by accident. I was just trying to get out of an abandoned house and a handler sent a bunch of the minions at me. This was one of the handlers who could appear more human. I killed him later—remember that first video of the fight at those restaurants? I think we were all just as shocked when I actually killed one."

"You didn't know they could die?" Douglas asked, leaning in closer along with everyone else.

"No. Dragons used to run from them. Everything we used as armor or weapons decayed. The secrets of how to fight them were known to only a few and had mostly died with my father. I had to rediscover a lot of what he and my mother knew."

"Does it feel weird? Being able to kill them the way you do and pulling magic life force from everything?" another soldier asked as the entire truck started to give me their attention.

"At first it did, but I'm used to it now. It only feels weird to try something new with magic."

"What *is* magic?" Douglas asked the question almost too

quietly to be heard, but a silence fell as soon as he did. Everyone wanted to know the answer and I felt the sudden anxiety of pressure to answer him.

"I don't know," I replied honestly. "Not really. All I know for sure is that it's a sort of energy that dragons harness and can then connect to each other. When we bring it together it can power several different objects... artifacts, I guess. A lot of what we know is limited. Someone wiped all the information we had, and we've been rediscovering a lot of it as we go."

The answer didn't really help any of them, but thankfully no one asked me another. Someone made a comment about how a shadow catcher rotted an entire car as it basically went over and through it to get to something else. I spent the next little while wondering what else had been lost to time and how this seemed deliberate. How much more could we do than we knew of?

There was no good answer, but I explored the connections I had, trying to move magic here and there and see if anything new happened. I also forced my ability to detect the demons as far as I could, wanting to notice company coming or anything else that held magic in it as we drove.

The hours ticked by, and I drifted in and out of sleep. The soldiers quieted as it grew later and later.

Finally we arrived at our destination. The trucks drove through some civilized areas before we drove along the coast and then along a sandbar that had been made into a road. The water lapped gently at rocks on either side of the single-lane road.

We were only just at the other end when they ground to a halt. I sat forward with a jolt and immediately got to my feet. I couldn't feel anything nearby, but I didn't know how close we were meant to be to Ben's intended destination.

Several soldiers pulled out flashlights and revealed some large concrete blocks across the road that stopped us from driving further.

"Everyone out," Lieutenant Douglas yelled. "We're continuing on foot."

There were a few groans as people started to shift, but it wasn't long before we were all on foot.

"How do you want to play this?" I asked Ben, hoping he had some idea of how we could find this needle in a haystack.

"I think it's on this island and there used to be a dragon city here. It would make sense."

I frowned, having hoped for a lot more than that. The island before us was shrouded in darkness. It was still a couple of hours before dawn, and everyone with me was tired. But we were full of magic and had come here to get an artifact piece before the demon did. I didn't feel as if we could walk away without at least trying.

"Okay, split everyone into even groups to go along with any dragon who feels semi-confident that they can feel for an artifact but exclude me, Lieutenant Douglas, and a few honor guards so everyone is happy I'm protected."

"What are you going to do?" Alitas asked. Neither he, Neritas, nor Flick looked very pleased about the plan. All three of them were likely to be the most confident of any dragons other than my mother at feeling for these artifacts, and I'd left her in Detaris with a significant percentage of our forces in case the demon went after the dragon city for another reason.

"I'm going to do a low flyover of the whole island while everyone else is doing a slower, gradual one over sections of the island they feel comfortable with." I wasn't sure exactly how to do what I'd just proposed but having Lieutenant Douglas with me served two purposes. He could radio in with his soldiers if any of them found anything or I did, and I was hoping he could be an extra pair of eyes to help guide which way I flew.

Alitas looked thoughtful before he picked out ten dragons and asked the lieutenant to pick out ten soldiers to ride with them.

"You're not going anywhere with a force smaller than that," Alitas said.

I nodded, knowing better than to argue with him when he was trying to make sure I stayed safe. It meant that the rest of the groups weren't quite as large with Alitas, Jace, Kryos, Neritas, Flick, and Cios having to split the rest of the forces between them. I didn't like it, especially when Ben opted to give each leader a quick overview, delegate a section of the island to them, and then join me as well.

We were going to be spread out over the whole island, but it was the only way to find this artifact quickly and get another of these pieces under our control.

After checking that my unit was all ready to go, I transformed into a dragon and waited for Lieutenant Douglas to climb up and strap himself in place.

It was strange to let someone strap a seat to me and even stranger to see other soldiers doing the same to dragons around me. But I knew it would protect the soldiers more if battle did come, and it would help them keep their seats while tired. It was worth a little undignified saddle-wearing on our part.

I got in the air as soon as I thought my group was ready, but I flew a few circles to make sure all the other groups were good to start searching as well. Some of them were taking longer to get organized, but all of them were going to be on foot and had to get an idea of what section they would be combing.

Only when I was satisfied that everyone was going to be okay did I fly onward. I started by flying low around the island, following the shoreline the entire way around. I had no idea if it was logical or not, but it seemed so to me. At the same time, I concentrated on feeling for anything magical that wasn't the weaponry artifacts we all carried with us.

I tried to spread my mind as far as it would go in every direction but up and flew low and slow enough that I hoped I would notice. I found nothing on my first pass around the island, and passed back over the trucks.

You good to go around again? I asked the lieutenant.

"Sure," he replied, unable to project his voice into my head the way I could in his. "I want to find this thing as much as you do."

It was all the encouragement I needed to keep going. The dragons with me had far less to do. They only needed to look out for danger and keep up, and with all of them working together, I was pretty sure that they would have no trouble keeping me and everyone else on the island safe.

I kept the shoreline about fifty yards to my left as I flew around again. The island wasn't very wide in places, and this was a large enough distance that I was already covering a significant amount of the island.

This time around, I couldn't fly quite as low. Too many trees were in the way, but I swooped down over the tops of them and did my best. Again, I went all the way around but didn't sense anything.

Growing increasingly frustrated, I went around a third time, focusing on the center of the island, and then flew over it a fourth time, zigzagging back and forth and trying to go over all the ground again.

By the time I was done with this fourth flyover, most of the groups who were also combing the island for the feel of an artifact had finished and were back at the trucks or heading that way.

I don't think it's here, I told Ben, the last dragon still flying with me.

I'm sorry. I was so sure it was.

It's okay. This still beats us all sitting around and waiting at Detaris. I'd rather be trying something. Is it possible it's nearby and we just need to be looking somewhere else near here? I flew back to the trucks as well, landing in the small clearing so the lieutenant could slide down and take the saddle off.

Possibly. I would need to look at my notes again and check if I made an error or not.

I transformed back to human form as soon as I could and ordered everyone to head to the hotel. If there was a chance that we were close to the artifact, I didn't want to leave and have to travel all the way back home.

No one argued with me. We were all exhausted and had barely slept all night. We were in no fit state to keep looking. Thankfully, there was a hotel big enough for all of us not too far north, in Bangor. We'd got almost the entire thing booked out for us and Reijo had offered to pay for other guests to be moved to different hotels to accommodate us.

Once again, I dreaded to think how much this was costing him, but it wasn't as if I had a treasury. At least, not that I was aware of. The dragon world didn't use currency of any kind. It was a very human concept. In the dragon cities, everyone was busy doing whatever needed doing, and I wasn't aware of anything like taxes either.

It was taking me a while to understand what that was truly like, but it had benefited me in the past. It was amazing to be able to forget about money and needing anything, but it was always a shock coming back to the human world and having to adjust my thinking.

The hotel was ready for us, and the rooms were held for several nights, just in case. The sun was coming up as we arrived, and they were quick to show us to the rooms and get us settled in. The soldiers had sent some people ahead to help organize everything. This was one of the times I appreciated the military efficiency and planning of the US Army.

Within half an hour of leaving the island on the trucks, I was in my own room, a large suite near the top of the building, and able to finally get some decent sleep.

So far we had found nothing, but I could only hope that Ben knew where to look next. For now, however, sleep was more important.

CHAPTER SIX

Sounds of chanting and yelling in the distance woke me up some time later. My head felt groggy, and I blinked against the light, as if my eyes were refusing to adjust. The dream I had been having slipped from my mental grasp as I tried to process what had woken me up.

Slowly I made out the words. People outside the hotel were chanting for 'dragons,' 'the queen,' and 'Scarlet.' I wasn't sure what could have happened, but I got up to go over to the window and check how many were out there. Neritas was sitting in a chair nearby and reached out to take my arm before I was close.

"Don't. You'll only whip them up into a frenzy again. They all want to talk to you."

"They?" I asked, still struggling to process what Neritas was talking about and what had woken me.

"Fans, I guess. Or protesters, in a few cases. The story broke on the human news that we were all here for some reason. Possibly for diplomatic reasons, scouting out a new city or looking for another old dragon one."

"They don't know but they're guessing?" I asked as I sat up and made myself decent.

"Something like that. Not sure who told them, but they've been getting slowly louder, and if they think you might be around they have moments of even more noise." Neritas bit into an apple that was already mostly gone and motioned to a fruit bowl in case I wanted something as well. I grabbed a banana.

"Do you think I should go talk to them so they go away?" I asked a few seconds later, concerned that the level of noise would disturb everyone else trying to rest.

"I don't know. It might make them worse." Neritas shrugged. "If you do go down there we should probably get Alitas and Flick at the least."

Although Neritas was right, I winced. I didn't want to wake either of them and drag them out of bed. I needn't have worried. By the time I had finished the banana, Alitas and Flick were both knocking on the door. The noise had woken them as well.

As I let them in, I noticed that several more of my honor guards were out in the hall and I had no doubt they, or others, had been there the entire time I had slept. Despite understanding their need and how they had sworn to do their duty in this way, I felt bad for them. I wanted them to be well and get plenty of sleep too.

I repeated some of my questions to Alitas, hoping he'd have more of an idea of what to do, but this was as new a situation for him as it was for me.

"It's up to you, but I will be with you either way." Alitas started sending messages to the other honor guards.

I made my decision in an instant. I would talk to them

to get them to quieten so everyone else could rest, even if I couldn't.

After gathering some more of the honor guard, we sent someone to go talk to the people first and let them know they would get an audience as long as everyone was quieter from now on.

Some of those who weren't so happy with me made a fuss I heard from up in my room still. The rest stopped chanting and did as we asked. It was an immediate improvement.

"Do you want anyone with you specifically, like Reijo?" Neritas asked, but I shook my head. These weren't politicians. They were people, and I had grown up around people. I should be able to handle this.

After taking several deep breaths to calm myself, I made my way downstairs. I could only do my best and try to answer a few questions.

"Scarlet! Your Highness!" Voices called to me as soon as I was out of the elevator door and the mob pressed forward.

Alitas and Flick both acted as crowd control, encouraging everyone to be quiet. Immediately they hushed, all of them staring at me. To my surprise, the person closest to me asked for my autograph.

I blinked, stunned, until Neritas handed me a pen and grinned.

"Have at it, Your Highness." The amusement flickered in his eyes, even when he stopped smiling.

Without missing another beat, I took the pen and scrawled "Scarlet" on the photo the lady was holding. It was of me and looked like a still from one of the battles I'd been in. The next person had a printout of me in dragon form. I moved past them, and the honor guards then encouraged anyone who had an autograph to step back and make space for the next person.

Some of them were sensible and moved away, but others stuck around, wanting to talk to me. It didn't take long for reporters to show up, and they asked even more pointed questions.

"Can you tell us why you're here and who is with you?" the first one asked.

"I'm on duty with the usual dragons who accompany me and some of the US military on a joint mission. I can't say much more than that. I do want to reassure everyone that we are working hard to keep everyone safe and defeat our common enemy. I'm sorry, that's all I can say on the subject."

The reporters seemed satisfied that I'd at least said something and moved on, asking me if I would be in the area long. I couldn't give committed answers, so I didn't. I made it clear I would be in the area as long as I had to be, and that I would be busy and would appreciate everyone's cooperation in not making a scene.

As I talked, I continued signing until my hand hurt and fewer and fewer people were coming forward. Eventually, I just couldn't carry on and I made my way back inside.

No sooner had the doors shut behind me than one of the hotel staff came up to me.

"Most of the party is eating in the dining area. Would you care to join them, or would you like us to send something up to your room?" she asked, enough kindness in her eyes and a motherly manner to the way she said it that I felt a little better. I was more exhausted than I realized, but I didn't want to go and hide either.

I opted to go eat with everyone else. It might be tiring, but I was going to make the most of being in the same room as the soldiers and try to win over as many allies as I could.

By the time I was sitting among them all with a plate of food to tuck into and a drink in my hand, I felt a lot better. The atmosphere was jovial despite the lack of success in our mission so far. And for now, everyone was on downtime. Except for Ben. As soon as I noticed that he wasn't there, I frowned.

There was no doubt in my mind about what he would be doing. He'd be finding us another location and trying to work out where he had gone wrong. But that pressure shouldn't be on his shoulders alone.

I wolfed down the rest of my food and grabbed some to take to him. I was pretty sure he wouldn't have anything and I was hungry enough to eat a second plate even if I was wrong. Before I could do more than get halfway across the room, however, he appeared.

"Scarlet, there you are." He wore the same clothes as the day before, wrinkled as if he'd slept in them as well, and in one hand he clutched a set of notes. "I was a little off. It's not far from here. I'm sure now."

I hurried to him and took the notes as I handed him the plate of food and pointed to the nearest empty chair. He sat, and the soldier closest to him got up and offered me his seat.

I stayed on my feet as I flicked through the new notes and then looked at the map he'd provided. It was easy to see where he wanted us to go. He'd circled it in a bright red pen.

Although I was done with the notes and sure that Ben had corrected his mistakes, I acted as if I needed to look over it longer, until he'd had a chance to eat everything I'd handed him.

"Let's go check it out," I said, not wanting to waste any more time.

Within seconds, the room went from inactive to the hustle and bustle of everyone getting ready to go. I joined them, helping the slower ones to get ready.

Lieutenant Douglas came over to me and looked at the map. Reijo was not far behind, and within another couple of minutes, the pair of them had worked out how to get there and where we could begin the search.

Only ten minutes after that, the entire team gathered in the foyer to go. So many of them were already packed and ready that I was impressed.

There were still a lot of civilian humans outside, and seeing our trucks roll up only made them more and more agitated and curious about what was going on. They grew noisier again and I was about to step out to get them to quiet down, sure that the few other people staying in the hotel wouldn't appreciate the noise and chaos, when Douglas stopped me.

"I think it's best if you let some of us in uniform go first. Then come out in the middle of the group so we can get you in a truck quickly."

I considered the alternatives, like me flying out of here along with some of the dragons, but he had a point, and I was still not at my best. When Ben almost staggered out of the dining hall to join me, I put out an arm to catch him and steady him as well. Some of the honor guards had also been up half the night protecting me, and I couldn't ask any of them to fly right now.

Despite that, Alitas picked out a few to take to the air above the crowds. I was sure they would love getting to see something like that. It just wasn't going to be me.

Although I was doing better after eating, it was so long since I'd had a decent rest that I still wasn't at full strength, so I did as I was told, waiting for Alitas to give the signal before I went out to the trucks. Neritas and Flick flanked me, with Alitas and Kryos behind and in front. I tried not to look too worried, but it gave the whole situation a more ominous feel.

The crowds pressed around the soldiers and dragons, but they let us through. As soon as each truck was full, the driver pulled off and got us underway on what would hopefully be the final part of this journey. It seemed strange to be heading off again, but the sun was slipping back toward the horizon, marking the end of another day.

It was strange to be driven through yet more crowds of people and it gave me yet another layer of appreciation for how many wanted to see who I was and talk to me. I'd spent ages signing autographs earlier but hadn't really processed the sheer volume of the crowd. If anything, it seemed as if it had grown, not gotten smaller, after I'd appeared.

I sat back and tried to relax, sandwiched between soldiers and dragons and about as safe as I'd ever be out in public. These were friendly crowds for the most part, but since being attacked in Detaris and bullied a few times, I still found this sort of thing difficult. It was made even harder when the majority of the time I was surrounded like this was because I was in the heat of battle and had a mass of enemies around me. The demons crowded in and attacked with a similar movement and press. It put me on edge, with my heart racing and my body tense.

"Do you think there will always be this many people wherever you go now?" Neritas asked. I glanced at him, the burly protector of mine who had stolen my heart, sitting forward with his eyes on the back of the truck and the opening that allowed us to see the crowds. He was equally tense. His shoulders were tight and his hands had curled into fists.

"I don't know, but I hope not. I hope I eventually become old news and a far more minor celebrity, if I'm even famous at all. Once everyone is safe again, I'll hide somewhere for several years or something." I shrugged, trying to sound as if it was a joke. This was strange to all of us.

As we traveled south along the coast, I tried to feel around me for danger. I felt vulnerable, out of sync with my body clock, and generally not at my best. We'd been so busy since leaving Detaris, and through the night we'd been active. After so little sleep and heading into another likely sleepless night, I was feeling the fatigue.

I drew on the magic connection I had to the isle of the ancestors a little. There was something about the magic that came from across the life and death divide that felt even stronger somehow. I used it to make myself feel a little stronger and dished it out in small amounts to the dragons around me.

After doing that, I focused only on trying to detect danger. I needed to protect everyone I was with, and I couldn't do that easily from here unless I used magic to aid me.

It bothered me that we still had no idea where the demon was, nor his army, but I felt as if all I could do was try to feel for danger and warn those with me. Danger could come from anywhere, at any time, and in any magnitude. The thought of that kept me on edge, even while the soldiers around me took the opportunity to get some more sleep.

We reached our destination about two hours after leaving Bangor. It was another stretch of coast that led onto an island—Southport Island. This one had a few human residences, but not too many, and they were spread out from each other for the most part.

We stopped our trucks just a few yards onto it and all got out. I encouraged everyone to form into the same teams as before. I knew this search would take a lot longer, but I was determined to begin somewhere. Ben was equally keen, handing out maps before taking dragon form and looking at me expectantly.

Feeling as if time was of the essence far more than before, I also transformed. It was still a little bit strange to be in dragon form around humans, but I was starting to get used to it and felt a sense of being kitted up for battle as Lieutenant Douglas put the saddle and other straps onto me.

It didn't take him long after another soldier came over to aid him. I waited only long enough for all the dragons in my unit to be ready to fly and carry the soldiers, and then I lifted into the air.

This island was a lot more easily defined, and houses and infrastructure across the entire island gave me a good sense of direction. It made it easier for me to fly around the edge of the shoreline and feel for the artifact piece. It had to be here somewhere. For Ben's sake as well as the rest of us.

CHAPTER SEVEN

The second time around the island, approximately fifty yards away from the shore and nearer the human settlements, I began to feel the strain. The aches from flying so much more than normal were settling in. I wanted to be done and find the artifact so we could all get some sleep and head home.

No one else appeared to be struggling the way I was, however. Many of them had gotten plenty of sleep one way or another, and the rest were on foot to be as close as possible to any artifacts in the ground. I tried to fly low down, keeping just high enough to stay above the houses and any other obstructions as I went around the island slowly.

Feeling out with my mind made me hyper-aware of all the humans on the island, as well as the animals and my companions. The more I connected with soldiers and dragons alike, the more aware of other possibilities I was. I didn't know if humans could use it, but they had the capacity to connect to magic as well, or at least be fueled and helped by it.

I had to stop myself from noticing the number of people on the ground, however. It was a distraction I couldn't afford right now. This had to be where we found the artifact part.

An hour passed as I flew in another loop, and then almost another hour as I looped around for the fourth time. As I circled to begin the fifth, my wings aching and Lieutenant Douglas growing less and less talkative on my back, I considered pausing. This would be our last run, if we made it, more of a flight down the middle than a circle. If I was exhausted, the dragons with me were going to be faring even worse.

I didn't know what to do until Lieutenant Douglas urged me onward. "We've only got a little further to go and we'll find this artifact. Think how amazing it will be to own another and be able to use its power."

The soldier's enthusiasm didn't just help me make my mind up, but it gave me a confidence boost as well. It *had* felt good to have the artifact on my arm, and even though it had appeared to be incomplete, there had been a clear boost to my strength.

It made me cross that the demon had three artifact pieces already. While he was already hard to defeat, he was using whatever means necessary to get bonuses and try to make himself even more powerful. I needed to do the same and hope that I had enough power to draw on and could get enough artifacts to make me the more powerful of the two.

If I didn't, I wasn't sure what would happen.

With Ben flying alongside me for the final journey, I tried not to notice how tired he was. He looked exhausted. Even in dragon form, he didn't look like himself. While this excursion had taken its toll on me, it had done even worse for Ben. I suspected that while I went down to talk to fans and sign autographs, Ben had been studying his books and the research he had to find the new location, sacrificing every moment he could rest.

As I got halfway down the center of the island, however, I was worried that we weren't going to find this item, and that could breed mistrust. If we weren't trusted completely by those with us, this trip could end badly. Not finding the artifact after looking for it in two places and taking a significant chunk of the US military from the base meant to watch us as much as learn from us wasn't going to help us.

I was about ready to give up when something caught on the edge of my mind. I immediately circled, hope flaring. I flew lower, nearer where it had been, trying to get a sense of it again.

"Found something?" Douglas asked. I heard the hope in his voice, but I didn't respond, wanting to be sure before I got anyone else's hopes up too much.

Unable to find it again, I landed and concentrated. As soon as I did, I felt the draw of something deep in the earth and what felt like the tiniest little device leading from it up to the surface.

There's something here. I projected my thoughts to every single dragon and every soldier we had with us. *I can feel the magical energy in something deep underground.*

Thank you, Ben replied, and I knew it was something he

only said to me. The relief was palpable even though I couldn't see him. No doubt he had been as worried as I was that this might end up being another dead end. But it wasn't. We had found something. Even if it wasn't an artifact piece, something touched by magic was here on this island. We had no reason to suspect it would be anything but extraordinary.

I let Douglas get down and take the harness off me before I transformed and walked toward the closest source of magic to the surface. Although I didn't know what it was for sure, I sensed a tunnel of some kind that led toward the artifact.

"I think there's something down here. A tunnel perhaps. There's a trail of smaller charged items on the way down to something bigger. It winds downward, a bit like a spiral staircase." Douglas came over to me as I lit myself up and directed the light toward the ground.

"Looks like a building once stood here." He pointed out dips in the grass and bushes that had the remnants of ruined stonework coming out of them.

As Ben came closer, he nodded and several more soldiers and dragons joined us, getting out flashlights as well. They fanned out a little, marking what they thought was the building outline with tape.

I nodded as I saw it take shape, almost as if I remembered it somehow. I couldn't—I'd never been here—but something still felt right about it. The other groups who had come in on foot began to join us as well.

"We're going to need some equipment," Douglas said as he bent down near me. "Something to excavate with."

"I'd appreciate it if we could do this in a way that will

preserve the building. Or what's left of it. There's clearly more underground." Ben joined us. I saw the concern on his face.

"This was one of your dragon cities, right?" Douglas asked.

Although I wasn't sure, one look at Ben gave me all the information I needed. "Yes. If we had a building here and there's an artifact in the vaults, then there was a great dragon city here once."

"Then it's your land and your stuff. I'm not going to tell you how to dig it up." He grinned at me as if this wasn't the exact response he should have given me but was okay with it anyway.

I got the feeling that a lot of the soldiers with me were of a similar mindset. As much as they were willing to follow orders, there was a reason they were the ones working with dragons and in an entirely new setting compared to the usual human conflicts.

They made several calls for me while I sat by the entrance and tried to consider what might be underneath me based on what I could feel of the magic devices. It seemed like a trail of some small devices. Perhaps they were lights, but that made less sense given that red dragons could create that without help.

I knew there was one not far below me, however, and I hoped that meant we could dig down to some kind of room. While I was sitting there, I also reached for the artifact with my mind. Although I cautiously connected to it, I made sure not to offer it any magic. Not before I could be sure what it was capable of.

Although I was still a long way away from it, I tried to

detect anything that might be protecting it as well, like a net or anything else that might make me want to be more cautious, like we'd found before. I couldn't feel any other magic items than the small ones on the way.

After a short while, we had drawn attention from the locals and the soldiers had to set up a cordoned-off area and bring the rest of us inside. I grew concerned as people started to build up despite the time of night. It was almost as if the fans from outside the hotel had followed us.

"Can we get some kind of tent and a way for everyone to sleep in shifts?" I asked Douglas when he came over to me again.

"We've already got supplies on the way from the nearest base. They'll be here soon. And we've requisitioned some equipment to excavate the site as well."

I thanked him profusely as the trucks all drove slowly up, encouraging the crowds to move apart and let them through. They parked them in a semicircle around the dig site and provided us with a little cover from all the people, although some of them then drifted around to the other sides.

Feeling exposed, I wasn't sure what to do. All I knew was that this was likely to be dangerous.

"We've got to encourage all these people to leave," I said to the team nearest me. Alitas nodded. By the frown on his face I could see he was equally concerned.

"I'll see what I can do," Reijo replied. "I think you should stay away from them and not give them any indication that you'll talk to them.

"And remind me to add a few small tents to the away kit so we can hide you from prying eyes no matter where we go." Alitas shook his head. "I can't protect you like this. It's too exposed, and while you're busy trying to figure out what this is, anyone could take a shot at you."

"The danger isn't going to come from humans but from the demon and his minions, and I can sense those coming too." I wasn't concerned about my safety so much as feeling studied and scrutinized.

"Humans will be a danger as well. While most of them love you, they will never all think well of you. It only takes one madman with a gun. And we're in the US. There's more than a few here."

Although I didn't want to admit it, Alitas had a point. While most people with guns in the US would never use them on someone out of spite, there were enough nut jobs who could get access. It wasn't wise to assume all human crowds would be safe for me. I didn't want to live in fear, though.

Thankfully, more soldiers arrived, Colonel Flint among them, and another truck full of supplies. Within twenty minutes, a tent was up around the dig site and I had some shelter from the crowds.

I stifled a yawn as the first kit was brought inside it. They erected it over me while I continued to sit on the ground, so tired I didn't want to move.

Douglas and Flint both helped me up and then offered me a seat nearby. By the time I was sitting in it, someone had shoved a sandwich into one hand and a drink into the other. I grinned as Flick immediately sought more for the rest of us.

By the time I'd finished eating, a very smartly dressed

man was in the tent, scanning the ground with a handheld device.

"This is fascinating," he said. "There's definitely a structure down here. And it has been here a long time. If we excavated here I think we'd find a tunnel that progresses downward."

I got up again and went over to him.

"Scarlet," I said by way of introduction. "Are you an archaeologist?"

"Yes. William…" He paused as if he was studying me and trying to work out if something made sense. Suddenly his eyebrows rose. "You're *the* Scarlet? The dragon queen?"

I nodded, fighting the urge to smile.

"Then this is a…" He looked back at the scanner in his hands and the floor below him.

"A dragon city," I finished for him. "Or it was."

He gaped at me, not sure what to say as he looked between the machine and me and then back at the ground.

"I need to get down there as quickly and as safely as possible. Will you help me?"

"Of course, Your Majesty. Whatever you need."

"Thank you." I moved to get the first spade or digger or whatever we needed to get started, but he reached out and stopped half an inch before taking my arm.

"I have a request. If I may?"

"I can't make promises, but I'll consider anything you have to ask as fairly as possible." I waited for him to tell me, wondering what on earth he could want from me.

"If we find anything really interesting and old that you don't need, can I keep it?"

The request took me by surprise and for a second I

wasn't sure what to say. "As long as it's not something we need for battles or to sustain anything important, I don't see why you can't have a souvenir in return for your help. I'd just ask that you run it by me first so we can make sure it's not harmful or something important in disguise. The last artifact piece, which is crucial in defeating the demon threatening us all, just looked like an arm strap with no rhyme or reason to it."

With this settled, he continued to map out the tunnel, proving I had been right about the possible devices on the wall and the reason they might be there. They were little lights intended to guide our path.

The soldiers came back with spades. William looked as if he was going to protest about how several people with no knowledge of archaeology and who were wielding spades could ruin the excavation, but Neritas stepped up to take one and the archaeologist thought better of it.

With no one else to stop them or object, the soldiers got to work, and I fed them a little magic to help keep them going as they did. Having several of them working at once soon gave us a large hole in the ground and the clear need to take some of the dirt out of the tent.

It was a fair way down when the first panting soldier paused. I took the spade from him.

"Rest. We'll all take turns if we need to." I scooped some of the earth out of the way. Magic could help everybody digging, but it clearly didn't make the body able to handle extreme fatigue.

Another twenty minutes of soldiers and dragons swapping out as soon as someone looked slightly beat had the hole growing large enough that we reached a stone covering several yards down. There was a ring laid into its center, and we spent the next twenty minutes or so trying to widen the hole to find its edge.

I kept the magic flowing, and my excitement built as I did what was necessary and what I was capable of on my part. We were so close to getting inside.

When we had revealed most of the stone, we attached a rope and used it to haul on the covering for whatever lay underneath. Before I let that happen, I checked it as best as I could mentally for traps. I wanted to be sure this was safe from my point of view and trust that the soldiers had everything else covered.

Finally, we were good to go, and the soldiers pulled back, taking the top of the rope. I gave them as much energy as I could muster to aid them. The length of the rope was enough that more and more dragons and soldiers could come along and aid in yanking on it, and even I joined in.

Several men stayed at the edge of the hole, each with a spade they'd shoved down the gap between the stone and the ground around it. The men continued to pull in short, sharp bursts as directed by Colonel Flint. More and more people got involved, but it didn't seem to want to give.

"Let me try to help a second." Jace went back toward it and used her magic. She had to lie on the ground at the end of the hole to channel her power into it.

I could feel her magic moving, more aware of it than I used to be. It was also something I could have done, but I allowed her the satisfaction of having thought of it and executed it. In a lot of ways, it felt good to be just another person in the crowd, helping with physical strength alone.

With Jace's modification and the maximum number of people possible pulling on the rope, the stone finally shifted and came up as we all eased back. It was heavy, and the stone was massive, emerging from the hole like a cork out of a bottle, but there was still some of it down there.

As we continued to walk back, tugging it up and out, it finally tipped toward us and let us haul it a short distance across the ground before it wedged in the dirt, too heavy for us to pull it further. We all dropped the rope and hurried over to the hole it had covered.

Someone shined a flashlight down there, illuminating a small stone room. We'd found our way into another dragon city.

CHAPTER EIGHT

With a tunnel to excavate, the camp came alive again in a whole new way. It was time to put together the team we were going to take down. I gathered the usual group, wanting to make sure it was made up of dragons who could handle the draw of any magic requirements, and a few soldiers.

The soldiers came with us mostly to protect our archaeologist and see if he could offer me any insights into what we might find. I wasn't sure how well this was going to work, and I knew that there was likely to be danger somewhere in here, so I didn't want to take the entire team again.

Someone had to be on the lookout for danger while we were down there. We hadn't seen the demon in well over a week, but he could come back at any point. I already worried the crowds mobbing our hotel had attracted too much attention.

I left Kryos behind to sense for danger, and Reijo in case there were any political issues he needed to help me smooth over, and then I made myself glow and lowered myself down into the hole with a rope. The floor wasn't too far down, but I was going to have trouble getting back up and out again without flying.

As always in these situations, I was going first, and Neritas, Flick, and Alitas came after me. The four of us had become almost inseparable, especially where danger was involved.

After that, we had our archaeologist join us. He lifted his flashlight and tried to shine it in the areas he wanted to see, but I motioned for him to lower it and made myself glow all over and gently brighten everything.

We were in a small square room with walls made of old stone. The ground had patches of dirt over it where our digging had shifted the earth and some had fallen in. Everything else was full of cobwebs, moss, and a strange musty smell. Off to one side was an opening that must have led down a tunnel to the artifact.

"Into the dark, we go once more?" I said, deliberately not sounding convinced. Of course we were going to go down there and try to get the artifact piece. It was what we had come here for.

Neritas came close to me before nodding, making it clear that if there was danger he would be right by my side. It was a comfort that I couldn't put into words. When Flick and Alitas came close behind, I felt even better. The archaeologist didn't appear to appreciate going next, but we didn't give him much choice as I walked deeper down the tunnel.

There were so many cobwebs that I raised my shield and used it to help clear a path forward. At the same time, I pulled my blade out and hacked at any tree roots that had broken through the walls and grown across. Thankfully, none were large or thick, and we still made decent progress.

It didn't take us long to reach the first magic item I'd felt. It was a small, smooth-looking stone set into the rock walls. It started to glow as we got closer to it although the light was dim. Almost instinctively, I fed it some more magic charge, drawing it from my connection to the isle of the ancestors. As it filled with charge it glowed brighter, showing more of the path ahead.

I reached the third of these stones, charging all of them as I went, when I felt something else approach my mind and the edges of my mental detection. Something strange was coming our way.

Pausing, I concentrated for a moment and tried to work out what it was. It didn't have a lot of magic potential, but it was coming in our direction and it didn't feel right.

"Don't tell me we've got company," Neritas asked when I frowned, confused by what I was feeling.

"I don't know," I replied honestly. "It could be anything."

"What?" William asked, no doubt very confused. "Why aren't we going deeper?"

"Trouble." I looked at Lieutenant Douglas behind him, who already had his radio in hand.

"Colonel, there could be incoming enemies…" His voice trailed off as he looked at me, waiting for me to provide more info.

"A little bit north of us, coming this way. There's definitely one." I stopped talking, knowing it was wrong the moment I said it. I felt more of them coming into range.

"Make that several, and several different directions, although mostly from the north."

"We'll get the men in place. Do what you need to and let us keep you safe for a while." Colonel Flint's voice crackled a little, not coming through entirely clearly, and I hoped that we wouldn't lose him on the way down.

I wasn't going to wait around for more encouragement to go deeper, however. With the dragons and soldiers still following my lead, I returned to shoving cobwebs out of the way with my shield and cutting small tree roots with my sword. We didn't make it past the first turn, where the tunnel seemed to bend as it went down as if it were a square tower. More and more of the strange presences turned up on the edge of my senses.

"I'm not sure about this," I said. "We've got even more incoming and they're forming a sort of line of attack."

"Is it *him*?" Neritas asked. "Could this be some sort of corrupted animal from his army again?"

Although I had my suspicions, I didn't respond. I didn't know how to.

If this was the demon, then I was in yet another difficult position, having to choose between saving and protecting an artifact piece, or protecting the people my entire race was meant to be looking after.

I was terrified of doing the wrong thing and froze to the spot, not doing either. It was an impossible choice. Both were my duty.

"We can come back for the artifact and guard the spot," Alitas suggested. It was a sensible suggestion, but in the past we hadn't been able to hold whatever the demon had come for, I didn't know if it was the right thing to do. The only time we'd managed to acquire the artifact was when we got there first. And one of us had still died trying to protect it.

On top of all that, having it would make me stronger. If I could get the artifact before anything really major got here, I could possibly use it to end the fight sooner. If I didn't, and he got to it, it would make our fight even harder. So far I hadn't been able to get back any artifacts that I hadn't claimed myself.

That understanding made my mind up.

"If we're going to claim this piece, we need to go get it ourselves. And we'll have to do it with as few dragons as possible. Can Kryos handle commanding the army up there with Colonel Flint?" I asked the dragon and soldier before me.

Both of them nodded, looking as determined as I felt. This was happening and we were all in completely.

Trying to ignore what I could feel of the enemy above me and incoming from almost every direction, I hurried deeper, leading the way and hurrying despite the danger.

I knew there was a chance the tunnels were unsafe, and a low-level anxiety settled in my stomach, tensing my muscles and making it harder for me to breathe calmly. Memories of being buried in a tunnel cave-in clouded my mind for a moment and I had to fight to push them away.

Now wasn't the time for me to fall apart. I had to hold myself together long enough to get this artifact and get out of there.

"Do you think we should maybe slow down?" Flick asked. He was normally the one to rush headlong into danger and take risks with a grin on his face.

He might have been right, but I sped up instead of slowing as I grew more anxious. If I was going to be buried again, it was going to happen no matter what speed I went. I didn't have time to be truly cautious either way. The fact that I was risking their lives, as well as mine, was a reminder I needed, however.

I stopped and looked between them all, considering my options. Up ahead I could feel the presences closing in. They were coming closer at a slower pace than I had expected. My forces and the allies I had, as far as I could tell, were holding still, protecting the area we had cordoned off and waiting for the enemy to come to us.

Given the demon liked to wear us down and overwhelm us, holding a smaller, more thoroughly defended area had more wisdom to it, but I also had to think of how long we'd hold it for. The truth was, I had a lot of the most powerful and experienced fighters with me.

"Neritas, stay with me. Everyone else, go back to the surface. Defend the area for me and I'll rejoin you as soon as I can." Alitas reached out for my arm, and I met his gaze specifically. "No arguments."

"What if you need magic to get through the door again?" His eyes searched mine.

"I am strong enough to connect to you all even from down at the bottom of this. If I need the magic, I'll pull it from you. Hopefully I won't." Although I spoke as if I had the utmost confidence in what I was saying, I didn't know for sure if I could reach that far. It was a problem I would have to tackle if I came to it.

Alitas didn't let go of me at first, but everyone else did

as I suggested and fell back. Even after Alitas left, however, William remained.

"This has already been an adventure my peers will be envious of for the rest of my life," William said. "I could easily go back. I don't need a trinket to remember it by if that's not going to be safe or possible. But I would like to stick with you and let the memory continue as long as possible."

"It might be dangerous. You could get caught up in a battle for your life."

"Sounds like I might anyway, and if you have another of those swords, I have some experience using them. I could help out in a pinch. I've always wanted to stick one of those evil-looking things. We're pretty sure they scared us off a dig a few years ago and killed one of our apprentices."

I blinked, not sure how to process the news that there were places the shadow catchers might have attacked before I'd ever been stalked by them and Anthony had needed to flee. It made sense, but I wondered why something like that had happened. I had a world of questions about what he knew.

Now wasn't the time for it, however. I felt the demons above getting closer and I was starting to feel the shadow catchers as well. Whatever was up there with them, there were a lot of different entities.

"Stay close to me and make sure you're paying attention. Don't get distracted by anything shiny or interesting unless you already know from me that it's safe to touch, and we'll get you a weapon if we can when we get to the surface again." It was the best I could offer William, and it allowed me to focus on the task at hand again.

Neritas gave me a nod, and I knew it was to acknowledge that he was thankful to be staying with me. After everything we had been through together and the feelings between us, I knew better than to command him to do something he wouldn't want to do. Not when one dragon wasn't going to turn an entire tide.

And in truth, I didn't want to be alone. This was going to be hard enough as it was.

We hurried deeper, although I went slower than I had been earlier. I tried not to let the fear in this time. Deflecting it made it easier to think about the task or even concentrate on the massive number of incoming enemies.

It wasn't long before I reached the end of the tunnel. There was a door, just like the last time, but this one was larger and I couldn't sense anything inside it. Or there was a net around the room. There was no handle, however.

"Do we need to be careful what we touch here?" William asked, looking at the carved stone around the entrance.

"I don't think so, but what do you want to touch?"

"The door and some of these stones. But not directly." William pulled a small pouch from his jacket pocket and opened it up to reveal several small brushes. "With these."

"Have at it, but be as quick as you can." I backed up just enough but kept my senses open in case energy came from anywhere.

Nothing happened as he brushed at the stones around the door, using quick, deft strokes to move years of grime and dirt. It revealed a script I sort of recognized. It was the ancient language of the dragons. Ben could read it and so could Anthony, but as much as I was learning, I was no master at it.

I stepped forward and made my hand glow even brighter to read it.

"It talks of a lock and a key hidden somewhere else and then danger to all who enter," Neritas translated a few seconds later. "Or something like that."

"That makes sense." William lifted the brush one more time and moved it over a small indent on the right side of the door. He revealed a perfectly hexagonal mark.

"So we need a key?" I wasn't sure where we would even begin looking.

"I guess so. Any idea where we might find one?" William looked up at me as he tucked his brushes away.

I had no idea, and it felt as if we were running out of time. The entities were close enough that I was pretty sure they would be visible soon, even moving as slowly as they were.

For a couple of seconds, I froze, not sure what to do now. I wanted to get through the door, but I also needed to join the fight upstairs.

Scarlet, we have a problem, Alitas said from somewhere above me. *The incoming are human. But they're... different.*

CHAPTER NINE

I turned and ran back up the tunnel, lamenting my choice. With everyone on the surface and no way to transform while still underground, I could only sprint as fast as I could to the entrance. It felt as if it took an age to get up there. I heard shouts and yells as I got close.

There was still a rope dangling down from above, and I grabbed it. Then I stared up. Gym had never been a strong point of mine and I didn't know if I had the fitness to climb up without aid.

"Let me go first." Neritas stopped me. "Both for safety and so I can help you up once I get there."

Although I would normally have insisted on being the first anywhere, I couldn't right now. We needed to do this in the fastest order possible. Even if I got up there before them, I would have to assist them and it wouldn't take any less time.

I watched as Neritas climbed, using upper body strength more than anything else to go hand over hand up the rope. The lower part swung back and forth but William soon stepped forward to grab it and help steady it. Instantly Neritas sped up and made his way to the top.

It made the task look easy and made me wonder if I was just being nervous about something I was perfectly capable of doing. After all, I was a dragon now and could use magic to aid in all sorts of activities.

"You go next," I told William as Neritas stayed at the top and bent back to give whoever tried next a hand. To make it clear I wasn't going to be argued with, I took hold of the rope at the bottom, a short way beneath where William would hold it to begin climbing, and waited.

If he wanted to go last, he made no allusions to it, but started climbing as well, leaving me in the tunnel by myself. It wasn't as easy holding the rope steady as William had made it look, but I did my best. William wasn't as strong or as fast as Neritas had been, but he had a better start, aided by me, and he had Neritas to help him up the last few feet.

Finally it was my turn, and I tried not to hesitate. Something was going on up there. It felt as if the dragons and allies of mine had shrunk back rather than held their ground, and I was eager to find out what Alitas had meant by 'humans are attacking us, and they're different.'

The thought filled me with dread, but I climbed anyway, mimicking the displays I had just seen. It made my arms and shoulders ache as I tried to pull myself up, and I was pretty sure it was going to rub the skin on my hands raw.

I kept going, however, noticing that the rope was also moving upward at the same time. Neritas and William had joined forces to pull me up.

It helped me to relax and trust them, and the speed I was ascending was faster than anything I could have achieved alone. Neritas was soon there with a hand extended to reach mine and help yank me up the last of the way.

With my armor on, I was heavier than he expected, and he grunted in surprise at having to take my weight for a moment. I relieved him as soon as I could and scrambled out of the hole.

As soon as I was on my feet I made my way over to where Alitas and the others in charge were. They were trying to do something strange, fighting the few shadow catchers who had made it to us but hesitating and shoving them instead of attacking with swords.

I sped up as I caught a glimpse of a human in the lamp lights coming toward Jace with a raised crowbar in his hands. Jace caught the crowbar and pulled it out of his grip before chucking it down behind her. Someone then shoved a shadow catcher into the man and knocked him backward.

"What's going on?" I asked, fearing the worst. These looked like corrupted people. People just like the coyotes and birds the demon had taken control of. If he could take control of people, then none of us were safe.

"It's exactly what it looks like," Alitas replied. "We're trying not to hurt them, but they keep coming and there's no way out. Did you get the artifact so we can try and run from here?"

I shook my head. I was grateful that he had taken the approach I wanted in not hurting anyone, but equally scared of what might happen if we didn't get out of this.

There was no doubt that they were doing their best to hurt us.

"What do we do if they hit our shields?" a soldier yelled to my right. "It seems to hurt them just like the other demons."

Everyone looked at me and I froze. I had no idea how to handle this situation. It had never occurred to me to have to fight a corrupted form of the very people we were meant to be trying to protect.

I had failed to see this coming just like I had everything else. It was yet another mistake I had made, and people were paying for it.

"Can they be saved?" I asked, the question tumbling out. "Can we somehow rescue them? Make them see reason?"

Thoughts of the handlers filled my head and how they had appeared to choose their fate and become corrupted over time. Fintar had been a dragon who could still appear like a dragon, and these humans felt more like him in their aura than they did anything else I'd encountered.

"I hope so," Douglas shot back. "Or this is going to be a rough war."

Again I froze, not sure what to do next as dragons and soldiers around me tried to defend themselves from an enemy they weren't sure they could fight mixed in with an enemy they were usually desperate to kill. It was an effective attack, and the group fell back. More and more of us were squashed into a smaller area, unable to even reach the enemy to fight.

The whole time, I could sense more enemies pouring into the area and it soon started to overwhelm my mind with all the unease and fear. This was chaos.

"Why couldn't you get the item? Can we get it quickly and then run?" Alitas stepped back and out of the fight, letting Jace close in beside Reijo and both of them take over the fight for him.

I shook my head. "Needs a key and I don't have it or anything close to it. If we had time we could blow the door or cut through it, but we clearly don't."

"Then I don't like to advise this, Your Highness, but we need to flee." He frowned as he spoke and I knew he would be feeling as conflicted as I did, despite suggesting it as the best course of action.

"Wait," Neritas had the frenzied excitement of a desperate idea in his voice. "Can you fight these humans the way you do the traps on the rooms and the strange, corrupted disks they throw back at us sometimes? Can you use magic to fight them?"

I didn't know and I wasn't sure we had time to try and find out, but I closed my eyes for a few seconds anyway and tried to concentrate on one nearby. As soon as I connected to them and tried to put magic into them, they collapsed, screeching and wailing in a pained and very human way.

Instantly, I stopped. "Not without hurting them, it would seem."

"We're going to have to hurt them anyway if we want to stay here. We have no other option open to us. If you're telling us that they're going to hurt and possibly die either way, then... I hate to say this as well, but killing them might be the biggest mercy." Neritas spoke quietly but firmly.

"I don't know how much they're genuinely hurting and

how much is them fighting me. We don't know what's been done to them. I can't kill them without being completely sure there is no alternative and they're already good as dead."

"If we had tranquilizers we could knock some out and take them with us." Douglas shrugged as if he didn't think it was a very good offer in terms of ideas, but it helped me know one thing: we still had a way to save them, and I wasn't going to kill anyone I could possibly save. Not even to get another artifact before the demon did.

I had barely thought of him when I felt the presence of the corrupted dragon enter my mind. He had arrived as well, and that could only mean one thing: he was here for the piece of artifact as well.

The choice was out of my hands now. I either became just like him and murdered innocents in my way or I told my army to flee, equipped myself better for the fight, and came back another time. It would make us less powerful and give him another weapon to use against us from now on, but it was the only morally sound option.

"Everyone to the trucks," I commanded, raising my voice and hoping that enough of my crew could hear me. "Try not to hurt the people and get toward the vehicle you came in."

"There aren't enough. Some of them have been decayed already." Alitas looked as if this was one of the worst pieces of news, but it was just another problem.

"Do we have enough dragons to carry the soldiers and fly out of here?" I asked. I realized that was a better option anyway after thinking about it for a few more seconds.

"Not who can fly for long. Not unless some dragons

take extra soldiers, and there's no way to get them into harnesses, or time to get them on. We'd be abandoning all of our gear, at the very least."

I looked around as I spoke, making objects within the perimeter of our fighting allies glow with light so I could see them better.

"Okay, then get as many soldiers as you need into the remaining trucks and load them up with anything worth saving, as much as it'll fit. Prioritize fighting and flying equipment that's harder or more expensive to replace. And start getting the dragons who are the average fliers in the center of our safe zone, to take a soldier each. Those of us who can handle it will take two soldiers and have to forgo the harness. Leave a few honor guard without so they can run interference, and let the slower dragons fly out of here as soon as we don't need them to hold the line."

Everyone moved to follow my instructions. Even Alitas seemed happy with this plan. I charged up the remaining trucks with magic, concentrating on helping everyone who had to move fast, lug equipment, or start transforming. As soon as I had done what I could with my magical energy, I rushed to the nearest part of the fighting line and stabbed a shadow catcher that had gotten through the line of people.

In front of me were people as far as the eye could see.

I tried to think of some way we could defeat all of them, but I was drawing a blank and I knew it wasn't going to come to me in the heat of the battle. This was a battle we were never going to win, and the demon must have known it. The scarier thing was not knowing where they had come from. How were so many of them like this and no one had reported any people missing?

A human came close to me. It had nothing in its hands, no doubt disarmed by Jace or someone else. It grabbed my armor and then shrieked and recoiled in pain. I felt the magic transfer out of my armor, hurting the person, but it only temporarily stopped them. They came toward me again.

Instinctively, I recoiled and slipped out of formation. Thankfully, Reijo had me clocked and shoved it away with a large spade. They then closed the gap.

With my armor on and charged, there was nothing I could do in battle that wouldn't hurt them, and for a second I stood, lost again. This was the worst situation I had ever been in.

Alitas brought me back to my senses as he gave the command for the next batch of dragons to come to transform. There was little I could do to help in any other way, so I joined them, waiting for the first couple to get in the air before I transformed and called three soldiers to me.

There was a little confusion when all three came rushing over and Alitas tried to send one of them away again, but a glare and snort from me stopped him in his tracks.

"Are you sure you want to be burdened so much?" he asked.

I nodded, not wanting to waste the mental energy on projecting my thoughts. The soldiers were more than happy to be getting out of this impossible battle. The trucks were almost fully loaded, and the dragons held the line as it shrunk.

Despite having three men on my back and being in the very center of the circle, I stayed where I was for a while, continuing to keep the trucks charged as they were readied to leave.

I'm going with the vehicles to escort them out if we can.

I didn't add that this was going to kill some of the human attackers, but it was either that or sacrifice some of the people on our side, and that choice was far less morally questionable in my mind. I had to get the soldiers who had trusted me with their lives out of here.

The demon was still a little way off and a long way up when our circle broke and the final few dragons hurried backward and up into the air. I kept the ground charged where they were to give them time to take off and then did the same.

Several humans wailed and screamed in pain, trying and failing to come after us, and I thought I saw at least a few fall, never to rise again. It was the best I could do, however, and no matter how much guilt I felt, I kept the area charged until all the dragons were in the air.

At the same time, I charged the ground in front of the trucks and made it glow as well. I moved it forward like an arrow that cut a path. Again, I winced at the number of people it was hurting, but they fell back and I had the satisfaction of popping several shadow catchers as well and seeing them turn into vapor.

It gave the area a strange foggy glow that added to the horror of the scene, but the two truck drivers kept their heads and drove along the path I had made them. I flew over them, weighted a little more by the extra person and their gear, but fresh enough and pumped full of enough adrenaline that I could handle it.

I let the ground go behind us and brought up the rear,

with the exception of the honor guards who were flying crisscross and around above us all and making sure that nothing easily dive-bombed us from above.

There were so many entities around, above, and near us that I could no longer make them out very well, but I felt them close in behind us and some of them entered the tunnels we had uncovered.

Trying not to worry about how spectacularly we had failed this mission, I flew to safety and off the island we were on.

CHAPTER TEN

By the time our hotel came into sight, the sun was rising again. I was exhausted and I was pretty sure that one of the three soldiers I was still carrying on my back had fallen asleep, propped up between his two companions.

The convoy had grown along the two-hour journey. More soldiers appeared to escort the civilians and dragons who could no longer fly, and police, other civilians who were merely curious, news vans, and other vehicles whose intent I could only guess at, all fell in the line somewhere.

When we reached the hotel, reporters swarmed the front, and civilians along with them. I circled a few times, almost not daring to land. This was a chaos of a different kind and in some ways more intimidating than fighting demons was.

We had easily left the demons behind. Their focus had been on getting the artifact more than attacking us, although we had needed to fight to get away from them in the first place.

I made sure everyone was okay and we had very few

injured. One of the honor guard was able to use a healing device on the few who were badly hurt in the back of a truck.

It was clear that the world wasn't happy we had fled our first major fight rather than fighting until our opponent was bested, and I didn't doubt they knew there were now enslaved people in the demon's army as well.

This wasn't going to be a fun moment. Although I thought I deserved some anger for how unprepared I had been, I couldn't have known this was coming this time. The demon had turned up at the exact moment I had discovered the artifact.

Yet again.

While we were flying back to the hotel I'd had plenty of time to think about everything, and once again I was struck by how often the enemy seemed to know where I was and what I might be up to. We hadn't seen the demon in days and then we finally found another artifact piece and he descended on us within twelve hours.

Someone was telling the enemy what was going on, and that meant I either had another handler in my midst or someone who wanted to be one. My mother had suspected that I had a rogue dragon in my party, but had not been able to pinpoint who it was. I had considered it on and off, but never very seriously.

The stakes were getting higher with every encounter, however. I couldn't afford to be relaxed about it anymore. I had to figure out who it was somehow. But I also couldn't tell anyone. Until I was sure that I could trust a dragon, I had to assume they were all betraying me. Could any of them win my trust back?

I landed with this thought in my head. I was one of only a few dragons left in the air. The soldiers were all safe inside along with the most tired of the dragons. Many of them were more exhausted than I had ever seen them before, but we had gotten everyone back to safety and the crowds were letting them all through.

As I shifted into human form, the crowds seemed to close around me. Neritas, Flick, and Alitas were still in the air and unable to land. Douglas was with me, along with two soldiers who were often with him in combat. They tried to form a protective triangle around me, but the press was strong and the three of them were as tired as I was.

"Can you explain why you haven't been protecting humans and they've been turned into zombies?" a reporter I recognized asked. It was exactly the sort of question I didn't want to hear and couldn't answer.

"Did you murder several people today?" another asked.

Again, I didn't reply, trying to join strength with the soldiers and push toward the hotel. The crowds pushed back as someone yelled to call me a murderer and then several others joined in, turning it into a chant.

Fear washed over me, making my breathing pick up as my heart raced and my mind fogged up. This was exactly the sort of press of people and chanting that had accompanied my beating at the hands of my dragon classmates in Detaris.

I was terrified and I began to freeze up, unable to run and not wanting to fight. I couldn't fight. These people weren't my enemy.

A roar overhead made many of them look up as a dragon swooped down low over all of us. Even I ducked, taken by surprise. And then it happened again. Neritas, Flick, and Alitas worked together in a swirl of tight-knit flying and low pass-overs to get everyone to back up from me and leave me alone.

Even then, not everyone pulled back and gave me space. Some people, especially the reporters and their cameramen, merely crouched and continued to bombard me with questions.

It gave the soldiers enough space to properly work with me, however, and Kryos and several other honor guards also came back out of the hotel toward me. Before long, I was well surrounded by a tight, regimented army of dragons and soldiers flanking me in a box. Most of them were taller than me, and the three dragons continued to fly and spin overhead, making sure that the crowds remained respectful and at a distance.

I exhaled and placed a hand on the shoulder of the soldier in front. Douglas had taken the central position ahead as the dragons wrapped around me from behind.

Within another minute I was in the building, and the crowds had fallen back for now. Alitas, Flick, and Neritas landed, yelling at everyone to get back unless they wanted to get squashed by a weary dragon falling from the sky.

It made the point that we were all exhausted, but I wasn't sure it inspired any confidence in us. They were pissed off, and lashing out at the humans wasn't going to help our issues, but I understood their reaction. I didn't like the thought of being in the middle of an angry mob either.

Thankfully, the US Army appeared to be on our side. Colonel Flint approached me and gave me the usual salute.

"I appreciate you getting all the men out of there, Your Highness. We truly weren't sure we'd survive that at one point."

"You've trusted me as your ally this far, Colonel. I may not be perfect, but I believe your motto is that you never leave a man behind. I'm happy to fight alongside you with the same mentality."

He gave me a nod and stepped back so I could walk past him, but before I could, there was the sound of breaking glass behind us. I turned to see that someone had thrown a rock through one of the hotel's glass doors. From where it lay on the carpet, I had no doubt that it had been aimed at me.

"Let's get you up to a room. Douglas, see her Highness isn't disturbed until she's rested enough we can make a new plan." Colonel Flint motioned to several of his soldiers. "We'll remind the people out there that you're an ally of the US Army and this operation happened exactly as we would have conducted it as well."

I nodded, letting my honor guard, boyfriend, and Douglas escort me away from everything and up to a room. although I didn't think I was going to sleep. There was a lot to work out.

As soon as we were all in my suite, I sank into a chair. Neritas brought some food over from the snack bar and made me eat, but my hands and arms shook as I lifted them up to my mouth. I was physically drained and I didn't know what to do.

Soon after we got there, Colonel Flint knocked on the door. Douglas let him in as if he had been expecting him, and he came over to all of us.

"I've made sure we're safe here despite the dissatisfaction of everyone outside. The hotel owner isn't happy about the damage, but I told him someone would make sure he was reimbursed for any damage."

"We can do that if the US Army won't," Alitas replied without missing a beat.

"That's appreciated. I'll suggest we split the cost, because it's a joint operation. No one should get their noses bent out of shape over that."

I nodded, not sure how to process such insignificant details over what had just happened.

"I'm more concerned about how this demon created the army he did and what we can do to stop him from harming more people," I said as soon as I could interrupt.

"As am I. I've ordered everyone to be armed with a tranquilizer weapon of some kind from here on out. And plenty of ammo."

"We're going to want plenty of those too. Can we get it arranged to acquire some as well? I don't want any more humans dying than can be helped." I shuddered, knowing some had died today and not wanting to ask my next question.

I bit the bullet anyway. "How many died today? Do we have any idea?"

"Once the demon and his army left, and most of the humans he controlled left with him, we had people sent in to look for the dead and at least identify them. There weren't any. They didn't leave anyone behind. We can only assume he either didn't want us to know or he has a way to make them rise again. Either way, it didn't sit well with the general public." Colonel Flint grew more somber as he spoke.

"It doesn't sit well with any of us either. We've got to find a way to heal them, save them, whatever is needed. And stop him from making any more of this human slave army."

I got up, intending to leave immediately, but I wobbled, instantly dizzy. Neritas gently pushed me back down. It was a clear sign that I was attempting too much, but I didn't know how to rest when there were people who needed me.

"Is there anything we can learn from here, or do we need to head back to base camp and the dragon city to figure it out from there?" Douglas asked, still sitting opposite me.

"Going back to Detaris would allow us to try and figure this out from a place of safety," Alitas replied. "We can't be attacked there, and you won't be hounded by the press while we work out how to stop him or fight him."

I nodded my acceptance. Going back to Detaris was the only real option for now.

"I'd like to make a statement of some kind before we leave. I don't want them to think we're running away from here as well. Can we let them know that we're doing everything to fix this, still working together, and we will have the ability to stop them the next time we come across them? Explain things like not wanting to kill them but not knowing how to not hurt them when everything we had was charged with magic that hurt any demon on touch."

"We can try." Colonel Flint reached for a stack of paper and pulled a pen from his top pocket.

Over the course of the next hour, we collectively wrote a speech, trying to put into it everything we wanted to say and all the ways we wanted to reassure the public while also keeping it short.

In the end, we had so many iterations and different directions that we had pieces of paper strewn across the bedroom floor. I picked up the piece containing the final draft, feeling a little better for having sat and rested. The food I'd eaten also boosted me.

"I want to deliver this personally, and then I think we should hand this out to whoever wants to have it, maybe someone from the media." I looked at all the people present in the room and didn't get an objection from any of them.

Douglas leaned forward and took a photo of the paper. "I'll get this typed up and sent out as soon as you finish reading it."

"The rest of us will go down with you and make sure you're safe, then we really ought to get a little sleep before heading back to Detaris." Alitas gave me a look that made it clear I wouldn't be arguing with the last part.

If this helped, I might finally be able to rest a bit. I was doing something, even if it was only reassuring a very worried crowd. I had no doubt that their reaction to all this was out of fear more than genuine anger. This new world was scary, and I didn't have the answers they needed to feel safe.

None of us did. But we needed to make them feel calmer somehow. I had to hope that this would work, but even if it didn't, it would make me feel better. I'd have tried.

Nerves set in as we made our way back downstairs and

toward the front of the hotel. The crowds there had dispersed a little, but they surged forward as soon as someone noticed me. Alitas had me hang back so he could head out there first, and Colonel Flint went with him.

I let them calm the people first and bring all the reporters forward. We were doing this properly. Only when Alitas motioned for me to go out did I move from my spot. I hadn't had time to memorize what I'd written, so I clutched the piece of paper between my hands and tried not to shake.

There were several heckles from the crowd as I stepped outside but they were soon quiet as well and everyone looked at me, waiting for me to speak. I felt the eyes of the entire world on me with the camera lenses feeding to all sorts of places live.

"Thank you for your patience in waiting for us to make a statement of some kind. I know that many of you are very worried about the events that happened in the early hours of this morning. In previous encounters with the demon, he has shown that he can corrupt the wildlife of our planet. In working with the US Army, General Miller, Colonel Flint, and Lieutenant Douglas as part of every decision and strategy we make, we hadn't foreseen any scenario in which humans would also be harmed and corrupted in this manner."

I paused. The image of the first one lumbering toward me and grabbing my arm was so terrifying that I couldn't breathe. Blinking slowly, I tried to focus on the words on the page I held, reading through them up until the same point again.

"When confronted with the people we had all sworn to

protect in such a way, none of us knew how best to handle the situation. We had never experienced anything like it before. It was easily agreed between all of us that we couldn't fight them. We don't want to fight them. Not if there is any chance that they can be saved and brought back to us. No matter what the demon has done to them, they started out as the loved ones of our people and they should be considered as such."

Again I stopped, but this time tears stung my eyes. I'd thought I would be strong enough to make this speech, but now it came to it, I was so emotional I could barely speak.

"We couldn't avoid harming some of them although we do not understand enough to know if they were truly in pain or merely angry at us. When fighting the usual minions of the demon, we charge everything on us—to defend us, and to fight with—so that a single contact with the enemy can harm it and protect us. When we prepared for this fight and before we knew that the forces would be so dear to us, we did as usual. This meant that a mere physical contact with the humans ran the risk of killing them. Our only option was to retreat, learn more, equip ourselves to handle this new development, and come up with a new strategy to try and save these people."

As I spoke, the crowd appeared to soften and relax. Something I had said was moving them, and it gave me the confidence to finish up.

"We haven't given up on them, and we ask that you don't give up on us. We're trying our best to protect everyone in situations we have never seen before. Thank you."

I didn't wait or give anyone a chance to ask questions,

but turned and fled back inside the building. Nothing I had ever done had been so difficult as facing a crowd like this and trying to explain my actions. I felt as if I had failed them and they knew it.

Somehow we had to put it right.

CHAPTER ELEVEN

It was a huge relief when Detaris came into view ahead of us. The US Army had helped us get back again and we'd all traveled as one group. We'd flown the last little way, but there hadn't been enough dragons to carry all the humans, so some of the soldiers had piled into a truck.

They pulled into the base camp outside Detaris only a few seconds before the dragons landed. We dropped everyone off and General Miller asked to have a debrief, but I noticed that several of the elders were also waiting for me. They were no doubt just as concerned.

"General, may I issue a formal invitation for you to join us in the chamber of elders in Detaris to debrief my elders as well as you and your personnel at the same time? This has not been an easy mission for any of us and I do not want to put anyone through explaining it twice." I had rehearsed the words several times along the way, grateful I didn't stumble over them now and that they still sounded natural.

He nodded and his aide came with him, as well as

several of the officers who had been on the mission. Everyone else on the base was dismissed.

It was a strange party that entered Detaris, and I offered to carry the general up to the elders' chamber myself, barely giving him time to appreciate being able to see the city in all its glory. It was the middle of a bright, sunny day, and there were few better times to be able to look upon the city for the first time. To his credit, he remained in business mode and merely looked it over before responding to my offer.

As I landed outside the elders' chambers, more and more dragons appeared, and the elders all gathered as well. We made the introductions swiftly. Jace came with us, and Elias and Sarai, the two oldest dragons currently alive, also arrived. They weren't officially city elders and held no recognized titles, but they were two of the dragons I most respected, even if I didn't get along entirely well with both of them.

No sooner had I landed than I reached forward with my mind and connected to the device that lived in the very makeup of the tower. To help the ruler of the city, a lie detector of sorts had been placed there. It had proved invaluable in the past, and I connected to it now.

Someone was telling the demon where we were and what we were looking for. It was imperative to find out who.

As always, I spent the first part of the meeting telling everyone present everything that had happened. For the parts I hadn't been present for and anything I had forgotten, Alitas stepped forward and added the rest. Then Lieutenant Douglas also came forward.

"I know that many of you are safe here in this tower and have not had to face battle, but I'd just like to implore you all to help us. Your queen has shown that she cares for us and fights like no one else I have ever met, but we do not know the hearts of any of you. We cannot fight this alone. We need your help. Please don't forsake us or act in a way that would see many of my race die."

"You make a very passionate plea," Brenta replied before I could. "Please be reassured that we consider our duty to protect this planet and the human race to be our highest and a great honor. We will do what we can. You have all spoken of some kind of tranquilizer weapon. We heartily endorse the use of this and a research mission into finding out what can be done to save these poor humans."

This helped all the humans relax and allowed me to do the same for the first time since I had got back. I'd feared that the elders would let fear override sense and they'd suggest caution.

"I think it's also clear that we need to trap this demon back in his prison as soon as possible." Sarai stepped forward. Her frail human form was almost a deception. In her dragon form, she was formidable, and even in human form, when you put a sword in her hand it was as if an entire century melted away from her appearance.

"We don't have a working gate," Griffin replied. "There is nothing to trap the demon inside."

"With the queen's permission, we would like to start trying to make an alternative gate and go to the old site. We also request access to the library here to see what we can learn of the previous maker and how it was constructed."

"Granted, for what it's worth," I replied. "Ben has been struggling to find anything that mentions any time before the demon was trapped. It's as if no history exists before then, except in memory and stories."

Ben nodded along to this but stepped forward as well when I finished. "I have found a few references, but they're in a particular personal journal and nowhere else. I think there might be someone still to find who might know more. I'd also like to try and find them."

I granted his request as well, grateful that everyone was trying to find their own tasks and ways to help. We spent the next couple of hours talking to the soldiers about getting weapons to knock out the humans instead of kill them and what we could trade for them. The general was being cagey with his promises, and it made me wonder if he'd been given some orders to distance himself in some way or if he genuinely didn't know if he could help.

My elders pushed for answers. Griffin was particularly keen to get details and specifics. The tension grew until I was preparing to intervene.

"This is all well and good, and I understand that you desire to have definites, but I am struggling to get these answers myself. There isn't usually a need for weapons of this nature. Wars do not usually involve such a massive desire to take prisoners and not cause major harm." The general expressed his frustration at being pressed before I could get a word in edgeways.

I stood to interrupt but Griffin bowed to the general as a show of respect and sat himself back down in his chair.

"Thank you, General. Forgive my eagerness. I just want to do my job as you do," Griffin, ever the diplomat, pandered to the general's ego just enough that it smoothed much of the tension.

"When the first human is sedated, I want to try and cure them or at least work out how they've been corrupted. I'll work with whoever is needed to try and research it. There is a chance that our magic can be used in a particular way to remove whatever has been done to them." I spoke to no one in particular, but it was the general who acknowledged me.

"We were hoping that you would make some sort of offer of this nature. It would cause public outrage and be a tragedy to let these people die in battle if they can be saved. Our best scientists in these areas are already on their way here."

I nodded at this information, not sure what to make of humans trying to explain our magic with science. The part of me that still felt human and recognized that I had been born and raised in the human world was very interested about the possibility that it could all be explained somehow. The more dragon part of me wanted to keep believing in magic.

Despite all these conversations, I still felt as if more could be done. It wasn't enough on its own and it didn't give me confidence. There were still five more artifact pieces to find, and it was more important than ever that we find some of them first. I expressed my concern that by now the demon had four of them stashed away somewhere and there was little any of us could do about it.

"We've talked about this before," Douglas pointed out. "What if you could find him and his lair instead? You sense the enemy, the artifacts, and many other things before the rest of us. Will you not at least try and find where he is hiding?"

"It's a possibility. I thought of this earlier today," I confessed. "I had two thoughts cross my mind. One, I don't feel it is time to share yet, and the other is that we may need to look for the demon's place of origin. With so many humans taken and corrupted, is there any location that is missing many people? Could we narrow down his location by gathering data on missing persons?" As I spoke, it was as if a light bulb switched on with the general and both Douglas and Colonel Flint practically beamed at me. It was something that clearly hadn't occurred to any of them.

"I will liaise with the relevant authorities and see if we can narrow down the area. You're right that this shouldn't be difficult and should be an obvious pattern," General Miller replied, still looking as pleased as any of us could be.

There was little more to say after that. I wanted to be in five places at once, trying to make the gate and its materials. Jace had spoken of trying to make it happen before, but knowing Elias and Sarai were fully on board with it helped. I wanted Ben to help locate the next artifact and wanted to be the one looking through the rest of Anthony's journal for clues. And on top of that, I needed to figure out who the spy was and whom I could trust.

It had been strange to be in a meeting and know that someone in the room might be lying. Being connected to the truth machine beneath the chamber floor hadn't given me any indication that anyone was trying to trick us or telling us anything that wasn't true, but I had tricked it in the past.

Even Ben had. In fact, he had been very good at getting

past it and knowing how to answer so the elders didn't realize he wasn't giving them all the information. The meeting was coming to an end, and on my second matter to think about, I was none the wiser. If the traitor was among us, I had no clue who he or she was yet.

And after such a thorough meeting, I wondered if I was right to even think there was a traitor. Could it still be magic, or a coincidence, or simply the stronger magic of the demon? He didn't come to Detaris and fight us. It was almost as if he knew some things that I didn't.

Not sure what else to do, I ended the elders' meeting and personally escorted all the soldiers back out of the city. More reporters and news vans had arrived and parked between the base and our city. Our shield still held to stop humans just walking into our city and kept it hidden from view, but it made it harder for me to fly out knowing that several news channels would be broadcasting my activity.

"It is good for them to see all of us working together and soldiers coming out of Detaris again," Douglas said to me as I landed and transformed, then eyed the news reporters with no small amount of trepidation. "Especially when the general has returned from Detaris in such a good mood."

"I hope you're right," I replied. For now, I was on the base and the reporters knew better than to film and broadcast footage from an active military base. It afforded me almost as much privacy as I got from being in Detaris.

There was no reason for me to stay, however, so I turned to go, preparing to jump, transform and spread my wings and fly over the tops of the heads of any soldiers nearby. Douglas stopped me from leaving.

"You never mentioned what the second thing to occur to you was. Given you've had such wonderful insights already into what we're facing and what might help, I'd love to know what the second thought you had was."

I looked back at him, wondering if it was something I could say. We weren't alone. Many dragons were waiting for us, having helped carry the soldiers. Alitas, Flick, and Neritas were with them. Could I trust this soldier? And if I could, was there any way I could let him know what I feared without letting the others know?

"Thank you for everything you did to fight alongside me yesterday," I said loudly enough that others would hear. As soon as I had finished speaking, I leaned in for a hug and whispered the rest. "We have a traitor in Detaris who is leaking my position and knowledge to the demon. I can trust no one."

When I pulled back from the hug his eyes were wide, but he recovered quickly and processed enough to consider my earlier words.

"You're welcome." He didn't let go of me right away. "I'm *always* here for you, no matter what you need or when."

It was all the acknowledgment he could give me, but I was willing to take it. I'd found one ally in all of this. There was no way it could have been the lieutenant, and we both knew it. It had to be a dragon and it had to be someone who had been in my world since the beginning. They had to be someone in Detaris, unless several were working together.

I remembered talking to my mom in the early days of meeting her and trying to narrow down whether anyone was betraying us or not. It hadn't mattered after a while. We had begun winning every fight, and only the gate and fixing it had remained elusive.

Now, however, I needed to find my mole. And I needed to do it fast.

CHAPTER TWELVE

The general had been true to his word. As soon as he got information on missing people that helped to pinpoint the area the demon had been operating in, he messaged to let me know. It was in Arizona, somewhere south of where I had been looking for the artifact in Nevada.

It wasn't conclusive data, because it turned out that a lot of people went missing from that area on a regular basis, but this was new and unusual, and in some cases whole families disappeared. This wasn't the usual kind of missing. They weren't runaways or drug addicts. No troubled teenagers or mothers who couldn't cope with the relentless pressure of being everything to everyone.

These missing people were people who should have been happy. People who had everything to live for, friends, family, and careers. There were no notes. Most people who left willingly also wrote goodbye notes. Something that explained why they were going and didn't intend to come back. Or there was a suspicious person or van sighting, or someone saw them talking to a dodgy-looking person.

From everything that I was looking at now, it was clear that these missing people had none of that.

"Thank you for finding this." It still covered a large area. This hadn't been done all at once. The demon hadn't arrived in a single town and corrupted all of them. He'd taken people at random from various places and he had done it over the entire time he had been out of his prison.

While we had been focused on artifacts, he had been just as concerned about building an army. And I was beginning to become greatly outnumbered. Somehow, I had to find the demon's hiding place and put a stop to all this.

"The government has already issued a warning to everyone in the state of Arizona to be careful whom they approach at night, to make sure they lock their doors and call law enforcement if they hear or see anything suspicious."

I tried not to voice my first thoughts. It wasn't going to do them much good if they didn't have a dragon to defend them or someone who had some understanding of the supernatural and how to fight it. It was better than nothing, however.

As I studied a map of the area that had been impacted and had a higher-than-usual count of missing persons, I realized it was still a very large area to fly over.

"I want to wait until it's nighttime and bring only a couple of dragons with me. Just the basics to confirm my feelings. I can outfly any trouble," I added, reassuring those who already looked as if they were going to object to such an idea. "As soon as I know I've found the demon or his lair, I'll come straight back here and we'll plan an attack."

Everyone looked at me as if I had grown two heads, but

Neritas stepped forward. "You know that you're not going anywhere without me, don't you?"

I grinned and nodded.

"And you want someone who can fly faster than anyone else. Just in case you do need backup." Flick looked at me with his usual smugness, knowing I wasn't going to say no.

Alitas folded his arms across his chest, but I shook my head. "You're needed here. I need you to make sure this city stays safe and everyone gets along. And if the demon appears anywhere else, take an army and save any humans you can."

Although he frowned, he accepted it and let his arms go loose again. "If you do this, you promise me to be careful. I'm not losing another monarch on my watch as captain of the honor guard. Especially when you're all as hot-headed and decisive as each other."

"I will be the model of caution," I reassured him as I smiled.

"I think at least one human ought to go with you. Just in case you need someone to make sure the cavalry arrives in other forms too." Douglas stood again.

"Okay, so... four of us." I looked between the three men that had decided they weren't going to let me go alone. I was glad that this was the group I had and I wasn't going out alone.

"It's a fair way away. I've arranged some transport to get us closer. It's in Arizona and near the Mexico border. It even used to be in Mexico, we think." Douglas pulled out his phone and showed me an older map of the area.

The area we'd be aiming for looked like it had once been another country and possibly part of a much different way of life, and my curiosity at what I might find grew even more.

But it also made me worried. This area might be part of one of the harsher climates in the US, but it was also somewhere where a lot of people lived still, and I didn't know if they were going to understand what was happening, or want to be a part of this fight, especially if lots of their loved ones were missing.

The humans alone could be more than a little angry.

Despite that, I didn't waste any time, accepting the lift and heading back to Detaris to get a proper away bag planned. I didn't waste much time, but let my mother and Ben know where I was going, asking both to keep an eye on their respective elements of my responsibilities, as well as Alitas.

It felt strange to leave again and only have Neritas and Flick with me. I couldn't remember the last time I had left the city with so few people. It was liberating. I wanted to be more incognito, and that had become impossible when I was constantly accompanied by an army.

We got into a small truck with plenty of supplies in the back. I checked it all and then looked at Douglas, who had taken the driver's seat, the only one of us who could officially drive on US soil.

He shrugged and pointed at the food crate over his shoulder. "I thought this time we could make sure we ate and slept well. Sometimes we don't get to."

It broke any tension between us as we handed out the popcorn and sodas and we all tucked in while we drove. It felt good to be able to be with friends and chill. Neritas and Flick told Douglas a bit about what it was like growing up as dragons and going to dragon school, and Douglas returned the favor, talking about what it was like to be a human instead.

Although I had grown up human, my life experience had been very different and not typical. Douglas could give them a better idea of normal for humanity.

"But this magic thing. Having magic and training magic. Is it really something mystical and strange? Can science really not explain it in any way?" Douglas asked when we had a slight lull in the conversation.

"Maybe. I don't know if it can. It's some kind of energy. It has a sort of charge and I can feel it, connect to it, and do complicated things with it that science can't explain. At least not yet, or nothing I've learned. Besides, I can change from a human into a dragon. How does that work if it's not a sort of magic?"

It was the lieutenant's turn to shrug. There was a lot that science would have to explain.

"And there's the telepathy," Neritas pointed out.

"We can only do that in dragon form. Don't ask me why."

"See, that makes sense. It's something in your dragon physiology that makes that possible. But seeing you hold that halfway form on one of the previous missions..." Douglas shook his head as his voice trailed off.

"That's not easy. Not all dragons can do it. It's as if the body fights against it. It wants to be one or the other."

"Understandable. Both forms are clearly stable, and you're not necessarily holding a stable middle ground."

Hearing his views on what we were and how everything worked served as an interesting counterpoint to everything

I was used to. He clearly had an appreciation for what we could do and had thought about how it fit in. It seemed to blow a lot of minds, finding that we were real, but he'd gotten past that and tried to work out what this truly meant for humanity, and from a good position. An inquisitive mind that wasn't judging but was genuinely curious.

I appreciated it and it made us feel like a solid group, all trying to understand and relate as we traveled closer to the possible location of the demon.

Along the way, I felt outward as far as I could. It was always easier when I was relaxed. It was strange in some ways. I didn't feel anything for miles and miles. After feeling shadow catchers dotted everywhere and hounding me prior to the demon escaping, it was so different.

There was no net of minor demons anymore. That made me even more nervous about the possibility that someone was leaking my location. Just thinking about it and remembering that my missions kept going wrong brought me back to my predicament with a bump.

I had to focus and figure out what was going on. Someone close to me couldn't be trusted. I knew that much. And of all the people, it was Douglas I doubted the least. He had only been involved for so long, and I suspected someone had been feeding the demon information a lot longer.

A part of me was angry that I hadn't figured out who it was earlier. My mother declaring that she couldn't pinpoint anyone in our group had put me in a place of comfort I should never have stayed in. Now I, and others, had paid for it.

As we traveled south, I tried to stay focused, letting the others talk for a while and doing my job. For now, it was enough to just be on alert and otherwise relax. This was a situation I had never been in before. I had never gone looking for the enemy, and never traveled without the intention of finding something I could bring back. This was purely scouting.

We stopped a few times to get food, but we used drive-throughs only and Douglas made sure that no one interacted with the general public but himself.

It was strange to be traveling so far without being recognized or seen by anyone, but somehow we managed it, and we were soon approaching the edge of the area where lots of people had gone missing.

The place was still a long way from Maine, and it was something that had been bugging me for the majority of the journey. I knew we could get people across the country in half a day, but did the demon have that ability? How was he moving his army?

I got out of the car to a rush of heat and the scorching sun, even later in the day. I knew that being in LA wasn't much better, but this wasn't pleasant.

"So how do you want to do this?" Douglas asked me.

"Preferably, I don't want to be seen, but I want to be low in the sky, so we need nighttime and we need a plan on how to sweep the area. Thankfully, I don't think I need to feel anything underground, so we can do sweeps wider apart than we did on the islands in Maine."

"Great, and I've got a GPS device that can map our journey. I can help you keep straight lines roughly the right distance apart." Douglas pulled out the handheld technology he was talking about and switched it on.

"Okay, then let's consult the map, make a grid and work our way through it, and we'll rest as we need to."

I pulled out the map and drew some boxes on it, estimating, based on our flight distances on the islands in Maine, that we could do each box in a couple of hours at most and would take a break after each one. It was a rough estimate, but it was good enough.

There was no way to be sure that we would find anything. A lot of the ground we were going to cover was wilderness, desert, and old tribal ruins of one kind or another. We were also right near the border. Not a lot of people wanted to live this close to the Mexican border.

We ate more food as we waited for the sun to set and for it to get dark enough that I felt comfortable flying. I grew more anxious as the time went by. I didn't like the pressure being on me to work out what was going on and who might be out there, but I had my favorite people with me. Somehow, I had to make this work.

With any luck, by dawn we would have found a demon lair and be back on our way to Detaris to get our army and attack.

CHAPTER THIRTEEN

It was good to be in dragon form again and flying. It almost didn't matter that it was a stealth operation or that I was flying back and forth on a grid directed by Douglas. I was in the air and stretching my wings.

The soldier was in his harness, and I had finally gotten used to having it on my back. It was comfortable in its own way. Neritas and Flick were flying out on each flank, both of them following along in my wake and effectively training as well.

All of us were relaxed, despite the seriousness of our task. Now that I had begun, I didn't feel so anxious about it. I was too busy focusing on what I could feel and making sure that I wasn't missing anything.

The quiet of night and the peacefulness of the area helped. It was wonderful to fly over a deserted area and focus on what I felt. Although I was meant to be looking out for the magical auras I could sense, I also allowed myself to feel the wind beneath my wings and blowing across my scales.

I breathed in the scent of the natural land and what few plants grew here, and I enjoyed the dim light and atmosphere. It was a beautiful, serene adventure.

As we flew across more of the area and it continued to get darker, I flew lower and tried to feel for anything. Still, there was nothing. We checked grid square after square, and nothing showed up. We'd done three and it was well past midnight when I wondered if we needed to change it up.

"I think we could do the grids about a third quicker if Flick and I spread out a little from you and you trusted us to feel for whatever might be out there as well. Let us give you more range."

Although I liked the idea, I was worried that they would need to be so much further out from me to have a range beyond my own that we wouldn't be able to see each other anymore.

I voiced my fear.

"Nothing to worry about there. We can feel each other the same way," Flick replied. "I always know where you are, as long as you're within half a mile. How do you think I worked out that you and Neritas had a thing for each other for sure? He stopped leaving your room at night."

My cheeks flushed as Douglas chuckled. It wasn't a relationship we'd confirmed with anyone specifically. No one had asked, but we didn't hide it, exactly.

"That makes sense. You two are almost never apart and you've got a lot in common. Similar temperaments, and I wouldn't want to face either of you in any kind of combat, ever. And that's after all the training I've had." Douglas shuddered good-naturedly. "I'm also behind this plan if it makes any difference. As much as I love being the lucky son of a bitch who gets to ride on a dragon almost every day of my life, I like a nice warm bed as much as the next fella."

I grinned at their enthusiasm and let all three of them persuade me to do it their way. It added so much to our range that it was easily going to bring down each grid that was left to just over an hour rather than somewhere between an hour and a half and two hours.

It would save us several hours across the night, and it meant that they were getting to properly practice, something I didn't have a problem with.

Although I was nervous about trusting another with a skill only I had possessed for a while, I kept telling myself that this was best for them, for us all as a race, and I should learn to allow tasks to be delegated to others.

We finished our break and got back in the air. We all wanted to get this done and hopefully find the demon. I was tired of reacting and not getting anywhere, but this wasn't a great plan either. It felt more like searching a haystack for a very, very small needle.

Despite that, we went through another grid, opted not to take a break, and flew through to the next. With Douglas directing me and both Flick and Neritas flying to stay on my flanks but so far out I couldn't see them, it felt a bit strange, but as Flick had pointed out, I could always feel where they were.

We were halfway through the second grid like this when I thought I found something. It wasn't the demon, but there was a small blip of power coming up ahead of us and slightly toward Neritas.

Although there appeared to be ruins and the terrain wasn't perfectly smooth, I hunkered down a bit lower and tried to get a feel for what might be there.

Only a few hundred yards later, when it was still half a mile or so ahead, Neritas also dropped down a little more.

Are you feeling that already? Neritas asked me as it came even closer.

I think so. There's something down there.

Another artifact? Flick asked, carrying on in line despite our excitement.

It feels as if it might be.

I made sure to include Douglas in the thoughts I was projecting and hoped that the others were as well, so he didn't get confused. But he made no objection as I shifted off the usual straight line and slowed while also heading right for the item I felt.

It didn't appear to be far below the surface, which was probably one of the reasons we had felt it so far out from its location. We didn't have to delve for this one.

There appeared to be more structures the closer we got, and I wasn't entirely sure they were all ruined and abandoned, so I kept a respectful distance above the place for a moment. I looked for signs of movement, but it was dark, late, and whatever area this was, it was a very long way away from anything.

I circled a few times, looking for movement or anything else that might tell me something about where I was and who might be impacted by me landing, but I couldn't see anyone. Of course, it was also the early hours of the morning and anyone living in this place would almost certainly be asleep.

Moving toward a more open area that was big enough to land in, I led my companions to a good spot and touched down. Douglas was quick to get down and hit the fast-release mechanism on the harness so it fell off me and allowed me to take human form within a few seconds.

By the time Flick and Neritas had landed, I was cautiously walking closer to the source. It appeared as if someone had carved huts and buildings into the rock, giving the place a strange, light forward and give us a sense of direction.

I didn't have any idea what to expect, but I moved as quietly as I could, just in case danger lurked. We passed several open-door buildings and I considered shining my light into them, but I was worried about what I would see. Some of them looked lived-in, with furniture of sorts near the doors although the light I dared to use often didn't penetrate further than a yard or two beyond the doorways.

When I went by a larger one, I noticed the scent of something that must have been cooking and a faint light flicker from within. I paused and waited for my friends to catch up.

"I think we're in some kind of village," I whispered. "Do you think we should try and wake someone or keep sneaking toward our goal?"

"Up to you, Your Highness. We're still on US soil, so whoever this is, they're some kind of tribe that is likely to speak our language and know they can't attack us legally." Douglas shrugged as if this was common knowledge and I shouldn't worry too much about it.

I tried not to think beyond the first part of what he'd told me. Whoever these people were, they were part of the

US, and even if they were a tribe of some kind, I wasn't going to be the first person to ever make contact with them. Despite this thought, they seemed more primitive than I would have expected from a place in the US, even if it was on one edge of the country.

"Is this an uncontacted tribe, you think?" Douglas asked after a few seconds, also keeping his voice low. It was in direct opposition to his previous statement and made it obvious he was growing just as worried.

"I didn't think there were any on this side of Mexico." I was willing to be proved wrong. It felt as if this was a tribe that didn't belong in the modern world, and that made this, in some ways, all the more exciting—and in others, very nerve-racking.

This was so unexpected. I had no idea what to do but I kept slowly walking. If nothing else, I figured that stopping in one place would be bad and moving toward the goal was at least progress of a sort.

Could I steal something from these people, though? If I had the chance, if they were all asleep, could I take what felt more and more like an artifact as I got closer?

I had no idea, but I opted to tackle that problem if and when I came to it. There were still a lot of other possibilities.

By the time we were three or four huts away from the artifact, we saw the first sign of movement. A man stood in the doorway of one of the buildings and it was clear he had been watching our approach. I hesitated, but then followed my gut instinct and bowed toward him.

"Are you the leader of this village? The aura I sense from afar has brought me to your people in a time of need."

He walked closer to me and I fought hard to appear calm, my heart racing as I studied him, looking for signs of anger or anything else negative.

"You have come at a very strange hour," he replied.

"I can only offer my apologies. I was trying to avoid those who would bring harm, and in darkness was the only way. We can return at a more convenient time if you wish."

He shook his head and looked at the three men with me, then he pointed out Douglas. "This man is a soldier. He is not like you three."

"No, but he's with me. I need his help and I trust him. He is a good man with a good heart." I was worried that this was going to ruin the entire conversation and he'd ask us to leave, but after a moment the man nodded and accepted my words.

"We knew of your coming. Is it you with the light blessing?" he asked me next.

"Light blessing?" I replied. "I'm a light dragon, if that makes any sense. I'm not human."

Again this earned me a nod, and I waited for there to be another question or something that might give me an idea of where his thoughts were going, but he didn't explain or ask me anything else. I didn't even know if this man was the person in charge or how to get back to talking about the artifact and how we might get hold of it.

"I am Chona, elder of this village. Come with me. I will show you what you seek and you will explain its reaction."

I lifted my eyebrows at the strange second part of the request, but he didn't elaborate and instead stepped out of his hut and motioned for me to follow him.

He led us deeper into the village and toward the object I

felt. It had some magic left in it and was active in some minor way as far as I could tell, but I wasn't sure exactly how or where or what it was doing and, just in case, I was loath to connect to it.

"Should one of us fly back to Detaris and let them know we found an artifact?" Flick asked.

I was about to shake my head when Douglas held up his phone. "I already let them know we found something but not the demon. I've got to check in every hour."

Although I frowned, I also understood him following protocol.

"Keep details vague if you can until we know what we're dealing with. This one doesn't feel like the others. I'm not sure it's one of the ten pieces we're looking for."

"Well, if it's not, it just means we've gained something else useful and still have a hunt to go on." Neritas shrugged and I had to admit he was right. Whatever this was, it was a discovery and certain to help us. All I had to do was get this village to let me have it and apparently explain how it worked.

But I had no idea how easy or doable that would be. It wasn't as if this situation came with a guide on how to navigate it, and I doubted there would be a do-over if I got it wrong.

As we went deeper into the village and came to the hut with the artifact inside, I paused. We were here and this felt strange. How could we be here and it be obviously out in the open? There were no protections, no traps. I could just feel it in the room ahead of us.

"This way. Let me show you what it is." The man continued through the doorway, seeming to not appreciate that I had stopped. I frowned, worried that I had done something wrong, and hoped that the others would keep up.

When I moved into the room, I gasped. This wasn't a dwelling but a purpose-built room for this object. It sat on a reed cushion in the middle of the room, on a sort of altar. Incense burned around the room and there were several other lights and candles lit. The item itself was also glowing, shedding a warm light that made the room look beautiful.

"This is stunning." I noticed Chona looked at it with a similar level of awe. In the light, I could see him better. He was wearing what looked like Native American garb from a couple of hundred years earlier, but muted, with no bright colors or adornments of any particular kind. Simple attire.

After taking him in, I gave my attention back to the object. It was a small oval inside a container. It appeared to have lots of little gems or reflective stones all over the surface, with the exception of what looked like a handle. It reflected back the light and made me wonder what it was for.

"It lit up," Chona said. "It doesn't normally do anything. But as you came closer it grew brighter. I knew something was coming, something was about to happen. I guard this, and then you arrived and—" He stopped and turned to me, the excitement clear in his eyes. "What is it?"

"I don't know yet. I wasn't expecting it to react to me either. May I get closer to it?" I asked.

"Yes, you may. I believe it likes your presence."

This was said with such simple conviction that I smiled

at him and moved toward the altar. I was careful not to touch or disturb anything as I got nearer to it and felt it more with my mind. It needed magic to power it. A slight draw came from whatever charge it had already.

It felt almost as if it had two separate charges in it. Both of them kept apart, neither interacting with each other, in the same way that I had been throwing charge into the other objects we had.

This was something new entirely and it was clear that it wasn't part of another artifact. This was entirely unique.

CHAPTER FOURTEEN

An awkward silence was developing, but I didn't want to break it until I was sure that there was a good reason to do so and I had enough information. And that meant taking a risk.

I carefully reached out with my mind, connecting to the object. At first, nothing happened, and I had the relief of not having magic sucked out of me on connection, something that had happened just enough times in the past that I worried about it now. Thankfully, it was a lot easier to hold this connection as well.

Something about this artifact felt familiar on one hand and yet strange and almost alien on the other. I didn't know if I liked it, but I was very curious about it. I let it have some of my energy, feeling my personal magical energy going into one of the reservoirs it carried. The other one, however, would only take energy from my connection to the isle of the ancestors, and even then, it was as if it was fussy about it.

It took me a moment to realize that it was only taking a

particular dragon color of energy in each well and keeping them separated, as if it were important to keep them on their own.

I tried to get it to do something else, but it seemed to need some kind of activation and greater control. The only thing I could do for now was to make it dimmer and brighter, as I could with any object.

"This does more than I can work out from here, but it uses the magic from the type of dragon I am and another, although I am not sure which yet," I finally explained.

My explanation seemed to be enough for our host. He was looking at me expectantly and with the same wide eyes he had looked at the object only a few minutes earlier.

"How did this artifact come to be here?" Neritas asked. He was the first one of us to think about some other element of the situation.

"It has been the honor of my tribe to protect it and look after it. The great ancestors were asked to do so. We were part of the Himuris tribe many years ago, but a great being visited us, one who could fly through the sky. He asked us to look after this item and told us that one day someone would return for it and we would know them by the way they could use it."

I blinked, confused about why a dragon would ask a human to look after an artifact, but I didn't deny that it appeared to have been placed here for someone like me to use. I just didn't know for sure what it was for, or what other color dragon was most needed to operate it. Not that it entirely mattered when I had my connection to the ancestors. I was able to fuel both parts of it either way.

"May I pick it up?" I asked, still wanting to handle this delicately.

"Yes, yes, please do, oh great one." Chona smiled. "It is yours. You are clearly its intended recipient. It will make the village proud to know our task is done, and done to the satisfaction of the great one. We will celebrate and feast. Please, please, let us join you in celebration and wonder and have this in the hands of its rightful owner once more." He motioned for me to go forward, the light in his eyes and beam on his face all the encouragement I could possibly want.

I inched closer and closer, still feeling for possible traps. In some ways, this tribal leader appeared to be too eager, as if he was compensating for something, but my mind could truly feel nothing else. And on top of that, the item itself was as easy to disconnect from as it had been to connect to.

There were no traps or tricks here. It was an artifact we had found in the middle of a village, and it was being given to me.

As I finally reached for it physically, I studied the container it was in and tried to work out how best to pick it up. Interestingly, it had something like a handprint on the top of it, with slight grooves where the fingers and thumb would sit on it to help it be gripped properly. It would sit in the palm of the hand, not much bigger than it, and only stick out a little way.

It was designed for the left hand, not the right, as if it was a tool that, once started, was just left to run. I took a deep breath and steadied myself, trying to stir up the courage to touch it and work out what it did. Something about this felt huge. I was finding something even more special than before.

Despite that feeling of taking a step toward something even greater than before, I took hold of it and lifted it up. It seemed to connect to me physically this time, suctioning onto my hand.

Everyone gasped, and Flick said, "You just disappeared."

"You can't see me?" I turned to the others.

"Nope. Can't see you but we can hear you. I'm not sure I can feel your magic in the same way either. It's muted, spread out and sort of thrown off. Like there's something here, but it's faint, and I can't get a pinpoint on anything." Neritas shook his head as if it was difficult to even try.

I was pleased about it. This was an amazing discovery.

I very carefully pulled it off my hand with the other one and then I watched the others find me again with their eyes, and all of them smiled at me.

If the tribal leader had been impressed before, he was practically ready to worship me now. I had vanished and reappeared before him, and I had used the device in his care to do it. This was something that no one had expected us to manage.

Without hesitation, I tried it again a few more times, putting it on my hand and taking it off again. Each time Neritas and Flick confirmed that I disappeared and reappeared. Douglas stood near the doorway, looking relaxed, but I could see the thoughts going around in his head and the concentration as he tried to figure out how he felt about this one.

I was careful to put it back in the container afterward,

understanding why it had a transparent box to nestle in as well. This also activated on being picked up.

It was interesting, as well. It could also be used as a lantern, and it looked inconspicuous when it was, like it had been designed in a time a thousand years earlier, when lights had been candles or oil inside metal containers. That alone would have fascinated Ben or Anthony.

"We should let the folks at Detaris know about this," Neritas suggested. "I don't really want to tell them. Just show them by sneaking into the elders' chambers and making them jump when we all appear, but—"

"We all appear?" Flick asked, picking up on Neritas suggesting we could all use it.

"Why not? It's a device. Even I can feel that it's modifiable. It's essentially bending light around the user. It should be able to bend light around bigger things, but I imagine it would use a lot more power to do that."

Neritas had a point and it made me want to pick it up and take a look at it again, but I yawned despite the discovery and the excitement of it. We had been up for a long time.

"Let everyone know who needs to that we've found an artifact, but not one of the ten pieces. And we'll get a little rest before returning with it." Douglas nodded as if he'd already done some of this, and it made me wonder what was being fed back to his boss by default. Neritas was swift to contact Detaris, and that left one matter. We were a long way away from the car, in another's village.

"You must rest and then celebrate with us," Chona interrupted our planning. "You cannot leave until we have prepared a great feast. I will get our tribe to begin this now. They will want as much time as possible."

I moved to stop him, not wanting him to wake anyone, but it was possible we had been talking too loudly or the villagers were very light sleepers, because I found many of them already awake and waiting outside when I went to follow.

The leader quickly spoke to everyone, using another language and talking hurriedly. At some point, he must have told them who I was because he beamed at me and the rest began grinning and clapping. After a minute or so more, he appeared to be done and the villagers all came up to me and touched an arm or my shoulders.

I let them, not sure what else to do. This was one of the strangest interactions I had ever had with people, and I didn't want to upset or offend anyone. As far as discoveries went, this was amazing. Knowing that I could make myself invisible at any moment and hopefully my friends as well made me feel a little safer. Invisibility would be a huge asset in my fight with the demon.

Although I wanted to rest, it soon became clear that I wasn't going to get to do so. Too many people wanted to talk to me and ask me questions. They didn't want to go back to sleep. All of the village wanted to party.

Thankfully, it wasn't long before they all hurried off to prepare food, and although one or two came to ask questions about foods and our likes, and Chona never stopped hovering nearby, he helped to bring my focus back to the object he had given me.

"This is a great honor," he said for the fourth or fifth

time. "Would you show me how it works again, show me your magic?"

I heard Flick chuckle as I nodded, wanting to play with it again anyway and knowing this would be the perfect opportunity. My hand slipped easily into the grooves, and I heard the gasp of a villager who noticed me disappear.

This time I tried to do more than just activate it, however. Focusing on what I felt, I tried to work out how to control it and expand what it could wrap around.

The field it operated over seemed to be a bubble, and I widened it slowly.

"Ummm... Neritas, I can only see half of you now," Flick said, mock concern in his voice. It was useful information and I carried on moving it until he was all gone.

"Wow, I can see you now," Neritas said, grinning at me as if this was perfectly natural. It was interesting and implied that the field was a forcefield bubble. I played with it a bit more, not sure how big I wanted to make it. As I'd grown it, the drain on the energy in the artifact had also grown, but it was still very little. The disappearing act cost me far less than I gained from the isle of the ancestors if I wanted to draw on it.

I was still experimenting with it, growing and shrinking it and starting to show Flick and Douglas alternative images and not just an empty space, when I felt something on the edge of my mind.

Pausing, I closed my eyes, worry filling me. Was this the demon coming after us again?

"What is it?" Neritas asked. He was the only one who could see me at that moment. Everyone else saw a replica of the small fire pit beside me.

I waited until I was sure before replying, "The demon is here."

Flick and Douglas both heard me and got to their feet, having sat to watch my antics. Douglas pulled out his phone and called for backup. Flick came toward where he thought I was, and I shut the illusion off so he could see me.

"We can't leave all these people and we can't defend them." I frowned as fear filled me.

"I'll fly to Detaris to get help as swiftly as possible." Flick moved as if to leave, but Douglas shook his head.

"The general will let Detaris know. Help will get here as soon as possible. Are we going to be up against corrupted humans?" Douglas asked.

I nodded, although I wasn't sure. What I felt was a mix of different entities, but I was fairly sure humans were among them.

"We need to get this village somewhere safer," Neritas said, echoing my next thought.

I nodded, not doubting that it was true, and hurried to Chona.

"The evil I feared would find me is on his way and he brings an army with him. I need to get your people and you out of here and somewhere safer. Will you lead them away?"

"Not if it will leave you in danger," he replied, not even hesitating. "Perhaps our next great act is to fight this evil with you. We are normally a more peaceful tribe, but we have had to defend ourselves before and you have great magic."

His faith in me felt misplaced, but I didn't want to put

his people in danger. My alternative was to leave and draw the danger away with me, but with just two other dragons and a single soldier, I didn't know how to do that either.

I froze, not sure what to do but aware, yet again, the decision lay on my shoulders and I had to figure it out or people were going to die.

"How wide do you think you can make this illusion field?" Neritas asked. "Can you hide the whole village and get us out of here and keep us out of danger until we can get backup? Sort of head toward the backup?"

"Unless I can also form a barrier, anyone who walks into the illusion is going to then see through it," I pointed out. It doesn't take long for there to be too obvious a group of people.

"Make some of the huts look like one big boulder and shelter all the people of the village inside. Then we can be in a more strategic place and just pick off the enemy, or you can make us invisible."

"For that, I might need multiple illusion fields." I frowned, still trying to wrap my head around the details. At least we were starting to form a plan.

The enemy was on its way, but I was going to keep the entire village safe if it was possible and put my life on the line if it wasn't.

I didn't need anyone else in the group to say anything for me to know that the demon had been led here. But was it by someone who stood with me, or by someone they had told?

I got the feeling that I was about to find out that distinction. Either this was going to work and I could trust the three men with me, or it wasn't going to, and I would have narrowed down my traitor's identity considerably. I just had to get through these next few hours and make sure I paid attention.

This might be the perfect setup to work out who my traitor was.

CHAPTER FIFTEEN

Chona helped Flick and Douglas get the villagers into the smallest number of huts possible, and I started working on the illusion, with Neritas as my guide.

Thankfully, we were still under the cover of darkness and I could get us hidden before the sky lightened and made us look more obvious from a long way out.

It helped that I felt the presence of the enemy from such a long way out that I had over fifteen minutes to get the villagers in two huts with the food split between them and get Neritas and me on one edge of the disguised area, within a space that would appear empty, and Flick and Douglas in another one. If the enemy got too close and came into the dome of illusion, we would kill them. Otherwise, we would wait.

The demon and his army kept coming closer, more cautious now that he probably couldn't feel us or the artifact properly, but we hadn't moved far from where we had started and I wasn't sure the illusion would trick anyone for long.

We were on the far edge of the village, where some boulders dotted the landscape already and the village was built more into the rocky bed of the ground than upward anyway. It was as unobtrusive as we could get.

Sound would still be a problem, however, and I didn't know how well the illusions would hold up under the light of day.

Everyone held still as we waited. The demon's army stopped about a hundred yards out from the edge of the village. I held my breath, aware that even if we protected the villagers, their buildings might end up decayed and rotted. They might lose their homes.

With the army at a standstill and the sky finally starting to lighten on the eastern horizon, I couldn't see very much of the army from where I was, but I could feel some of the ones up in the air coming our way as if they were trying to copy my attempt to find an artifact the last time and do a fly-by.

Although I had the assurance Neritas had given me that we couldn't be felt in the same way as normal, I was still worried that we would be noticed.

The demon was the easiest to feel from where I was. His presence was always the strongest. He flew by about twenty feet to my right and several hundred above, not even slowing or stopping. He couldn't tell where we were or what was going on.

We all kept as silent as possible as the demon flew across again. No one moved, and I barely dared to breathe. Because the artifact had magical charge in it already, I hadn't bothered to give it any more, but after about fifteen minutes of holding this area under the illusion, I started to worry that it might run out.

I wasn't sure it would be wise to charge it right now, however. I wanted to be sure that it wasn't going to draw attention. Magic was always easier to notice when it was being moved from one place to another and I didn't want to run the risk that something like that was noticeable when this didn't appear to be.

More minutes ticked by as the sky began to change from the starry dark of night to the dark blue of the incoming dawn. I was facing east and enjoyed the changing view as best I could.

The longer this went on, with the army not moving and the demon flying past, the safer I felt, until I wasn't worried.

If anyone had asked me how this trip might go and how well we would evade capture and survive, I wouldn't have thought it would be like this and I wouldn't have expected to find the perfect artifact for the situation I was in.

None of it made me feel any better about the humans who had been corrupted, however. They were all out there and I could feel them. I had to hope they could be saved and the team on their way to help us could also help save them. I wanted to save them. All of them.

The demon finally gave up flying overhead and stopped moving. I felt him land somewhere in front of us, a little further off than his army, but I couldn't see him once he landed.

He was too far away to make out, but the feeling subtly changed a few seconds later and then a human strode forward and out of the edge of the army, coming so perfectly toward me that I felt as if he saw me clearly. It made me take a step back, aware that this was the first time I had seen the demon take human form—an average, good-looking male.

In human form he was a little bit taller than me, dressed in a suit that could have come from any good men's store in any city in the country and somehow able to wear it in such a way that he didn't look overdressed but just right for how well-groomed he was. Women everywhere would have swooned over him.

With a shock of red hair not that dissimilar to my father's, he could have even been a relation of mine. But I had to remind myself that he wasn't, not even close.

Here and there I could tell that he wasn't quite human. His eyes showed no color and his fingers were slightly elongated. He also walked oddly, as if being a human wasn't something he was familiar with. As he came closer, there was the obvious smell of rot and decay.

I almost gagged on it and had to lift my hand to my mouth and nose to cover them from the stench and force down the desire to gag.

Although he glanced in my direction, there was no indication that he had heard my movement. He focused more on the dwellings on either side of himself and walked into one. It was strange to see him in this way and I was still trying to process what I was seeing, or if there was anything I should be doing about it.

I couldn't see him for some time, and I worried that he was up to something I didn't understand or that he was on to us and waiting for one of us to make a move or talk or give ourselves away somehow.

Although his army was made up of humans and shadow catchers, they didn't move the way they normally would. All the people were very regimented and controlled, and the shadow catchers swayed gently as if they were mesmerized. Finally their leader reappeared again.

As he held up some smoking embers that should have burned his skin, I could have sworn if I wasn't trying to be silent. It was evidence that someone had been there. We were likely to be hunted now.

"They haven't been gone long and could have hidden in here somewhere. Search the place," the demon commanded. His voice was familiar and sounded very like the one I'd heard in my head every time I had approached the gate.

It bought us some time, but it was likely to lead to discovery if we weren't careful and everyone got too close. I held where I was to watch what happened next.

Our allies were no doubt on the way here, and we hadn't gone as far away from Detaris as some of our adventures had taken us. There was a chance that we would be able to stay hidden until help arrived.

And on another positive note, no one in my group had betrayed our position yet, indirectly or otherwise.

There was still time for this to go wrong, however.

I watched as two of the usual tentacled handlers moved up through the army into the village as well. They were the only full demons that seemed to be able to control if it decayed whatever they touched, and they weren't harming anything right now.

Although I wasn't sure they would afford the huts the same courtesy once they got inside, I hoped this was a sign that these villagers weren't about to lose their homes. I already felt guilty enough that I had led the demon to their doors.

Instead of finding the demon's lair, I had brought him to a peaceful tribe. It was shitty enough as it was.

The handlers seemed to take their time, going into each dwelling one by one. The sound of furniture breaking and items being smashed came through the open doorways. Every time there was a very loud bang, I expected them to punch a hole through a wall, or someone in the huts to make a loud noise.

Thankfully, the tribe was silent. They comforted each other and remained huddled in their groups. They had a few kids and I worried about how they would react as the demons came closer and made more noise, but so far so good.

Another hour slipped by, and I needed to shift. I used the noise from the handlers going through the huts to scratch itches and change how much weight was on each foot. I didn't dare sit down or stop watching what the handlers or the rest of the army were doing.

Most of them had stopped in a rough circle around the village, but they weren't entirely static and the circle wasn't perfect. If we needed to make a run for it, the northeast was the best option. Of course, that was because it was also the most difficult terrain, but I hoped that I would have some more dragons by then or could keep using this illusion device.

After almost two hours of use, the artifact had used up about a quarter of the magic inside it. Enough that I knew I was draining it and needed to be careful, but not enough for me to decide to take the risk of topping it up yet.

The sun was starting to appear on the eastern horizon as well, making it harder for me to see what was going on with the light in my face, but I could still feel.

The handlers continued to come closer and were at the huts nearest us by the time another hour had passed. I could feel the demon pacing back and forth by then. We had used the noise they were creating to get drinks, relieve our aching feet for a moment, and have a very hushed conversation about how much longer we might have to wait for help to arrive.

Because it had been passed on that we had civilians with us and were struggling to protect them, I learned that they had split forces, sending ahead a strike team and getting them to meet up with other dragons who were closer. Soldiers were also on their way from a much closer army base, one that had received some of the charged weapons we had created already.

It was all the solace we had, but we still had to wait a little while longer. The enemy was barely more than fifteen yards from us now.

We'd pulled back until we were close to the illusionary boulders, hoping that no one came too close, but the demon himself reappeared before they had finished with the final two dwellings near us.

"Have you found them? Where are they?" he asked, the anger clear in his voice.

The handlers didn't respond in intelligible sentences but came out of the dwelling, waved their tentacles around, and made strange sounds with what passed as mouths.

"They have to be here somewhere. There was no way for them to leave, and that dumb red dragon who calls herself queen isn't that magicked-up that she can teleport them out of here. I felt her. She might have learned how to hide herself, but they're here."

I listened, grateful for being able to overhear, get to know my enemy a little better, and make him mad for once. But I also felt my temper flaring. This demon had been directly responsible for so many deaths and the pain of many others. I wanted him dealt with.

As I waited to see what the handlers did next, I watched him close his eyes, almost as if he was trying to do what I did sometimes and feel for me. I focused on the same thing but I wasn't about to close my eyes. I needed to see how close they were getting to the illusion and if we were in danger of being discovered.

I could easily feel the aura of the demon and his mind trying to reach out and connect. From this close, I could also see the connections he already had running out from him to all of the handlers. They were his minions in more ways than one.

On top of that, I could feel the artifacts he carried. He had only a couple of them on him, not all four.

The handlers didn't move, almost as if they had been told to hold still as well. Their tentacles were frozen in midair.

His connections and mind felt out toward me and I shrank back, but it was as if they came close and seemed to slip by. The artifact I held was hiding my magic aura as well as the visual trace of us.

He continued to probe for some time, feeling down and

around the entire area, and his brow furrowed more and more as he still didn't detect us.

He opened his eyes and looked around the area again. I held my breath as he gazed my way once more, as if he could almost see me and wasn't convinced that the large rock surface in front of him was real. It soon passed, however, and he walked away again.

His fists were clenched and he moved with more stiffness than before. We might have been in a pretty bad predicament, just four fighters surrounded by an entire army, but in that moment I was smug. For once, I was screwing with his head, and not the other way around.

Despite my glee, I knew this couldn't last forever. If he kept looking, at some point a handler or he himself would try to climb the rocks or get too close for us to remain hidden, or a child or adult in the village would make too much noise.

We needed the cavalry to arrive, and we needed it soon.

CHAPTER SIXTEEN

The handlers had begun to get more clever, feeling out and decaying structures and possessions. And they had shadow catchers helping them.

"We're not going to be able to hide much longer. We might want to consider a way to get everyone out of here," Neritas whispered, so close to my ear that he barely made a sound.

"How?" I asked, so worried and stressed out by the comment that I spoke louder than I intended. "If we so much as move, we will get overrun before we can get anywhere."

I noticed that a handler and several shadow catchers were looking our way. The latter swayed and seemed to listen, much the way they had the very first time I had encountered them.

Although I couldn't give Neritas a plan for what to do to get away, I knew he was right and there was a good chance we were going to need to try our best to get ourselves out of this situation and in the air with as many villagers as possible.

Thinking about it for a moment, I considered everything I was capable of doing. Maybe we could draw some of the monsters in and pick them off? But we were going to need to be very careful how we did it. I needed to wait for the right moment.

Not long after I thought this, the demon launched himself into the air again and flew around, back in the form I was used to seeing him in. He circled several times, coming in closer from the perimeter of his army. I waited for him to fly overhead several times before he moved on.

Eventually, he flew up higher and further away, as if something had distracted him and he wanted to go see what it was. At the same time, the handlers paused their searching and the shadow catchers acted on their own for a few seconds. I could only hope that this meant the reinforcements had arrived.

One handler immediately came our way again. I nodded to Neritas and Flick, getting Douglas to watch our back as we moved toward the area of our illusion where the handler was closest. I began to form a dark patch, not pitch black but darker than the surrounding area.

At the same time, I reached down and picked up a small rock. As the handler and the shadow catchers near it separated and the minions set to attacking one of the dwellings further away, I dropped the rock.

It bounced and skittered across the ground, drawing the handler's attention. The creature raced toward us, coming partially into the illusion. As soon as it did, I extended the illusion bubble and made the area pitch black so it couldn't see us. Neritas, Flick, and I sprang into action, stabbing at it while I kept it wrapped in darkness.

The creature let out a couple of screeches and flailed about, drawing some more attention our way, but we killed it quickly while it was handicapped, already tired from doing its master's bidding. All three of us were practiced against this type of handler.

As soon as it was dead, the carcass half-burned away to vapor and the rest a heap on the ground, I got all three of us to step back and pulled the illusion back to the smallest circumference that would still hide us.

It revealed the dead handler to the rest of the army, which confused another nearby handler. The second was more cautious, coming toward its dead brother but far more slowly than the first had been to investigate. Several shadow catchers came with it, but they were still a fair way behind when Flick and Neritas let me know they were ready to go again.

For a second time, I extended the illusion field just far enough to bring the handler in with us, made it pitch black around its head, and the three of us rushed in to kill it. The creature was no more capable than his companion, and we soon dispatched that one as well.

Two of the shadow catchers were very close to our illusion field when we killed their handler, but without a leader to guide them, they froze for just long enough that the three of us could fall right back again and bring our bubble back with us.

It was only as we got back to our starting positions that I noticed one of us must have stepped in some handler blood and it had left footprints on the ground coming our way. On top of that, the demon was on his way back to us, finally disturbed enough by losing two handlers that he was returning.

The sun started to burn off the demon ichor and it began to vaporize and fade, but I didn't know if it would be gone in time. The demon was flying fast.

Only a second later I felt the first new friendly presence also heading in. Some dragons were on their way, though I couldn't be sure who. I wasn't familiar enough with the energy signatures they gave off, but I could tell it was a variety of colors and plenty of them were strong and brimming with magic.

I considered connecting to them, but I worried that it would draw attention to us again and I didn't know what reinforcements to expect. This could just be the dragons from a few of the closer cities. While they might be able to do a little to help, if I drew them into the center of this fight I could get them killed as easily as everyone else.

The demon landed again, dropping from the sky much the way Flick did. He studied the corpses, taking in the destruction, and then let out a loud screeching roar of anger. His entire army seemed to drop to the ground, momentarily stunned by whatever their master communicated through their connections to him.

Slowly they all got back up and shifted into a different army formation. More of them came up toward the village while others turned toward the incoming dragons. We weren't going to be able to hide much longer.

"We really need it to be nighttime again," Neritas whispered. "And some help getting everyone out of here."

I looked at him. His words had given me a brilliant idea.

He was a genius and had stumbled upon the exact sort of thing we could now do.

I took a small step sideways, closer to Flick. "When I make it really dark, Flick, I need you to get into the air, get to those dragons and guide them all here. Between you, get the villagers out of here and somewhere safe. Find the nearest human soldiers and work with Douglas if you need to."

"What are you going to do?" Flick asked me. We didn't bother to be as quiet now that the game was close to being up and we were about to go on the offensive.

"Work my magic and show that smarmy, arrogant demon what this queen has learned to do lately."

Flick grinned, and the gesture was infectious as I pulled out the tranquilizer gun that the US Army had loaned me. It didn't have a lot of ammo, but the weapon was for an army to use and I was just one person. With any luck, the few humans I would be able to sedate would help us figure out how to save the rest.

Neritas came to my side again, exactly as I'd hoped. I hoped everyone was ready, as Flick and Douglas hurried into a hut each to tell the villagers that the plan was changing. We didn't have much time and Neritas and I were going to have to hold off a lot of demons and corrupted creatures as soon as this started.

At the same time as I pulled all of the yellow dragon energy out of the artifact so it could only control light and dark, I pushed the illusion net out far enough to encompass all of the entities I felt. I plunged everyone into total darkness.

The chaos was immediate and complete, as the demon

stopped flying and trying to figure out where we were. I knew that he could feel us, but the dragons in the sky were close enough to him that he didn't come rushing toward me straight away, still undecided.

He continued to circle, and his army became essentially blind. Anywhere I could sense a shadow catcher within a certain radius, I charged the ground around them and tried to smother them in magic.

I lifted my gun and used a strange combination of magic and natural abilities to make sure my bullet hit the target. Within seconds, humans were collapsing while the shadow catchers roasted where they stood. It wasn't an easy thing to do, and it required me to pull all the magic I could from the ancestors for a while, use my own magic fast, and suck it from the armor, weapons, and dragons around me.

It was an all-out blast of energy and unsustainable, but I didn't have to hold it for long—just long enough that everyone with me could flee and find the relative safety of more allies. Flick and Douglas didn't waste any of the time I bought them. Flick was soon rushing off to guide in our help, while Douglas got the villagers ready to be airlifted out of there.

Neritas didn't try to brute-force the magic as I did. He focused more on shooting the humans I hadn't and supplying me with more magic and filling in where I might have missed something. He provided the perfect backup for the situation I was in, allowing me to focus on the overwhelm and letting him pick off what I didn't catch.

Very soon, dragons were flying in and Douglas was

calling that the soldiers had arrived as well and set up a temporary hold point.

"Get the villagers behind the line of soldiers and take a couple of dragons who can use magic to hold the ground in front of them," I commanded.

"They're all armed with tranqs as well." I heard the grin in Douglas's voice as Flick landed again, already having taken his first person to safety.

The demon in the sky didn't take too kindly to having dragons fly across his army, and he brought in the sky creatures to harry everyone, but Jace must have been up there because she quickly took over. She flew hard through the birds and tore them apart. I tried to make a charged area of air above the dragons carrying villagers, helping to protect them, and eased off the charged land on the ground now that the plan was working.

All the handlers on the ground had grown more cautious after watching just two dragons slaughter or knock out a significant percentage of their army in minutes. I kept up the pressure just enough, but I knew I couldn't do this much longer. The magic was draining too fast from every source and the connection to the isle of the ancestors was dwindling, as it always did when I drew too much.

I felt for the positions of all the dragons and dared to glance toward Flick as he came back.

This is the last run, he said, anticipating my question. *Fly away with us and get this artifact out of here.*

I almost didn't need to, however, as the demon gave up and flew away from us, calling his army back with him. I'd killed and neutralized so many of his fighters in a short space of time, and so many were still wrapped in darkness they couldn't see that he had no idea where I was.

A few seconds later I felt another element in my favor. More dragons were flying in from the north—the rest of the help I had sent for. I held onto the darkness for a little longer, but rather than charge any more of the ground, I let the army flee.

Though I backed off to preserve my energy a little more, all the dragons under Alitas attacked, and the soldiers that had just arrived hit as much as they could with the tranquilizers. The weaponry didn't work on shadow catchers, but it knocked out even more of the humans and even took down a handler when they hit it with a lot of shots at once.

I turned off the illusion artifact and stowed it away as the enemies flowed through the village. I focused on taking out easy targets, rushing at the shadow catchers with my sword and fighting alongside Neritas so we could clear a path between our forces again. The village was in tatters and there were unconscious humans everywhere, but we had survived until help arrived.

Even with the demon's army retreating, there were so many of them and the US soldiers were so keen to get some payback that many more shadow catchers died and we kept even more corrupted humans from fleeing with the demon.

It wasn't until we finally stopped, surrounded by vapor, unconscious people, and the remains of a couple of handlers we had run down and finished off that I realized how exhausted I was. I collapsed where I stood on the hot desert sand.

Neritas sat beside me, also panting and looking drained. He had given me a lot of his own magic and never left my side. I leaned into him, grateful for his presence. He slipped one arm around me, partly leaning back and partly propping us up. For now, it was enough and everything we needed.

CHAPTER SEVENTEEN

As the demon army fled from my mind and more dragons arrived, someone handed me a sandwich and a cup of coffee. Neritas was offered the same a few seconds later and we munched, the silence still soothing between us.

I looked around as I ate and drank, noticing the upset villagers as they returned to the wreckage of their village, and Alitas working with Colonel Flint to get everyone safe and reunite all their families. As far as I could see, only a few dragons were sporting injuries and Flick was already healing them.

For a few more minutes I hung back, letting my people handle everything while I rested and tried to work out what was needed first.

Temporary shelters popped up in a matter of minutes, courtesy of the US Army, giving the villagers and many of the unconscious humans shelter from the sun. It wasn't enough for how many humans there were, and when Alitas went to help a soldier move one under a raised tarp, he pulled his hand back with a hiss of pain.

Even from where I was sitting, I could see the rotten flesh that even the briefest of touches from the corrupted human had caused him. It was as if he'd tried to grab a shadow catcher with his bare hand.

I got up, determined to go to his aid no matter how tired I was. Although he was attempting to be stoic about it, the pain was clear on his face. He quickly warned everyone else not to touch the bodies, and they were all left out in the sun a little longer.

As soon as I reached Alitas I began healing his hand, not an easy process with his kind of wound and no device, but I relieved the pain he was feeling and helped lessen the damage. He breathed more easily within seconds, and after a couple of minutes, I had repaired most of the damage.

Thankfully, he had only grabbed the human lightly and let go fast or it could have been a lot worse, but it made me wonder how we were going to help these people. At some point, the sedative would wear off, and if we didn't have them back to normal by then, they were all going to attack us again.

I moved toward one and Alitas grabbed my arm. "Don't get too close to them."

Although I appreciated his concern, I knew I couldn't ignore them. We had to help them. But if they were like the shadow catchers now, I wasn't sure how to save them.

"Let me try a few things and see if we can save them," I replied, but no sooner had I said it than more soldiers arrived with more vehicles, bringing supplies.

They started erecting more tents, and a couple of scientists or medical professionals came up. The message not to touch the humans was passed around, and the soldiers tried to usher everyone away from the unconscious corrupted humans.

"I'd like to try and get one of the people onto a medical table and examine them before they wake up," a woman said as she came closer to me. We were standing beside one of the bodies closest to the tent.

"You can't move him," I replied for the soldiers who were listening to her orders. "If they rotted the flesh on Alitas' hand, then they will also decay anything they are touched with or placed on. All you can do is erect tents over them so they don't burn in this sun."

"I am not leaving patients to die or otherwise rise again and attack. I have been tasked with understanding this disease they have been given and it is my duty to see them healed and our understanding grown." She lifted her chin higher and made it clear I had an argument on my hands.

"We're on the same side here. I don't want to stop you from doing your job. You are going to have to do it on the ground, but I will assist however I can." I tried to motion for the nearest soldiers to bring the next tent and erect it over the area of humans, not beside them, even if they had to be careful how they put it up.

No one changed their plans, and I sighed as the doctor ordered her equipment anyway. Thankfully, the soldiers who came up to aid her refused to touch the person and reiterated what I had told her. There was no way she could do what she wanted.

Almost as if she was determined to find some way around it and show me up, she knelt beside the body and pulled a stethoscope from her pocket. I rolled my eyes as she tried to put it on the man's chest and listen for his heartbeat. I knew she was just trying to help, but this wasn't going to work.

As I'd expected, the part she pressed to the corrupted human soon decayed away, rusting and falling apart. She let out a squeal and quickly leaped to her feet.

"You really might want to let me try and get the corruption out of him *before* you do your tests. I know you're here to help and you have your orders, but we need to make this safe for you."

She gulped and pursed her lips but eventually she gave me a quick nod. If nothing else, she understood why I was there. Alitas and Neritas tried to get me to stop.

"Are you sure you have the capacity for this?" Neritas asked, beating Alitas to the verbal protest.

"I have some energy left and I will take this gently. You're both here if I need anything," I tried to sound more confident than I was.

This was such a new situation that I had no idea how to handle it, but that didn't mean I was going to give up. I was meant to protect humanity and I hadn't kept the demon from these people. It had to be me who tried to put this right and save as many people as possible.

I closed my eyes, just a few inches from the body, and concentrated. Although I reached for a connection with the human, I didn't attach to it at first, trying to get a feel for the magic within him. He didn't have any inside the same way a dragon did, but then humans didn't normally have anything magical in them.

No matter how many times I had tried to connect to the soldiers and flow magic in and out of them the way I did a dragon, or even sense where they were, it wasn't the same. I could help them run faster or combat fatigue by pushing magic into them and help heal them by speeding up what their bodies did, but it wasn't something they could store. I was using it on them, not giving it to them.

But this human felt like an energized being, in the same way, the demon and the handlers and shadow catchers felt energized. The opposite sensation of dragons. I knew that as soon as I connected to this human it was going to drain magic from me, just like the portals spewing out shadow catchers or the traps around artifact pieces.

Somehow, I needed to do this in a controlled way. I needed to not tear apart or kill this person as I healed it. As such, I made sure that I wasn't connected to anything but the isle of the ancestors. With the connection being much slower and smaller, I hoped that it would stop this person from being able to rip energy from me at speed.

Concentrating on nothing but this connection, I finally let my magic touch the man and slide into him. It tried to suck more out of me, but the pull was one I had begun to get used to and I fought it despite the discomfort I felt. As my magic met the corruption, it seemed to fight until my energy overwhelmed it.

"It might be working," Neritas said beside me, his voice distracting me a little but not so much I couldn't keep the flow controlled.

"Only sort of," Alitas replied. "He's beginning to look more hurt as the corruption recedes."

I felt the damage Alitas was talking about and encouraged the body to heal itself. The body's response seemed to be sluggish, but I used magic to simulate the natural healing as best I could, and it responded. I kept the decrease of the corruption slow and steady, healing what I could along the way and fighting hard to keep the man alive.

After a little while, Neritas got the gist of what I was doing and began helping. He healed while I focused on the corruption. It made the task easier and allowed me to work faster.

About ten minutes in, the man gasped and sat up. Immediately he reached for me and grabbed my arm.

"Where am I?" he asked as I tried to work out if he was hurting me or not. I eventually settled on not. His grip was tight and pinching but with no decay.

"You're in the middle of the Arizona desert with friendly soldiers and dragons. The demon took you for a while, but you're safe now. We're healing you but we're not done yet. Can you give me a few more minutes to finish the job?" I asked, trying to sound as casual as possible.

His eyes went wide, and his mouth opened and closed several times as he tried to process what I'd said. I took the opportunity to heal him further and cleanse the last of the corruption from him.

"There, he's all yours and will hopefully be okay," I said to the doctor who still hovered nearby. Someone ran up with a new stethoscope for her and she used it with a lot more caution this time.

I moved straight onto the next human, repeating the process, a soldier on hand as soon as I was done to explain to the human what was going on. Not all of them woke up. Neritas healed without also combating the sedative in the tranquilizer, but they hadn't all been knocked out at the same time, and some were bigger than others and needed more to knock them out for longer. None of us wanted everyone to wake up in a mass panic, so we let them stay sedated as long as possible so the staff coming in had a chance to get in control of things before they were overwhelmed.

While I worked, more dragons landed and tried to help too, but very few of them had the strength to slowly fight the corruption. After a few attempts, most of them simply provided magic to me and acted as guards and protection while the soldiers helped to organize and guide me to the next best people to help.

More shades popped up and people who were healed were taken into tents and looked after. Now and then someone handed me food and drink, but it was quick snacks and gulps of water between people. I was on a clock, and some of the people took a lot more healing.

Some who had far more corruption in them were a lot more damaged, and the healing process was far more taxing for me and Neritas. Several dragons stepped in and we called for more medics as well. One of the corrupted humans didn't make it, despite everything we tried to do to help him.

Hours slipped by as I helped person after person and used more and more magic. It was exhausting on top of everything else, but every time I thought of stopping, more dragons arrived with at least a little more magic for me to use, someone handed me some more food, and I looked out over the humans who were still corrupted and in need of help while I hurriedly chewed.

Neritas didn't leave my side and Alitas was never far away either, though they were almost as exhausted. Eventually I reached the end of the array of people and pulled the last of the corruption out of a young woman who couldn't have been more than eighteen or nineteen. She didn't wake up when I was done, but she was breathing easily.

I walked away when no one guided me to another person, and Alitas immediately wrapped an arm around me to help keep me going.

"They've already set up a tent for you to sleep in and get some rest. You've saved all these people. You've fought back corruption, Scarlet. Do you have any idea how monumental this is?" Alitas' voice was low but excited.

Although I was almost too tired to care, I smiled at him and felt Neritas lean in closer as well. Both their eyes shone with pride as they looked at me. Was this really so huge? All I had done was try to fix the mistakes of my past.

The people had needed someone to save them, so I had done everything I could. It was what I was meant to do.

When Alitas escorted me into one of the smaller tents and I saw a few beds laid out and several other dragons resting, I exhaled with relief to be out of the limelight and public focus and get to sit down. I was beyond tired at first. So much adrenaline and stress pumped through me that I needed to calm down before I could sleep.

I spent the next few minutes showing the other dragons the artifact I had found, how it worked, and getting debriefs from everyone as well as sharing my story of what had happened.

It was a relief to hear that the general had told Detaris of the trouble we were in and offered every help to get the dragons here quicker. Colonel Flint had handled everything else, having been stationed closer and able to get in the air and get his squad here even faster.

With the combined efforts of the US Army and my dragons, the response had been swift, but we had all given everything we had to the fight. It didn't take long for Alitas to hand over the safety side of things to a fresh honor guard and encourage the rest of us to get some sleep.

I still took a little while to drift off, curled up on a camping bed against Neritas with him cuddling me from behind. He fell asleep easily, as he always did, but I stayed awake, worrying. The demon was making an army of humans, and if I was one of only a few dragons who could help save them, were we ever going to win?

There was no way to know, but I wasn't about to give up. As soon as I was rested I was going to get back to work and do everything I could to stop him.

CHAPTER EIGHTEEN

As soon as I was awake I was aware of an array of sounds and smells. I opened my eyes to see Neritas, Flick, Alitas, and several of the other dragons in the tent helping themselves to some hot food. It looked like a stew, plus plenty of sodas, water, and all sorts of other snacks.

I sat up as Neritas headed my way with a plate. Although I had no idea how long I had been asleep, I felt a lot better and joined them all at the small makeshift table. Everything was army-issue pop-up furniture and gear, but the food was decent and I wolfed down the entire plate before getting a second helping.

Once I was done and we had discussed the state of everything so far, Alitas sat back and frowned, looking at his phone.

"What?" I asked, my stomach sinking.

"While we were all sleeping, the demon didn't rest. He's flown all the way over to the coast of Europe," Alitas explained.

"Flown? With his human army as well?" His words, like

the whole situation, didn't make much sense, and my still slightly sleep-deprived brain struggled to process what I was hearing.

Before long there were shouts outside and we rushed out of our tent toward the main hub that had been set up. I was admitted, along with several other official-looking soldiers. I spotted Douglas and hurried up to him.

"What's going on, Lieutenant?" I asked as soon as I was close enough to get his version of events.

"Captain," he replied with a grin. "Our success here today got me promoted. But as for what's going on, the demon has hit somewhere again. Somewhere out of US Army jurisdiction, and he's hit hard."

"With corrupted humans as well?" Once again I asked about the humans, not sure how he could have gotten an army so far so fast.

Douglas shrugged and motioned for me to follow him. The colonel was pulling up a news feed from a foreign station on a large monitor, and several soldiers and other personnel had gathered around. They parted for me and Neritas, and Alitas and Flick came right after.

We watched live on the screen as the demon brought in an army of his usual forces, humans as well, and attacked what appeared to be another human settlement at first. People ran screaming, and even the news reporters didn't want to get too close.

No one moved for several more minutes, until a dragon appeared from behind some kind of force field near an open area of a river. The dragon flew high up into the air, trying to make a run for it. Another followed it, and another after that.

"There's a dragon city there?" I asked Alitas, turning to get information from him.

"So it would appear," he replied. "But no one checked in and told Detaris that there was trouble. They didn't know about this until I told them."

"Who told you?" I was aware that this wasn't a good conversation to be having in front of all the soldiers and human staff, but I didn't care. Dragons were running away and leaving humans to fend for themselves, and I wasn't anywhere near the demon and his army.

"One of the honor guard in the human world let me know. He saw it on the news like the rest of us." Alitas frowned, catching on to what I was thinking.

"How quickly can we get there?" I asked no one else in particular. The captain placed a gentle hand on my shoulders.

"No one could get you there in time. If this is happening live in Europe, there is nothing that any of us can do."

"I can't do nothing," I replied, not hiding my frustration.

Neritas put his arm around me. "You have already done an amazing amount. Think of all the people you have saved in the last day or so. All the people *we* saved. This battle is far from over, and no matter how many artifacts he collects and pieces he gathers, we will find a way to beat him."

"Neritas is right," Colonel Flint said, joining my group. "The last time this foul creature was defeated, it sounds as if dragons stood alone, but now you have humanity on your side, and we might not be perfectly effective on our own, but we are trained to fight and many of us consider it an honor to fight alongside you."

I nodded, grateful for the words of encouragement on some level and not sure I could keep watching the live show of what the demon was doing. Despite that, I didn't look away. Something about making sure I witnessed it brought me some comfort and made me feel like at least the innocents' deaths didn't go unnoticed.

I was going to make this demon pay.

Somehow.

"Why don't we go see how all the people we saved are doing and see if any of them can be helped with some more healing and then head back to Detaris to figure the rest of this out and train everyone we can how to remove the corruption?" Flick suggested.

It was a far better idea than standing around helplessly when I had no way of getting to a fight in time to change its outcome. Focusing on what I could control was a far better way to be a leader, but it wasn't always easy. I also knew that we should keep trying to find his lair, but we had the same problems for now and Ben would still be focused on that task for me.

I let the others lead, finding myself flanked on all sides by my fellow dragons and soldiers as we all went to check on the humans. One of the largest tents had been turned into a field hospital and research facility, and several doctors and nurses with white or blue coats over their army fatigues moved back and forth between beds full of people.

A few were sectioned off away from the others, and I knew that these would be the hardest hit and the ones most in need of our attention. We went straight to them, fanning out and healing them a little more.

It didn't make any of them completely better, but the medical staff, including Dr. Hargreaves, the doctor who had been the first on the scene, soon arrived and took vitals and measured the improvements we'd made to their health.

There was one particular man who was alive, but barely. It had been touch and go when we'd finished removing the corruption within him and healed him enough to be transported into this tent. Both I and the doctor went to his side now.

"I'm keeping him stable, but there isn't much hope for him recovering," Dr. Hargreaves said. "Not with what we can do."

"When it comes to healing, we only use what the body already has available to it, but there's a chance that it can do something the body isn't doing for some reason. Give me a moment." I closed my eyes so I could focus, wanting to be sure that I didn't screw this up. I also pulled out a healing device this time. It made things easier and helped target the right parts of the body.

As I tried to repair whatever I thought was wrong, and explored with the device, I found very little that actually needed fixing until I got to a small part of the brain. It was almost as if the corruption had fought with some of the cells. I wasn't entirely sure how to proceed, knowing that the mind was more complicated than just repairing cells.

Stopping for a moment, I relayed this to the doctor and tried to explain what I was seeing. She asked me several questions about the part of the brain and what might be damaged, to work out if it was what was keeping him in a coma, but without medical training I could only help so much.

Eventually we both agreed that me trying to heal the damage was the only thing that could be done to help him anyway, and as long as I couldn't make it any worse I ought to try. I concentrated again and got to work, taking my time and trying to heal him slowly. I noticed that once I got past a certain point, the body appeared to take over naturally again, healing more of the cells and replacing them on its own as it would have done normally.

Something had been stopping the body from even trying to heal itself and I had got it going again. I could only speed that process up so much, however, and I soon had to stop.

When I was done the man was still in a coma, but I once again told the doctor what I thought had changed.

"It sounds as if he might wake up, then, at some point?" Dr. Hargreaves asked.

"I think so, but I don't know when and I'm not sure if it will be with anything remaining of his mind. I healed his body, but the personality and many other elements may already be gone."

Silence fell between us as we both looked at the man. It wasn't a pleasant thought, but we could only wait and see.

"If you've got a moment, I'd like to show you something else I've discovered since I got here. It's still early days and I'm not sure what can be done with it, but I think it could help." She tipped her head toward a small desk she'd set up in one corner of the tent and a bunch of equipment she had around it.

Although I wasn't sure I'd understand what she was working on, I followed her eagerly. If there was something she could do to help save these people, I was going to embrace it with open arms. As Douglas and Flint had both made clear, humanity was going to help in the fight this time and, in some ways, might well be able to help save themselves.

At her desk, she motioned for me to take one of the stools. Neritas and the other dragons had finished up in the curtained-off areas by now and joined us. The doctor didn't appear to mind gaining even more of an audience as she showed me the blood samples she had taken from various patients before we'd slept.

"I sent a few off to be analyzed as soon as possible, and due to the nature of this situation they were processed fast. They found something remarkable that may help all of us." Dr. Hargreaves paused for dramatic effect, almost as if she hoped that one of us would demand more info, but after glancing at us briefly, she continued. "There are antibodies against something entirely new. We think it is whatever the creature uses to control the humans."

"Their bodies are fighting it?" I asked.

"Yes." Her eyes shone as she turned to me. "Yes. It would appear so. See?"

For the next few minutes, she showed us the lab results and what was found, matching up blood samples with different people and a rating system she had already given them for how hurt they were once I'd originally cleansed them. It was clear that the worse the corruption had been and the more damaged the individual, the more antibodies their bodies had created.

"This is all fascinating, and I can see how this is positive news. But how can it be used to help?" Alitas asked, waiting for the right moment and gently cutting through the scientific explanations. "What can we do to save all the corrupted humans currently in the demon's army before they're so damaged that we lose them as well?"

Dr. Hargreaves didn't show any sign of offense at being asked such a blunt question and smiled as she turned to us all. When she was sure she had the attention of every dragon, she put her hands together and finally explained.

"If there are antibodies, then we can take them from one person and give a concentrated dose to another. We can literally help the human body fight this, and fight before it takes too much of a hold. It might mean that a single injection or even a shot similar to a tranquilizer dart could give the people the creature has taken a fighting chance to recover on their own."

I blinked, struggling to get my head around what she was telling me.

"We might even be able to give people protection ahead of time. Not just help people recover but also stop them from being taken control of in the first place. Like a vaccine of sorts, if it will make it easier to understand. If nothing else, it's highly likely to make them able to resist longer and give you and your dragon allies time to get to a place and then help."

"Thank you, Dr. Hargreaves. You're right, this is wonderful news. Whatever you need to make this antibody cocktail and get some kind of advance protection, let us know and we will aid you in getting it."

"Please, call me Alice." She beamed and it made me

wonder how rarely anyone was ever given funding for these sorts of things. Had we just made her day in more ways than one?

I had no idea, but she had just given me hope. If there was a chance that we could protect people before the demon even got to them, we needed to take it, and then we could focus on saving the ones already taken. But it could take a while.

Judging by the brain of the human who had been corrupted for a long time, the people already corrupted may not have a lot of time. I needed to get to them and try to get them back on their feet and human again.

Armed with more knowledge than the last time I had been in Detaris, I opted to head back to the dragon city. After standing beside them in battle and not being betrayed, I felt as if I could go back to trusting Neritas, Flick, and Douglas. My traitor wasn't one of those three or we never would have remained hidden and safe until help arrived.

I still didn't know who the traitor was, however. And now I had to find yet more artifact pieces. The demon had half of them and I only had one, plus an artifact no one had been looking for.

Before I left the area, I found the villagers and Chona to check that they were being well taken care of. They were in a group of tents, some of which had been erected over the more broken of the dwellings the village had lived in.

"Are you all being looked after?" I looked around to at least see that there was plenty of food and water and that everyone looked warm and calm.

"Yes, we are. Many are sad for what they have lost and

the beauty of our home being gone, but after seeing the evil you fight we are glad that we could aid you and feel that it was an honor to have hosted you. You protected us, hid us, and your friends risked their lives to get us out of danger. We will rebuild and know that in our time of need, the gods sent you to us and saw fit to let us all live."

It was a relief to hear that they were all fine, but I continued to ask questions and check what details I could to be sure. I promised to send what aid I could from my own dragon resources and finally walked away.

This mission hadn't been anything like I'd expected or hoped it to be. In a lot of ways, it had been far better.

CHAPTER NINETEEN

Although I felt better for being in Detaris, I always felt as if presenting everything to the elders after a trip out of the city was like having to explain my actions to the principal of the school. It always seemed like a good idea at the time, but in retrospect and thinking about it all from a more detached position and vantage point, it made me question everything I did.

On top of that, General Miller also wanted to know everything, and while Captain Douglas could fill him in, there were certain questions and elements of the situation that only I could put in.

Thankfully, the elders and General Miller agreed to hold a joint debrief again in the elders' chamber on Detaris. The question of who the traitor was never left the forefront of my mind, but I still had to keep that piece of info to myself. I wanted to tell Neritas and Flick but that couldn't happen yet.

Instead, I spent what felt like another day telling everyone what had happened. I had to show off the new device several times and explain how I'd used it to protect the village. The Detaris elders were particularly interested in knowing who might have left the artifact with the village, when, and why there was no record of it in our history.

It was a small hangup that I tried to move past as swiftly as I could. I didn't want to dwell on something I couldn't control and didn't really matter. Thankfully, General Miller appeared to agree and didn't want to talk about it, focusing instead on the enemy's moves.

"My biggest concern in all of this is that while we were still trying to work out what had happened, the demon managed to get an army partway around the world to the coast of Europe and pinpoint yet another place where a charged artifact piece was. I want to start focusing on two things—taking away his army, and putting together a much larger, better-equipped, and more efficient team of dragons and humans around the world, who can show up where he does and stop him or go hunt him down for once."

I'd gotten to the point where I knew that finding the last few artifact pieces first was unlikely, and until I found the traitor among us, less worthwhile.

"I think we can all get behind rescuing those humans and going on the hunt for the demon. I have a feeling that more countries are going to want our help than the last time you spoke to the ambassadors as well," Douglas said, speaking in the elders' chambers for the first time. "And I know that we are also eager to have more charged weaponry. We've used a lot in the last week or so."

Douglas was right, but I was at the point where my two meetings could no longer overlap.

"What of the other artifact pieces?" Brenta asked as I was about to end the meeting and let all the soldiers go. I groaned inwardly, having hoped that no one would notice my lack of mentioning them.

"I'm sure that those researching their locations will still do so, but so far none of them have been determined soon enough and we cannot afford to wait if we are to protect humanity." It wasn't a bad excuse to give, and I hoped it would satisfy her.

Either way, Brenta let it go, and I was allowed to move on and end the meeting for now. I had plenty I wanted to put into motion, but none of it could be done in a single mass session anymore.

As most of the people walked or flew away, Brenta hurried over to me.

"You have not been entirely truthful with the elders." She kept her voice down, thankfully. "What are you not telling us about these artifact pieces?"

"Something I need to keep to myself for now. I promise that I will speak of it as soon as I can. If I do so too soon, I could risk many lives and even get the dragons with me killed."

Brenta studied my face, and I was sure that she didn't want to agree.

"I know it's not something simple to ask for, but for the sake of a lot of others, I need you to trust me until I know more. All I have ever wanted to do is protect those I care about. I care about this city, I care about dragons, I care about humanity. And on top of that, my pride wants to see this demon beaten."

"Even if I cannot be completely sure of your motives regarding the dragons in this city and worldwide, I trust that last part. But whatever is going on, I insist on knowing as soon as it does not hamper the overall goal of beating this demon and putting him back in the ground. Our people are dying and losing their homes."

"And I will give everything I've got to stop it."

She nodded, hearing the conviction I spoke with. Brenta and I were never going to see eye to eye on a lot of things but there was at least one thing we agreed on, and I knew in that moment there was no way she was a traitor either. Still, I said nothing. Even if she wasn't the traitor, she might inadvertently tip them off if I told her anything. I didn't trust her to know how to handle what I knew so far.

With all that said, she let me get on with my task and even came with me. Refugees from several of the dragon cities already hit hard had filled up the rest of the towers and there were now more coming in from Europe. I was pulled from one meeting about the greater problem into another about the city itself.

"We might need to expand the borders of the city onto the land toward the army encampment," I told Brenta and Griffin when I looked out over the city. "It's the swiftest way to get more housing."

"It would be outside of the city shield and visible to the human world," Brenta pointed out.

"Yes, which is not ideal, but they know of us now. I will also need to talk to General Miller about us getting closer to his base. But I need somewhere to train more out in the open as well, and I promised that our training would include some human soldiers. We could put our military forces out there and give the vulnerable more room in the city." As soon as I finished speaking I snapped my mouth shut.

Surprise filled me at how easily I had suggested a solution that not only furthered our other goals but was likely to be accepted by the US government with ease and considered even to meet one of their requests.

Was I beginning to show diplomatic tendencies? A glance at Alitas showed a slight smirk on his face. He gave me the smallest of nods and I exhaled with relief. He thought I was on the right track too.

Over the course of the next hour, I tried to address all the other issues and then excused myself. It was exhausting to be in meetings almost as much as it was to fight sometimes. All I wanted to do was take the fight to the demon again, and that couldn't be done until I knew we could save as many humans as possible.

I made my way over to the army base next, taking a contingent of the best dragons with me to train, charge up the weaponry the soldiers had, and figure out what our next move was from a military point of view.

Douglas met me at the gate, always smiling and walking with me deeper into the camp. The base was larger again, with another permanent structure almost finished, but I also noticed that some of the humans who had been lingering outside Detaris when we had tried to keep hidden were back and had set up camp a little further down the road.

"The general wants to talk to you," Douglas said.

"Good, because I also want to talk to him."

Although Douglas lifted an eyebrow, he didn't ask questions and merely stuck with me, acting as my official escort in the US Army base yet again.

It always felt strange to have grown up in the US as a human yet now be treated like I might be a threat to the human world, but the army base was slowly relaxing and treating me like one of them. They did the bare minimum to satisfy protocol and didn't worry about the rest.

Several soldiers greeted me on the way through, all people I had fought alongside. I left most of the dragons who had come over with me outside, talking with their military counterparts and the people they were used to flying into battle with, and headed inside with only Alitas, Neritas, Flick, and Douglas. It was becoming a very normal group.

The general had a proper office now and it was large enough to admit all of us. It looked as if he intended to dismiss Douglas at first but then opted to let the man stay.

"Thank you for coming over here even though we've just had a meeting over there." He motioned for all of us to take a seat.

"I have something I want to talk to you about as well, so it's no trouble. Makes it easier on both of us." I didn't sit but leaned against the window, taking a peek at the view from where he sat. It included the city, or where the city would be if it was visible from this far away and it would include whatever we did to extend it.

He'd built his office building so he could keep an eye on

our comings and goings, something I would never escape. I would need to always work with the general.

"Shall I go first?" he asked. "Or would you like to?"

"You can. I've had a lot of meetings and haven't had time to properly formulate what I need to say." I opted to be frank. It seemed like he was about to ask me for a favor or present me with a problem that he felt needed fixing. I might be able to make this work in my favor.

"Very well. Did you notice the people who have begun reappearing and camping out along the road?" he asked.

I nodded and finally moved to a chair to sit down. The rest of my group, with the exception of Alitas, was already seated. The captain of my honor guard stayed on his feet, moving around the room and checking for threats, something everyone was used to him doing.

"Well, they and many others, who have at least not made their way here yet, wish to sign up to fight the monster attacking everyone and his army, especially if it means they have a chance of getting loved ones back or to exact revenge. As you can imagine, some of them are quite insistent."

"So sign them up," I replied, not sure exactly what the problem was. "Isn't the army always looking for more recruits?"

"They don't want to sign up to my country's military. They want to join yours."

I blinked, not having expected that response. A thousand questions ran through my head. I didn't have the capability to train a human army and knew very little about the US Army system. Why was the general even telling me that?

For a few seconds I thought about it, not bothered that I kept everyone waiting.

"How many people are we talking here?" I asked.

"Several hundred at least. Some of whom are citing that they've fought with you before." The general spoke so matter-of-factly that I was even more shocked and confused. I'd expected him to say ten or so, maybe. A few of the people waiting outside. But hundreds? That was an entirely different matter.

I didn't know what to do with this knowledge.

"I'm going to have to think this over," I eventually said, having no idea where to begin. Could I take on a human army? Did I have the resources? There were so many questions to answer and elements to consider.

"Then that would, for the most part, bring us back to why you came to talk to me." General Miller sat back and waited for me to say something.

"Detaris needs to grow, pretty much immediately, due to the many refugees we have taken in, and that means doing it onto the land in front of the city. In the past we would have just made our shield bigger, and had someone in some position of power influence whoever is responsible for rerouting the road make it appear as if even more of the cliff had disappeared. Or, alternatively, built over the sea—but that takes time."

"So this is more of a courtesy, in that you're warning us you're going to take more land before you do so?" He didn't sound entirely happy about what he was saying, and I realized that my earlier words had sounded like a threat.

"No. I know this is the wrong course of action. But we do need more land, fast, and if I am going to provide for all my refugees, that is the only way I can do it. I wanted to discuss with you what the options might be, seeing as it appears to be land that you have under your authority on this *new* army base."

The general nodded, relaxing as he understood that I was presenting him with a problem I needed help solving more than insisting upon anything.

"We've set up a base on land you felt was part of your city's expansion plans in a time of crisis, and now that crisis has happened, and because we've learned of your existence and in the spirit of cooperation between our two races built a base near your city—"

"Without consulting or checking with us," I added, interrupting him.

"Without consulting you, or checking the land was entirely without prior claim," he amended. "Because of this, you are asking us to *cooperate* further and make way for some more of your buildings."

"Exactly," I finished, pretty sure that he had just massively helped me.

"I'll put something like that in writing to my superiors and give them my recommendation that we work with you to perhaps create a joint military base here, perhaps with the road diverting around the back of both bases to give you more space and to give you back some of the land you feel already belongs to you."

"Thank you, General. We are very grateful that you would do so." I smiled gently and gave him a brief sitting bow.

"I might add that if you did decide to take on these willing human volunteers to join your nation and its forces, it would be a good space for them to train alongside our troops and help to continue the cooperation happening between us."

"That would probably be a good thought to add," I replied, trying to keep the grin I wanted to show at bay. It wasn't going to be a done deal, I knew, but with any luck, everything would work out and I would have the land I needed for the city.

CHAPTER TWENTY

When there was work to be done and politics involved, I had expected it to take weeks, but only two days after standing in the general's office telling him I needed more land, I was standing on the ground we would be using, discussing where the road would be dug up and where we would build houses.

It wasn't going to be easy to smooth everything over entirely, and there were still details to work out, but the dragons had begun arriving from the city attacked in Europe and they had nowhere to go right now. We needed some houses and we needed them now.

I'd talked at length to the elders, and then alone with Alitas, Flick, Ben, my mother, and Neritas about the humans' desire to join us. There was some reluctance among the elders, and Alitas had reservations, but everyone else could see the benefit. It meant that we were going to try it, but it was a secondary concern.

With dragons helping, it wouldn't take a huge length of

time to get buildings up, but again Reijo seemed to be financing our element of it from somewhere. My mother insisted it wasn't a problem, and it made me wonder how wealthy he actually was.

"Red! Haven't seen you in a while," Jace said right after landing nearby. She had also offered to be involved after I'd messaged her about humans wanting to join us.

In a lot of ways, I couldn't think of anyone better from the dragon side of things to oversee something like that, but she'd also been working on the problem of getting me another gate made.

As soon as she was close enough, I hugged her.

"Tell me everything I've missed," I said as we stepped away from the chaos for a moment.

"There's nothing really to tell. I'm sorry, Red. Making this new gate is proving harder than we thought. It wasn't just a piece of metal. It was far more complicated and a lot of it is broken now. The demon knew what he was doing."

"It's okay. Don't give up, and in the meantime, we'll fight him every way we can. If need be, we'll find another way to trap him," I spoke with as much confidence as I could fake. It wasn't good news, and she knew it. This war wasn't going well. We won the occasional battle, but all of us knew that, in general, we were losing.

As she backed up and I saw the slump in her shoulders I knew I had to refocus her. We needed hope.

"The scientists in the human world are trying to help us. They think that with our magic and the antibodies they found in the corrupted humans, we can keep humans from being corrupted and we might be able to make everyone immune to his corruption. We're going to beat him one way or another. But I could do with your help here. You know how to handle a ragtag militia. And..."

"The applicants are a little ragtag?" she asked, lighting up a little more.

"You could say that. Some of them can be a handful. Alitas would like to be a part of the interview process too."

"Naturally. None of us want anyone alongside you in battle who is here for the wrong reasons." Jace smirked. "We can't lose your red ass when we need you most."

I grinned back and shook my head before we were joined by Douglas and several other soldiers to continue with the work. It didn't take long for the group to figure out what we wanted and where. A barracks and room for more dragon towers were my biggest concern. Feeding everyone came next.

"You'll need an officer or two and some spare rooms for meetings," Douglas pointed out as he came closer to me.

"Do you mean an *office* or two?" I asked, not sure I'd heard him right.

He didn't reply at first but smirked slightly.

"I take it you'll be the commander-in-chief of any military formed?" he asked as the others drifted off to measure the land and work out the best place for the dragon towers to be erected.

We wanted them to be made up from the rock using an artifact that the dragon city kept in the vaults, and Ben thought he had discovered the perfect one. It had been used for repairs mostly in the past and had been forgotten along with the other items I'd already taken from there, but with enough time and magical energy, we thought it could be used to make a tower.

That was the biggest reason I was present. If this could be done with magic, it would save a lot of time. And if any artifact was to be tested, it was on me to test it. For now, I was happy to let everyone do their parts, however.

I was no architect, and I had no intention of making planning decisions about where a tower would sit best. I was here to provide the magical safety net and figure out how to use the artifact in the first place. Not to mention that there was still some political smoothing out to do.

While there had been agreement that a joint base was a mutually beneficial thing to do, I hadn't been given express permission to build homes or spread out in quite the way we'd decided to.

"You're up to more than you've told the general, aren't you?" Douglas' words were barely above a whisper.

I considered not telling him, but I knew this was a soldier who had my back and I decided to see what happened. After a brief pause, I nodded.

"I want to join you. If you'll have me?"

Still processing what he was asking and not sure exactly, I took a moment to respond.

"You want to join my army?" I asked, only remembering to keep my voice quiet at the last second.

"Yes, if you'll have me. You could do with some experienced human combatants, no matter how good Jace is."

I exhaled. He had a point, but I was pretty sure that his defecting to join me wasn't going to go down well. And I felt guilty at my eagerness to say yes.

"The general has me spying on you. If I stay in this role, I will have to tell him something. And I don't want to do that. You're the one risking your life out there every time. You have from the start."

"Are you going to get in trouble if you do?" I looked away from him and watched the others move about the area so it didn't appear as if we were talking about anything of consequence.

"Maybe. I honestly don't know. I figured that at worst I could live in Detaris in one of your low towers and you guys can give me food and let me live out the rest of my days with one heck of a view. At least, after we've won this little war."

"You think we're going to win?" I asked, admitting that there was a little doubt about that too.

"I do. You're not going to give up. Sooner or later, you'll win."

His faith in me made my mind up. While I wasn't so sure how this would turn out, I knew it was important to have plenty of people around me who had faith in me and our shared goal. On the bad days, they would keep me going.

"Okay, if that's truly what you want to do. I don't think I could really stop you if that's what you want anyway."

"Then it's settled. I'm your guy. I'll be your veteran in this new army of yours." Douglas grinned as if I'd just told him it was Christmas and sauntered off after the others.

I watched him go, not sure what to make of what he'd just said. He'd told me that the general wanted to spy on me, and I got the impression that whatever Douglas would have found out and told him, it was something he'd find out either way. Someone would act as a spy in his place anyway, and we were on the same ground now. It would be easy for them.

As I shifted to involve myself in the current work again, I got closer just in time to see them mark out where the first tower would go. They were swift to mark out the other buildings with ropes and stakes, planning out the first extension to the city. It was surprisingly efficient, and it didn't take long for someone to hand me the artifact.

It looked like a strange box with buttons all over it. Alitas was soon near to hand, the usual protective nature coming out in him. Neritas put his hands on the box as well, making it clear he was in this with me. I grinned, grateful for the backup these days. Having another powerful dragon around was always a good idea.

We connected to it gently together and I felt it wanting to suck hungrily at the magic I had. I drew in some from the ancestors, going slowly and helping to control the flows. I also fed some to Neritas, feeling the magic pull out of him and wanting to make sure he didn't run out.

In case danger threatened and we had to fly out, I didn't want either of us drained. Even if this project took longer to build, I was going to make sure that we had the energy to fight the demon and his army if it came to it.

Slowly the box filled up with energy and started to feel warm in our hands. When I was sure it had enough to begin working, I tried to figure out how to activate it. There were so many buttons on it, and it had such a complicated-looking arrangement that I didn't know where to begin.

"Were there any notes on this?" I asked out loud.

"Something about the sides being responsible for different parts of the construction." Ben shrugged as if this was all the explanation he had.

"Well, the foundations would be good." Neritas slowly turned it in his hands and looked at the engravings all over it. Eventually he stopped with one side facing up. "If the symbols in each corner are anything to go by, I'd start here."

Not sure what else to do, I slowly pushed a button. Almost immediately the ground began to shift and shake. I stopped and looked up at Neritas.

"I think it's going to require some directing." He took over, being a bit more gentle and experimental than I had been. It was easy to let him take control. I didn't try to fight it, for a moment merely learning the subtleties of it.

Just like a lot of the other artifacts we had used, it could be mentally controlled and had a physical component as well. We had to be close to what we were building and build it up around us. It took some time and repositioning —of ourselves and the few people sticking around to help us. It also meant that we had to go slower on certain elements of the build to make sure we didn't destabilize anything.

After an hour or so we had foundations, a clear smooth rock floor to the first room of the tower, and the beginning protuberance of rock walls. If we had wanted to make a building out of other materials, like bricks and wood, it would have also manipulated those and required far less magic.

As it was, it was sucking up loads and it felt as if

nothing could feed it entirely but my connection to the ancestors. And that could only provide me so much at once.

We took a break while I slowly filled the device back up again and then we passed it around and Neritas showed others how to use it and let them take on the workload. I wanted to be involved, but I had a lot of different things to focus on, and finishing the tower wasn't an activity I absolutely had to be part of beyond fueling the artifact.

With others taking that role on, I got back to training. I had other dragons charging the weaponry to be distributed, and that earned me another shipment of tranquilizers and guns to hand out to my dragons, as well as some other army-based supplies for the field. Everyone in Detaris who fought had the kit they needed now. The rest was heading out to dragons who came from other home bases. I needed as many prepped dragons as possible.

Some were also stationed in Detaris for now, training with me and the others to be prepared in battle strategy and take the knowledge back with them. I couldn't be everywhere at once, as evidenced by the recent chaos in Europe, and I had a delegation of European ambassadors showing up later in the day, no doubt to demand answers.

I wasn't looking forward to that, but I did love training.

As soon as all the dragons and soldiers had gathered in the courtyard on the base, I began the lesson. We were using the illusion device to make some shadow catchers and play with what the army could see, and it was surprisingly effective. It used up some magic, but it gave everyone a chance to figure out some tactics and it meant I could lose myself in the flow of fighting and teaching.

It wasn't until I was showing one of the dragons from another city how to get a good thrust with the swords we had issued out that I realized how far I had come and how much I had learned. I'd been fighting shadow catchers for so long now that I hadn't appreciated how much stronger and faster I had become.

Another technique I demonstrated pulled the sleeve back from my wrist and revealed several of the scars I had there. It reminded me of my mother's arms and how I had seen her the first few times she had fought beside me. These days she saw less combat, staying more involved in the politics and the running of Detaris when I was taking the risks, but we both preferred it that way.

I knew the city was in good hands and that she understood both sides of the dragon lifestyle far better than I did.

As Douglas stepped up to help me train the soldiers, I grinned and let him give instructions. For now, he was a captain in the US Army, but I didn't doubt that as soon as my side of the base was built, he would be a very different sort of captain.

For a little while I watched him, noticing how a lot of the soldiers responded well to his commands, and the respect they had for him as well. It made me wonder how many of them would follow him to my side of the fence when the time came. I considered that I may come to regret saying yes to him if too many followed.

The general was not a man who would appreciate the majority of his forces walking out on him and joining an ally. But equally, I could see how much I was going to need someone like Douglas if I took on humans of my own. I was going to have to be careful with the whole plan.

Either way, the decisions had been made. All I could do now was hold on for the ride.

CHAPTER TWENTY-ONE

I exhaled as I considered the meeting I was in. The ambassadors had been as impossible as I had feared, demanding to know why they hadn't seen more support during the attack the day before.

"We understand that you were here in the US and on the opposite coast to Spain," the Spanish ambassador said, getting more irate. "But you promised us that your cities in our countries would protect us as well."

"Again, I made no promises. You all stood in this very room and asked me to remove my cities from your countries. Some of you even told me that you would not recognize our sovereignty in your nations and that you wanted us to leave." I looked pointedly at the French ambassador as I said this. She had been surprisingly quiet the entire meeting, and I felt it was a little unfair to do it, but she had been the most vocal before.

Several of the men and women shifted as if they were going to argue with me further, but I was done with this meeting. It was time to wrap it up.

"Now, with all that said, I still see it as my race's duty to protect this planet and all life on it as best as we can. And it is clear that our system wasn't ready for an attack on a different continent. We are doing everything we can to remedy this. More and more dragons are being trained to fight and are being sent around the world in an effort to improve protection for everyone."

"That is not likely to be enough. The dragons present all fled at the first sign of difficulty." The Spanish ambassador wasn't letting it go, but it had been his country that was attacked and a part of me couldn't blame him.

"I am aware of that as well. They were a small, peaceful community, not trained in combat. We are sending more of our trained dragons to Europe as soon as we can. And today we also agreed to take on human soldiers and train them too. Many have applied to join our forces, and from now on we will deploy both together and ensure that we have even greater forces to protect each area."

This finally seemed to settle them down. Either that, or they were shocked to hear that people wanted to join our nation of their own free will. It felt strange to me to say it and I knew it would take them a moment to digest the information.

"We have other plans, of course. I'm not interested in sitting around and waiting for the enemy to show up where he wishes, but I can't speak any more than that about ongoing operations. We recently had a very successful mission, shortly before the Europe attack actually, and rescued many humans from his captivity as well as gained a powerful artifact that had been lost, which will aid us further. In any war, there are casualties and setbacks, but I'm confident that this war, we shall win."

I stopped speaking, not sure where my confidence and passion had come from. I hadn't been confident earlier in the day, and I wasn't even entirely sure now, but they needed calming down. If they lost their heads it wasn't going to help any of us.

Thankfully, they seemed to accept this explanation, and although they asked questions about the artifact and how everything was progressing in terms of protecting humans from the corruption, I could redirect them for most of their answers to somebody else. I knew no more than they did, and besides, I wanted the answers as well.

If humans could be protected and this serum could also help save the corrupted, then I wanted to have it in our arsenal as soon as possible. I knew the general had similar feelings, and if I wasn't about to poach one of his best men I'd have trusted he would give some to me immediately. As things stood right now, I didn't know what would happen.

I could only worry about so much.

Now that the ambassadors seemed somewhat placated, I left the meeting and made my way back to Detaris. It had gotten dark while I had been inside but I could easily see the work that had been done on the dragon end of the base now. The road was already entirely rerouted and a large tower stood in one corner.

There were still a couple of dragons working on it, and I paused with Neritas nearby to give the box a little more magic. I didn't know how much longer the builders were planning on continuing, but I didn't want them to be held up by the need for magical energy. Our city needed the space and I didn't want to wait any longer than we had to.

Before I could leave the base, General Miller appeared. He had been lurking in the shadows to one side but stepped more into the light as I approached.

"They've thrown that up and moved the perimeter of this base far faster than I'd have thought possible," he said as he came to my side.

I looked up at the tower alongside him, the moon casting just enough light that the outline of it could be seen. We watched it grow for a few seconds, both of us admiring how easy it appeared.

"I won't deny there's some marvelous benefits to your way of life and whatever this energy is that you can all use."

Yet again, the general didn't use the word magic. It always amused me. In a lot of ways it wasn't magic, but that didn't mean it wasn't the best word for it sometimes.

"There are downsides too. But it definitely helps to get these up fast. A lot of dragons and humans will need them over the coming weeks." I tried to sound casual about it.

"You're going ahead with accepting human recruits into your army then?" He tried to sound casual too, but a single glance between us made it obvious he had failed.

"Yes. I think so. It makes sense when there are fewer dragons in this fight than there were the last time the demon was free. We need to find a way to protect more people, and faster."

He nodded and pulled out a small vial. "I didn't give this to you."

"What is it?" I asked as I took it.

"The antibody serum the scientists are hoping will stop

people from being corrupted and help protect them. They managed to isolate the antibody part very quickly. They're going to start giving some to the teams here to use in battle in emergencies, but it's still experimental and months away from formal approval. If your kind can do wonders building this sort of construction faster than us, I wondered if you could speed this up and make it safer as well."

I didn't know if it was possible, but I appreciated the general taking the chance on me to see what I could do to help. The trouble he could get into for having done it was huge, and I quickly tucked it into a pocket.

He moved to walk away and end our little clandestine meeting, but I stopped him.

"I think it's only fair that I let you know something that happened today," I said, launching into it before I could change my mind.

He paused and gave me his attention.

"Your Captain Douglas volunteered to be in my army and help train my troops. Said he'd defect."

"Did you accept?" he asked.

"I didn't see any sense in refusing."

"Then you know as well as I do that he's not been my Captain Douglas for some time. He's been one of yours since the moment he first flew with you. I can't say I blame him either."

"I promise I won't poach anyone else as far as possible."

"But we both know that you won't say no to any volunteers either."

"I can't afford to," I shot back, knowing it was the truth and hoping that the general would understand.

He appeared to deflate, his shoulders slumping and his head lowering. "I won't encourage it either, but I would understand the hearts of any who follow you into combat. Besides, we fight on the same side."

The general really did walk off this time and I got the feeling he did it before he could tell me that he would have followed me into battle as well. The general and I might be of different races and technically working on different teams, but we were allies, and we understood each other.

With the vial in my pocket and Neritas still at my side but giving me peace and time to process, I continued back to Detaris. I wasn't sure I had done the right thing in telling the general what was going on, but his offering had made me feel as if I owed him something.

And in war, I was willing to do what was needed to get some firm allies and keep them. If he had prior warning that his soldiers were likely to defect to me, he might stop some of them, but he would consider my warning and the chance of keeping his troops a victory, when he would have seen losing any and the surprise of it a defeat before. At least, I hoped that was how I'd just made it appear.

If nothing else, I had something new—a serum that might save some lives. I planned on getting it to the right dragon to get more of it made and study it ourselves. Although science wasn't something our dragons focused on in the same way humans did, I was sure it could be of help.

As soon as we were in the city and sitting down with the usual team, I produced it, but I didn't tell anyone where I had got it from.

"If you'll trust me with it, I think I can get a contact of

Sarai's to make more of it and study it," Jace offered immediately. "Can you get more?"

"I don't know, but if you think you can get it replicated, our source seemed to think that it could be used in combat and emergencies already. I'd like to have some to hand, just in case."

She tilted her head to the side and looked thoughtful for a moment. "I'll do my best. If I can take it with me tonight, I might have some answers by morning."

No one argued as Jace took it and hurried off. She never stayed in Detaris long, still not really feeling welcome, and I never put pressure on her to stay. I hoped that her being able to stay on the base would help keep her around, especially if there wasn't much progress with the gate, but I also understood her need for some freedom.

With everyone else settling in for the night and no sign of Ben, I opted to go over to the library and find him. For a few weeks it had become an almost nightly routine, but the last week or so had been so crazy that I hadn't had a chance, and I missed it. The library had been somewhere I had started to go to escape everything and think.

Ben was also one of the best listeners I knew. In a similar way to Anthony, he could be nearby and doing some task while I talked and then he would give a pointed bit of advice with zero judgment at the end of it. And then he would almost forget we'd had the conversation and never be irritated if I didn't take his advice.

I left everyone else in the royal tower, flying the short gap between the two by myself. No one feared for my safety in the city anymore. They had once, but not after uniting the city against our common enemy so well.

Ben was sitting at the small table, scribbling away almost furiously when I joined him. Before I could speak a word or ask how he was, he lifted a hand as if to silence me.

Wordlessly, I slipped onto the nearest chair and waited. He had Anthony's journal in front of him, a book written entirely in code. We'd found two copies of it so far, and it had led us on a journey about who I was, what was happening with the demon, and then shown that Anthony had been preparing for all of this because he had suspected it was coming long before it had.

Not that it had helped him much. Ben and I had found him dead, killed by shadow catchers, as far as we'd been able to tell.

I watched him as he translated another page, wondering what had unlocked this, when he sat back and looked up. Tears were in his eyes, and he shook his head when I opened my mouth to speak again. Although I put out a hand to take the page he'd translated, I hesitated when I noticed that he was reading it again and more tears were sliding down his face.

It was only at that moment that I noticed they were the very final pages of the notebook. Whatever he had just translated, I got the impression that it was going to explain some of Anthony's last days and why he might have died. I wasn't sure I was ready to know that either. Not if it was having this much of an impact on Ben.

Slowly, he calmed down and I waited, placing a hand on his knee instead of anything else. He put his over mine, something we had done many times in the past. We sat together in the flickering candlelight he had been working by until he sighed.

"I'm sorry, Scarlet. This was tough to read."

"That much was clear, but it isn't your fault. I'm sorry that you had to find it now and were alone at first. I know Anthony meant a lot to you."

"You're here now. Do you want to read it or have the cliff notes?"

"Cliff notes, if it means I won't cry as much. I'll read it later when I can handle the emotions. It's been a long day."

He nodded and gathered himself, and I wondered if I had put the burden on him to spare myself for a second.

"It looks as if he was betrayed. Someone in Detaris knew that he was guarding you. They've known who you were all along... And they're probably like Fintar, some kind of handler." Ben shook his head again, closing his eyes as tears threatened to fall once more.

"Does it say who?" I asked, barely daring to breathe. I'd suspected there was a traitor for so long that I wasn't sure what to say now that Ben was confirming there was one.

"Not directly. Someone very high up in Detaris. They're never mentioned by name, but there's a few ways we are likely to be able to tell. Anthony talks of several possessions of theirs and some information only they know."

"How high up? Are we talking as high up as an elder?"

"Almost certainly." Ben stood as he spoke.

"Then let's go find out. It's late. Everyone will be asleep. If there is evidence, I'm sure we can find it. Especially if you know what we're looking for."

"I do now." Ben scooped up the translated journal page

and the journal itself, tucking both into his coat pocket out of sight.

For a second neither of us moved, frozen in place by the enormity of what we were about to discover. We were about to find the dragon responsible for getting Anthony killed and possibly many others since. Finally, we would know who our traitor was.

CHAPTER TWENTY-TWO

As we flew up to the elders' chamber I felt the nerves building inside me. What if we didn't find any concrete evidence and we were left guessing again? I had to hope that we would, but doubt gnawed at my mind. If nothing else, I was grateful that I was alongside Ben. I hadn't liked doubting him either. Or anyone else.

Now all the fears would hopefully come to an end. We would know, could put a stop to their informing the demon of anything going on, and make sure that we had more of an advantage going forward.

I'd been frustrated that Ben had been finding me locations only as the demon found them. Almost in every case, the second Ben had told me that we had a new location to try, the demon had found out too.

So many questions ran through my head, but I tried to push them away as I landed. I was getting ahead of myself. I didn't know what we'd find and I wasn't actually sure where to begin looking.

Although I had been in the elders' chamber many times,

I hadn't actually done more than sit in it, eat now and then, and talk, but Ben strode in with confidence as soon as we landed. I hurried after him, letting him take the lead.

There was a small door at the back of the room and Ben headed through it, again acting as if he knew exactly where to go. I wasn't about to argue as he made his way up a small flight of stairs to a small room above the main chamber. There were few windows up here, but a small light came on as we walked into the room, a storage area.

"The elders in the city have this area as a sort of private chamber, normally just for them, but in theory you are allowed to access it as well. And... I'm with *you*, so..." Ben grinned, his first sign of mirth.

"What are we looking for?" I asked.

"Several possible things." Ben pulled out the pieces of paper with the translation. "Anthony mentions them being able to communicate in almost real-time, so a phone or something else like that. They might have some reference books stolen from the library. Anything an elder shouldn't be hiding from the city would be a good start."

I nodded and looked around the room, not sure where to begin. There were wardrobes, cabinets, and trunks, all seemingly scattered throughout the room, and many of them locked or fastened with padlocks. To some degree, it made me want to fetch Neritas. He had broken into several places around the city, but no one had thought to look in here. It was normally guarded by default, with elders always present in the chamber below.

"How do we know what belongs to whom?" I asked as Ben lifted the lid on a trunk, breaking an old lock with ease. It made a bit of a noise, but it didn't slow him down.

"There's a sticker on each item or some other kind of marker. They've each got one. Of course, not all of them are obvious. But this is Brenta's, and I don't know about you, but I kind of want to start there." Ben looked at the contents of the trunk: several items of clothing at the top, including a scarf I'd never seen her wear.

Of all the things I had expected to see in one of these containers, clothing hadn't been it. Why would an elder need to hide clothing from prying eyes or store it away from their normal belongings?

Ben had similar thoughts and lifted it out. Underneath were a bunch of books, and for a second I couldn't move. Had Brenta been our culprit all along?

I partially wanted to believe it, but I also couldn't bring myself to. Brenta was annoying, and had accused me of all sorts of things, but it had all been in the name of protecting a city she genuinely appeared to love.

As Ben crouched to look closer at the books, I knelt beside him, needing to see for myself as well. There were several books that contained histories, some of them possibly books that would have helped us, including a genealogy book and a magic book that Ben also put to one side.

The next one in the pile made us both gasp. We recognized it almost instantly. It was the third and final copy of Anthony's journal. Brenta had one, and judging by the dust on it and how far down it had been in the trunk, she had owned it for some time.

I was the first to recover and I very gently picked it up and flicked it open. Ben pulled his out and we compared them, flicking to random pages and making sure all the contents were the same. There were odd mistakes that set them apart, as all three had been written by hand, but otherwise, they were identical.

Not even hesitating to consider the ramifications, I put the new copy into my bag. I wasn't leaving something like that with Brenta, whether she had been able to translate it or not.

"It looks like we have found our traitor," Ben said when he saw that the next book was a history of dragon artifacts.

Although it looked like it, I wasn't entirely convinced. This trunk had been easy to open and in plain view. On top of that, Brenta was who we would *want* our traitor to be. If she was a spy, she wasn't a very good one in many ways.

"I think we need to keep looking. We haven't found any evidence that she or anyone else on the elders' council has actually betrayed anyone."

Ben exhaled but nodded. "You make a good point, as much as I hate to admit it. This isn't enough to convict anyone of anything. Although, if we are in the elders' chambers, we could ask her. She wouldn't be able to lie."

"If we can be more sure, then I would be willing to try that," I replied.

As Ben carried on looking, I moved to the next trunk and pulled it open. It was almost empty. Its owner had only stored a few precious items that appeared to be heirlooms. No trace of magic or anything suspicious. I opened a few cabinets and found what appeared to be diaries and personal notebooks. I even found some charcoal drawings that showed one of our elders was a very talented artist with a taste for the erotic.

It struck me as something that a city elder might want

to keep hushed, but nothing that ought to bring anyone any shame. Again, I moved on, Ben finally having gone through the rest of Brenta's trunk and found nothing more than some other books that appeared as if they might be useful.

The door of the next cabinet was almost stuck, something holding it shut that made me wriggle the opening and try the lock in many different ways.

"Need me to pick it?" Ben asked.

"I think so. It's not budging, and almost everything else has been unlocked or easily forceable." I waited patiently as Ben came over to me, pulling out some thieves' tools. I wasn't surprised he had them, having seen him do something like this before, but it still struck me as strange to sit back and let him.

If I hadn't known I could trust Ben, I would have considered that he might be the one who had been a traitor, but if it had been him, I didn't think he would have brought me up here.

It took him several minutes to get the lock to pop, and then we found the cabinet was still stuck anyway. Ben wriggled it some more and then I heard a crunch, and it came open, almost breaking entirely.

For a few seconds, I wasn't sure what I was looking at. Papers, notes, and clippings were shoved inside a bit haphazardly, but then I felt the item within. Something with a very low-level source of magic was in among the chaos. Worse, I hadn't felt it until Ben had opened the cabinet.

"This is lined with something that hides magic." I pulled the door almost closed again. "I can't feel it when it's shut."

It was perfectly true. No matter how much I tried with my mind, there was something on the cabinet that prevented me from feeling the magic. And that only made me more suspicious.

Slowly I pulled out the papers, finding that a lot of them were letters. They had been leafed through many times, and they had finger marks on them and coffee stains here and there, but that wasn't what stood out to me most. They were all in Anthony's handwriting. Whoever had been keeping belongings in this cabinet, Anthony had been writing to them.

None of these were in the same code as the journals, but they weren't in the common dragon language. They were all written in the ancient tongue.

"They're about you," Ben said. "Almost all of them. They're about you and what you were doing. That you had no idea who you were still, and many other similar things."

I gulped. Whoever owned this cabinet was far more likely to be our traitor. And even if they weren't, they had some serious explaining to do. Anthony had given this person information that should have been used to crown me earlier if nothing else. Almost too nervous to continue, but knowing I must, I pulled all the letters out of the way and handed them to Ben.

"Who uses this one?" I asked, hoping he'd look while I continued to reveal what was underneath all the hastily shoved-in pieces of paper.

There were a lot of different items. Most of them were from the human world, including money in stacks and what looked like a passport and driver's license. This was also someone who had a human-world persona.

"It looks like it's Griffin, I think," Ben said a short while later, looking at the etchings on the side of the cabinet. There had once been a sticker, but it had been peeled off and something else carved into the metal. A glance at the ID confirmed it was Griffin, his face on both the passport and driver's license.

It wasn't until I shoved the money aside that I found the item that used magic. A small, stone-like thing. I almost didn't want to touch it, wondering if it would suck at my magic.

"Do you know what it does?" Ben asked when he noticed what had caught my eye. I wanted to answer, but the truth was that I had no idea, and I wasn't sure that I wanted to find out.

Slowly, I focused on it, reaching for the connection before I realized that it wasn't powered by the usual magic.

"It's either a trap or it uses corruption." I pulled back with my mind.

"That could be proof enough," Ben said.

"Not alone. They could be keeping it in here until it can be cleansed."

"Possibly, but it's a good indicator that something is up and gives us a reason to question Griffin. And you and every other elder is going to know if he's lying."

Ben had a point and it felt as if it was enough to give us a reason to call him in for questioning. Using one of the scarves, I went to pick up the item and swept up all the other items on that shelf as well.

"What's going on in here?" Brenta's voice broke through the quiet as I moved. I almost dropped the strange stone, and it slipped in the scarf until it was near one end.

"This may look strange," Ben began.

"Very strange." Brenta's eyes shifted to the trunk, and it was clear she knew it had been opened.

"I'm sure you remember me saying that I had something I wanted to keep a secret." I stepped forward, rewrapping the item in Brenta's scarf.

"I do. I think now would be a very good time to explain."

"We have a traitor in our midst. Someone who betrayed Anthony to his death and has been telling the demon and his forces where we are and where the artifact pieces are as soon as we have found them."

Brenta came closer to me to look at what we'd found. Without hesitation, Ben showed her the letters from Anthony. She quickly scanned through several of them, her mouth forming into a thin line as she did so. As soon as she was satisfied with those, she came over to see what I was holding.

It didn't take her long to look over the rest.

"These things would suggest that Griffin has some explaining to do," she replied eventually.

"He does. But I think we should be careful how we handle this." The beginning of a plan was forming in my head. "If he's the traitor and we out him but don't harm him or keep him here, then he's left with only one place to go, especially if we keep his money and his human world ID."

"Straight to the demon." Ben looked at me as if I had just said the most brilliant thing ever.

I nodded, not sure I liked the strange look in his eyes.

"If you follow him, I would like to join you," Ben said,

but it didn't sound like a question, and the look on his face made it clear that he would brook no argument.

"We'll need to be careful. He'll be expecting you to want revenge. I'll have Flick come back for you and everyone else if I find the demon. That's the best I can do and offer." I knew it wasn't what he wanted to hear.

He looked at me, gritting his teeth as if he was trying to figure out the best way to tell me to go screw myself without actually saying it. Brenta shifted between us and looked from one of us to the other and back again.

"I understand that both of you have ideas on what to do, but Griffin has not been proved guilty yet and there is more to discuss before we call him before the elders and get to the bottom of this situation. While it does look conclusive, I will not condemn a dragon who has served the city many times without at least hearing what he has to say for himself." Brenta gently ushered us toward the door as she gave Ben back the letters.

Although I wanted to argue with her, I knew she had a point. We needed to go through this the right way.

"If he is guilty, we might not have long to get organized."

"Can you fly out immediately?" she asked me. "If he does make a run for it. Could you follow?"

Trying to keep my cool and consider the answer properly, I didn't reply right away, instead thinking about it and making sure. Eventually I nodded. "If you give me two minutes, I can make sure that I'm ready to go."

"If I don't go with you, Alitas is going to want more than Flick to be with you," Ben pointed out.

"There's no way Neritas would let me leave him behind

either. But we would wait for you to join us to attack anyway. If I fly out, everyone who can fight needs to be told to get ready as soon as possible." I considered what I would need, wanting to make sure my armor would be with me, even if I wouldn't be able to wear it. This wasn't going to be the easiest task, but we would make the most of it.

If nothing else, it was likely that we had found our traitor. Now all we had to do was get him to admit it.

CHAPTER TWENTY-THREE

Pacing across the chamber floor, I waited for everyone else to be assembled. All the evidence sat on a small table beside my throne. The more I thought about what this might mean, the more angry I grew. Griffin had fought alongside me so many times I hadn't once considered him to be a threat.

The dragon had clearly been playing a long game, however, and had managed to keep his activities so well covered up that no one had suspected him. When I had been considering possible traitors, I hadn't thought of someone so innocuous.

Of course, I had to keep reminding myself that he might not be guilty and it was better for me to keep my head and not assume the worst. All the questions and thoughts I had could be considered when I knew one way or another.

I sat on the throne as people started arriving. Many of them were yawning, not dressed as immaculately as they were during the day. It was very late, and many had gone to sleep already, including, it would appear, Griffin. We had agreed that no one would tell him what was happening.

Only Brenta, of the elders, had been told the exact plan for what we were doing. Neritas had said he would tell Flick, and Ben wanted Reijo and my mother to know before they walked in. Everyone else simply believed that something had come up, perhaps a new danger, and we'd all been summoned to discuss it for an immediate response. It was the only way to make sure Griffin cooperated and the whole event unfolded naturally and with as many witnesses as possible.

"This is very late for an elders' meeting," one of the other women pointed out. I didn't disagree with her, but I didn't respond, not sure I could say anything without giving the situation away.

"It's very important. News has come to light, and Scarlet didn't want to act without consulting us. I for one am grateful for the opportunity to do my duty and be included in this conference." Brenta gave the woman a pointed look, almost as if the complaint itself offended her when this was part of an elder's duty.

If nothing else, it discouraged everyone else from saying a word as they all gathered.

Others showed up as well. Alitas had made sure plenty of honor guards and city guards were present, no doubt to protect people if Griffin had any surprises up his sleeves. I wasn't going to stop him from being careful. Normally there were a lot of dragons present at our meetings. I didn't like to shut anyone out.

Until my mother walked in and came up to me, I felt like a fish out of water.

"Neritas just told me," she whispered. "I know this won't be easy on you. Your father had to do something similar once. Do not blame yourself. That'll make you more angry than calm-headed, because of your imagined guilt. Handle this with dignity. You have caught it now, and that's all that matters. It will stop, and you can prevent more death as soon as you know."

I nodded, grateful that she understood what I was feeling without me even needing to say it. After giving my shoulder a squeeze, she went to her seat as well. Griffin was one of the last to appear, having been summoned last. No one who knew what was going on wanted to be in the room with him for a long time.

As the rest of the elders appeared, Flick, Reijo, Neritas, and Ben were also admitted. Neritas and Flick stood on either side of my chair as my honor guards.

Only when I sat did the meeting officially begin and all eyes looked to me, very few knowing why.

"I am sorry to have summoned all of you to the chambers at so late an hour, and I'm sure many of you were dragged from your beds. This matter wasn't one that could wait, nor was it one that I thought I should handle alone."

For a few seconds I wasn't sure how to continue and the pause only made the tension in the room even worse. I needed to think of some way of phrasing it that made sense and gave Griffin the benefit of the doubt.

"As all of you know, I discovered I was a dragon when Anthony went missing. He had been watching over me and our lives were peaceful and relatively easy. Then, suddenly, everything changed. We have known for a long time that Anthony was conversing with people, some of whom ended up being allies—such as Reijo, who was supporting us financially, and Jace, who has helped us fight the demon numerous times. Another contact of his has come to light."

There was a ripple of movement as everyone reacted to this. Even Griffin lifted an eyebrow and gripped his seat a little tighter. I didn't look directly at him.

"There is evidence that Anthony was in contact with one of you. That one of you already knew exactly who I was and why I had been hidden away from the city," I added.

"So you have brought us here to question us?" one of the younger elders asked, his voice wavering slightly as if he expected to be tortured or at the very least uncomfortably interrogated and was trying to sound brave and fearless despite being quite the opposite.

"Not exactly," I replied, not sure how best to proceed. A part of me hoped that Griffin would have the honor to at least offer up an explanation. That we might have made a mistake and he could explain.

And then Griffin's gaze landed on the pile of letters by my side, still hidden by Brenta's scarf, and he took a deep breath.

As he stood, everyone gasped. No one had suspected it was Griffin. Of course, very few of them knew that this was a betrayal yet either.

"I believe it was me he was conversing with. When he left to be in the human world, no one knew exactly why, and I wanted to make sure he was okay. He was a good friend. I have a few letters, not many, but I kept them in a safe place after his tragic death. They don't say much, however."

"No, some of them don't, do they?" I connected to the artifact that detected a lie and noticed that he was also already connected to it. At once, almost everyone did the same. "Others do, though. And that's not all you have tucked away, is it?"

Immediately his eyes narrowed and he changed stance, going from the slightly placid older man look he normally had to something entirely different. He scowled around the room.

"If you already know what I have, why do you ask?"

"You know why I asked. Don't deflect." I stood and lifted Brenta's scarf to reveal the mound of letters and the strange artifact I'd found in his cabinet. "I want you to tell me what you know so we can be sure what you speak is the truth."

Griffin let out a laugh, and not the kindly chuckle I was so used to hearing from him. This one was full of scorn and hate.

"You think you are so clever, but you're still nothing but a child in charge of an army of old fools. You can't stop him. No one can. The corruption will take over until all this world belongs to it. It is easier to give in and let it. More peaceful. It isn't so bad to let it have the occasional sacrifice."

"Sacrifice? We will not sacrifice anything to anyone. It is our duty to protect this planet and all those on it." I stepped forward again, more angry than anything else. A glance at my mother checked me. I took several deep breaths while Griffin looked around the room, searching for some support.

Every elder kept their chair, cold expressions turned on the dragon they had once called friend.

"You don't deny it, then? That you betrayed Anthony to his death and told the demon's forces where we were?"

"You already know, don't you?"

"I want to hear you say it," I replied, noticing he was still skirting my accusations, answering my questions with questions and being evasive.

"This is a joke. I do not have to answer you. I will not bow to a child who thinks herself a queen. You will lead the dragon race to ruin in the name of honor." He turned to go toward the door and leave, but Alitas and Kryos stood to block his way.

"Griffin, you are not free to leave these chambers until you either confirm or deny what it appears you have done. Did you betray Anthony?"

"You will think I did, yes," he replied—again, not technically lying.

I growled, unable to think of a better way to phrase it. Somehow I wanted him to admit it. While I tried to calm down, Brenta stood. She didn't get any closer to Griffin, but he did give her his attention.

"Did your actions lead to the shadow catchers finding him and hunting him?" Brenta asked.

"Yes." Griffin lifted his chin higher, as if he was proud of this.

"And have you been telling someone else where the artifact pieces are when we've discovered them?"

He frowned and scowled at the question, clearly not

wanting to answer it. He looked between me, Brenta, some of the other elders, and the guards on the door.

"Yes," he finally said, looking back at me. "You don't deserve to wield that power. It's an affront that you even have one of them."

Again, he tried to leave and Alitas blocked his way, but I shook my head and waved my hand.

"Let him go. There's nothing more to ask. He's betrayed us all and freely admits it." I watched as the guards moved out of the way and he launched from the open doorway. Closing my eyes for a couple of seconds, I followed the feel of his magic, still not sensing anything evil about it or any defect to the usual dragon magic.

Whatever Griffin was, he wasn't a handler. I kept track of him as he moved around the city, however, and grabbed my away bag so I would be ready at a moment's notice. I'd stowed it behind the throne and Flick and Neritas had done the same with theirs, making sure they could fly with me.

We would take advantage of it being nighttime and also let Griffin get far enough ahead that we wouldn't be able to physically see him. I could still feel him.

After flying out of the chambers, he flew to his home in the city, no doubt to pack up a few belongings. We had his passport, money, letters, and what we were assuming at this point was a communication device.

The elders all got out of their chairs as well and came rushing toward me to get me to explain what had just happened. One of them went to touch the stone and my mother stopped them.

"I wouldn't do that if I were you." She covered it back up with Brenta's scarf.

"I'll cleanse it if I get the chance, but don't touch it until I can. It might hurt or corrupt any of you," I added.

No one argued with me, and Brenta also joined the group, encouraging them to ask her or Ben their questions rather than me.

"Are you sure you should follow him?" Brenta asked me when everyone had quieted and I was still feeling for Griffin's presence, my bag on my back.

"I have to take the chance that he will lead me to the demon. He has too many artifact pieces and I need to try to take them back. This is our best shot at being led to him. And if nothing else, at least we are getting rid of our traitor. I'll learn *something* following him."

"Be careful," she replied. "We'd like you back in one piece. I've never been comfortable with our leaders being the ones to face so much danger."

"We're at war and I have trained for this. You run the city just fine without me." I smiled, starting to feel like I might have managed to thaw Brenta with this latest development. She had trusted me and I had shown her that when the time was right I would tell her everything. Maybe, just maybe, we were starting to get along.

I didn't get to think much more than this and hug my mother and Ben one last time before Griffin shifted again and came out of his tower. He was one of the better fliers, and he flew up high very swiftly. Following him would no doubt give us a workout.

As soon as he started moving away from the city, I motioned for Neritas and Flick to come with me.

"One of us will come back here as soon as we have a position on the demon's lair or any other news of importance," I told Alitas on the way past him.

"I should be coming with you."

"You're needed here. In case Griffin doesn't lead us to the demon and he targets somewhere else. Take the army wherever it is needed and keep training it in the meantime."

"Training? You had definitely better not be gone long enough that I have to do any of that." Alitas gave me an unexpected hug as well before he finally stepped aside.

I led Neritas and Flick into the air just in time to follow Griffin southeast and away from the city. We were almost a mile behind. In the daytime it wouldn't have been enough, but during the night with only a small moon to light the sky, it was perfect.

Can we kill this guy if he doesn't lead us anywhere useful? Flick asked as soon as we were away from the city ourselves. It was a surprisingly aggressive statement for Flick, and it took me a moment to properly process it and consider.

No, I eventually replied. *Not unless he poses an obvious threat. He might have done some despicable things, but he's just lost his home for passing information on. We don't know for sure what else he did or didn't do.*

All we know he is guilty of is giving the wrong person information. We don't even know for sure that it's the demon. But we should find out. And then if he does do anything that threatens anyone I care about ever again, there won't be any hesitation or checking for permission. I will kill him. Neritas' tone stayed almost perfectly even and matter-of-fact the entire time he spoke.

I didn't doubt that he meant it, but we had no idea how far we were going to have to fly. Or where Griffin was taking us. All we knew for sure was that if it was to the demon, we were about to start another battle. And this one would be on his home turf.

CHAPTER TWENTY-FOUR

It was almost dawn when Griffin finally slowed. The horizon ahead was beginning to lighten. We had flown over more of California and a lot of Arizona. Then Griffin had turned south and back west for a while, coming close to the Mexican border and not far from where we had found the last artifact.

If the corrupt elder was leading us toward the demon, then it would make sense to be going in this new direction given where the demon had come from when we had been defending the tribal village. We weren't far from there, almost as if Griffin was using it as a marker along the way to navigate by.

Griffin had found whatever he was aiming for, however, and he lowered to the ground, coming in slower. I slowed as well, not wanting to get any closer to him and risk being felt by any other presence or the demon. As Griffin landed, so did I, stretching my mind out to its full potential so I could keep an eye on him but not be right behind him anymore.

We turned back into humans as we landed on the edge of a suburb. It was quiet, and the night air kept us in darkness a little longer. There were a few street and house lights, but we avoided those, passing the back fence of a yard and finding an alley to stop in. Flick pulled out food from his bag loaded with snack bars.

I carried drinks, and quickly pulled them out as well and passed them around.

As soon as we had refreshed and rested for a couple of minutes, we moved closer, finding our way in the dark. Griffin was also moving on foot. I wanted to keep the distance between us, but I didn't want to lose him and my range in this form only stretched so far.

It felt strange to be trailing a man we couldn't see and I could only sense, but it wasn't long before I could also feel the telltale sense of the demon's corrupted creatures. There were some flying around Griffin before much longer, and as we got closer I felt even more.

"We've found him," I whispered. "Or at least a significant part of his army."

"That's good enough," Flick replied. Although I was tempted to send a message via phone to the city, Reijo and everyone else who knew the plan had warned against it. The demon was corrupting humans and that meant there was a chance that human technology could be traced.

I didn't like the idea of Flick flying all the way back to Detaris on his own, but he was fast enough that with any kind of head start he could outrun anything, and we'd juiced him up with as much magic as we could. All three of us were fully powered, fueled with all the magic the ancestors could give us, and on top of that, I had the invisibility artifact to make sure that at least Neritas and I stayed safe until help could return.

We watched Flick fly away and I continued to feel the connection I had to him, right until the very last moment.

"How long do you think he will be?" I asked.

"At least three hours until he gets to Detaris. It took us almost four and a half to get here at Griffin's speed. Even with Flick flying back in a direct line, he's got a trek ahead of him." Neritas took my hand, making me feel slightly better. At least I still had him by my side.

We had become a couple so naturally and gradually that sometimes I almost forgot that's what we were. I couldn't have asked for a better partner in my life. He understood me, understood what I had faced, and he'd been on my side since the moment we had met, even when I had feared otherwise.

That didn't mean I didn't worry for Flick, however. We'd flown a long way and he would have to make the trip three times in total. I had no doubt that he would return with the army we needed, making sure he wasn't left behind. I just hoped that didn't put him in danger if this became a war.

"We should get closer, scout the area under cover of your illusion device and find out as much as we can so we can plan a battle before anyone gets here. Hit him where it hurts." Although Neritas spoke the way he would about the demon himself, I wasn't sure he had been referring to the large monster this time and not Griffin. Either way, I was all for the plan.

I pulled the wrapped illusion rock from my bag and unwrapped it so I could begin manipulating it. I didn't make a very large illusion around us, just enough so we could move unseen and look like an empty space. In the night, this would be easy to maintain, and I was also sure that I could keep us hidden even if the demon came within ten yards of us.

As the sun came up I didn't doubt it would be harder, just as it had been the previous time. More important than any deception, however, was how well this device hid our magical presence.

Before we carried on and followed Griffin toward the heart of the demon's forces, I made sure the device had all the magical energy it would take. We did not want to run it out and I hadn't thought to test it to see if anyone else could sense us inside, like perhaps my mother. We would have to make do and hope it lasted.

With it only powering a small illusion to hide us, I didn't think it would run out for a long while, so I felt safe enough holding Neritas' hand and making my way closer.

The demon and his minions were still a good distance ahead as Griffin moved deeper into his army and we approached.

Ten minutes later I felt the demon himself. We had come away from the more residential area of the nearby city. Several times we wandered over dirt and sand where the ground was hard and dry from the heat in the area.

Finally several natural rocks and mounds of sandstone rose ahead of us, and I felt an army of creatures sitting on them. Most of the creatures looked as if they were birds by their outlines in the early morning light. The sun wasn't up yet, but the world was beginning to get brighter around us and there was no doubt we would be visible now if it wasn't for the artifact.

I didn't let go of Neritas, though both of us were moving slower and with more care. Several times we had to shift to one side when a shadow catcher, handler, or even a corrupted human came lurching past or close enough that they would have cut into our illusion and seen us.

Griffin was somewhere in the middle of the mass. The feel of him had changed slightly and made it harder for me to pinpoint him specifically. I didn't know if Neritas could feel it as well, but I got the impression that he was following along when he pulled a face and paused for a moment.

While we were surrounded by birds, wildcats, and other creatures full of corruption, I didn't dare to whisper anything to him. The hands we held were our only form of communication.

Whatever was happening to Griffin, he was becoming more like them and I wanted to rush closer and kill him before he did. This wasn't right. Griffin was a dragon, and if Griffin could become corrupted, there was a chance that all of us could. And that was a scary thought.

As we got closer to the heart of the area, I noticed that it seemed to be a cavern network. It started as rocks that formed two natural walls with no roof, but then disappeared into the ground and had either been dug out by the demon or had been a natural cave network that he had taken over.

Neritas gave my hand a squeeze and continued to walk deeper, but I hesitated and pulled him back a little. If we went in there and someone tried to walk through our space, we would be seen. He lifted his sword and made it clear we would be killing anything that got too close.

It made me nervous, but I saw his logic as well. Taking out some of the demon forces while we were impossible to see and find wouldn't be a bad thing. I could sense a lot of entities ahead of us, however, and it made me worry that the demon would be able to work out exactly where we were too fast and we would be noticed by so many of the lesser demons that we would be overrun.

Still, Neritas kept walking. If he was nervous, I couldn't tell. He kept going, almost leading me now, and I didn't doubt that he was heading for Griffin. Now that the dragon felt corrupted, he was going to make sure that the traitor died, and I was much more okay with that idea than I had been.

Now and then a corrupted creature got too close to us, but we moved efficiently and as a team, trapping and killing whatever entered our field of illusion before it saw us. I used the same darkness trick I had before, putting us in complete darkness briefly so we couldn't be seen even if it did get past our illusion.

It was draining me of magic faster than I'd have liked, but it was allowing us to get deeper without appearing to be detected, although the deaths were beginning to cause panic and unease among the troops.

After we had killed our first shadow catcher—and not just a corrupted creature—I felt a shift in the dynamics of the army, almost as if this was something more linked to the whole and therefore immediately noticed. We pulled back toward the edge of the cave and I shifted the illusion to bring the wall out slightly. The cave was dark and it helped hide us as we slowly crept away from where we had killed the creature.

With nothing but vapor left and us getting further away from where we had killed it, the army didn't have much chance of finding us. Still, we were still more cautious from then on in. The demon himself began to move, but he left the cave network on a route that didn't go past us.

A lot of the creatures and minor demons went with him, running past us and away. Griffin was slower, almost as if he lingered, moving around a small chamber not far from us.

For a few seconds I was torn, but as soon as there were significantly fewer entities between us and whatever Griffin had become, Neritas set off again, and if I was going to keep him safe, I had no choice but to follow. I ran after him, keeping up and killing anything else that came too close. It wasn't easy, but Neritas wasn't giving me any choice.

I wanted to call out to him, but I couldn't. It would alert everyone to our presence. He was so fixated on getting to Griffin before the traitor could get away that it took everything to keep up with him and kill whatever noticed us. My heart pounded, as I expected to be caught at any second, but the cave network continued to empty and Neritas kept running deeper.

Eventually he reached Griffin. The traitor was lying on his back in the middle of a small cave. He was breathing hard, covered in sweat, and his skin had taken on a strange hue. The cave was dimly lit but still dark enough that my illusion easily held up.

As soon as I could, I squeezed Neritas' hand, hoping to get his attention and get him to slow down. I wasn't sure I was ready for this. I wanted to see if we could save him first. See if we could pull the corruption out of him. I reached out to connect, wanting to win the man's heart back.

Neritas shook his head at me before he moved forward, taking me and the illusion with him. I needn't have worried we'd be caught, as Neritas snuffed the light and made the cavern pitch black. At the same time he brought the sword he was carrying down and cut Griffin's head clean off.

I stopped, almost dropping the artifact responsible for our illusion. It had taken all of half a second for Neritas to use his sharp sword and end Griffin's life, and the dragon hadn't even seen it coming. For a moment neither of us moved. Neritas was panting and exhausted, having used magic to give himself extra strength to strike with as well as control the dark and move fast.

I was stunned.

This wasn't an attack we had agreed on together. While I had been considering it, I hadn't made my mind up yet about it. As Griffin's body remained where it was, and very little vapor coming out of anywhere, I also wondered what had made him choose to serve the demon. Was this something that had seemed logical to him? Or had he been tricked?

I'd had so many more questions for him.

There was so little in the way of decay that I also worried that it would be obvious we had killed him, but Neritas seemed to have this under control as well. He moved the head back so it appeared to be attached to the body and then waved me over to him.

"Can you make it look as if we're where Griffin is?" he asked me, his voice a small whisper that only I would hear.

"I might be able to, but then they'll know we're here." I had no idea what Neritas was trying, but I wasn't sure I liked it.

"Trust me," he replied. "It's not perfect, but it's the best solution we can come up with in the situation we're in."

I fought back the desire to tell him that we wouldn't be in this situation if he hadn't killed Griffin so rashly, but it was an unfair thought. The truth was that I wouldn't have gotten answers. I'd tried already. All hesitating would have done was make us even more likely to be found and caught.

Not sure what else to do, but willing to trust Neritas, I made an illusionary *us* exactly where he said and then moved to stand on the other side of the cave with him.

"Now we need to make just enough noise that we attract a single shadow catcher. Maybe two." He didn't bother to hide his voice.

"Just one or two." I used the same volume. "That's oddly specific."

It was a random statement and meant little, as at least one entity outside the small cave noticed the noise and came back to investigate. Two shadow catchers dove toward the illusion of me and Neritas and attacked them as we both raised our swords. They rushed straight over Griffin, decaying his body and rotting it as they did.

Only then did they realize they had been tricked, and

by then it was too late. I darkened the entire area again and Neritas and I fought one each.

Within a minute they were both dead and Griffin had been slithered over so badly that there was little left of him and no way to tell how he had died. Our activity drew the attention of another entity, however, and the magical signature of something even stronger came through the cave network toward us.

I grabbed Neritas' arm to warn him and pulled him to the side of the cave as I shifted the illusion again to make us look as if we were part of the wall. It took a few seconds and made me fear we were detected, but the creature on its way didn't speed up.

We waited for a few more seconds before one of the tree-like handlers walked in. As it moved to Griffin to investigate, I tugged on Neritas and pulled him slowly around toward the exit, covering it with the illusion that it was a wall and standing in the gap together. I also made it look like a wall from the other side, making sure nothing else would come in here and disturb us.

As soon as we were in a good position, Neritas made the room dark one last time. With it being a handler and blinded by the darkness ourselves, we were both much more cautious, and I put the illusion device down, wanting to use both hands to fight.

We attacked limbs and hacked at body parts from as far away as we could. I still took a couple of hits to my armor, and each smack almost knocked me off my feet, but Neritas was more cautious.

Eventually we killed it. The body turned into mist for the most part, except the main part of the torso, which landed near what was left of Griffin. With the way they had both died and everything left behind, we had managed to make it look as if the two of them might have fought each other.

If anyone came across them now, there was a good chance someone would think Griffin had beaten the handler but been so spent some shadow catchers had finished him off before he could get away.

"Come on," Neritas whispered, being as quiet as possible again. "Let's get out of here and wait for the cavalry to arrive."

CHAPTER TWENTY-FIVE

As we headed toward the light outside, we had to slow again. There were more creatures and a couple of handlers, as well as humans waiting outside. And it was a lot brighter. While we had been inside and moving around, hunting Griffin and tidying up our mess, the majority of the army had prepared to leave.

Some of them were staying behind, guarding the area and acting as lookouts, but more were leaving, following a trail of entities I felt heading west from here.

I wanted to follow them, but for now we were essentially stuck. If we wanted to keep under the radar, we were going to have to move slowly, making sure our illusion held as we did. We stuck to one wall, and Neritas kept his sword out and a smaller dagger in the other hand to help him swiftly kill anything that got too close.

While I led us at a slow pace, I controlled what everyone else saw and kept an eye out for threats coming our way. Inch by slow inch, we made our way from the entrance of the cave network and along the left edge of the rock wall until we reached an area that was more open again.

Although I lost track of time, I didn't lose track of the army. The last part of it was ready to move out. Out here again we could still feel the demon with the army around him and helped by him in some way.

"Should we follow?" I asked as soon as we were far enough away I dared to speak again.

"You should stay here, or Flick won't know where to go from here." Neritas tucked his dagger in his belt a moment before he squeezed my hand. He then shifted to pull away from me despite us being out in the open.

"What are you going to do?" I didn't let go of him, wanting to make sure he was safe.

"Someone needs to follow the demon, and I can feel him from almost as far away as you can. I'll ping you my location at regular intervals."

"That could let him know he's being followed."

"Which is why we're going to get you safely away from this army first and then I'm going to follow with the illusion device. Only way to go after him. But you're needed here to reclaim and clean those artifacts. Then you can bring your extra powerful self to help me. It's the only way this makes sense."

Although I wanted to argue with Neritas, he was right. I bit my tongue and considered the alternatives quickly, but if I left him here to await the rest of the army, I wouldn't be doing what was needed and I would risk others dying to get artifacts. It only worked if I stayed and kept myself hidden, something I could do far more easily, even without the artifact, than anyone else. This was the safest plan for Neritas too.

"Promise me that you'll be careful?" I asked when I finally accepted his conclusion.

"As long as you promise me the same. My life is only complete with you in it, my queen." He smiled, and his eyes were full of intensity when he kissed me.

I kissed him back, pouring as much passion into the connection of our lips as I could possibly convey. I wanted to make sure he knew how I felt in the hope that he would come back for more.

Eventually I had no choice but to hunker down behind a rocky outcrop in the shadows and to one side of the camp and let him take the illusion device. He waited until the army was starting to move off, letting the main demon get far enough away from us that he wouldn't feel my power as we separated, and then I watched Neritas slip away from me until I was outside the illusion field.

It was as if my mind slipped off the connection I'd had to him and couldn't find it again, even though I knew it must be there somewhere.

The sensation was strange enough that it made me sure something was there, but I didn't know if it was a feeling I would recognize if I wasn't looking for it. With no way to know, all I could do was hunker down and wait for the backup to come.

With everything we had done since Flick had left and all the sneaking around and in and out of the lair, several hours had passed, but there were still plenty more before I had any hope of seeing some allies again.

Being alone felt strange. I knew I should have felt

vulnerable, but so little was left of the demon's army and I was so well equipped with weapons and armor that I was fairly sure I could have cut my way out of any situation involving these levels of enemies. Despite that, I stayed hidden. There was no sense in tempting fate, and with the rocky outcrop where it was, I could easily make it extra dark underneath it and keep myself hidden from view.

It left me only one thing to do: worry. About Neritas, about Flick, if we'd done the right thing with Griffin, and especially about how we were going to save everyone and stop the demon from turning entire cities of humans into his personal slave army.

As I waited, I also considered where the artifacts might be. I was pretty sure that the demon had taken some of them with him, no doubt choosing the best ones for whatever he was taking his army to do. If there were any here, I hadn't felt them, but I hadn't been looking for them either.

Griffin had been my sole focus, and then Neritas. Now I had very little else to do, and Neritas was right—it would be worth risking this even if all we could do now was take some of those items. While I kept myself hidden in shadows and the remaining demon guards milled around thinking they were safe, I felt out with my mind.

There were still a lot of entities, and it made it hard to figure out what I was feeling. Corrupted artifacts weren't very different, especially when someone like the demon had been using them and filling them with his version of energy or charge.

It took all my concentration to figure out that there were three in a small space deep in the ground. They must have been off another branch of the cave network to the one Neritas and I had gone down.

I considered going after them now, using my magic and making a path. With everything I had charged and my connection to the ancestors, there was a chance I could do it, but I held back. With an army it would be easy, and hopefully I would then find something I could use to chase after his army faster.

While I was hiding, Neritas must have touched down somewhere, because he sent me a ping to let me know his location. He hadn't gone that far yet, but I was able to work out he'd traveled almost straight west. If nothing else, it gave me a direction to take my army after this. Maybe his plan would work after all.

After about four more hours of waiting and the sun shining and beginning to come around enough that I had to shift position, I felt the first sign of dragons with my mind.

They were a smaller group, flying in fast, and they pulled up when they were still a little way from me.

Scarlet, I think that's you I can feel in the shadows under that rock, Flick said into my head. *Hope you're okay. If you think you can do so safely, want to come flying up to us?*

The last part was a question, but I didn't move right away and I wasn't in dragon form to be able to reply. I had to wait and think, feeling for the full forces. My army started to mass a little beyond Flick, no doubt trying to keep out of range of what they thought was the demon and his entire forces.

I waited only a few more minutes and then used magic to propel myself out of the shadows at a run toward Flick.

At the same time, I leaped into the air, transformed, and flapped up.

After so long in a cramped space it felt amazing to properly stretch out, to fly and push my body to its greatest speed.

The demon is no longer here, just remnants of his army, I told every mind I could sense or see. Douglas was riding with someone else on Flick's back. *Follow me. We're going to slaughter them while he's away and then steal his artifacts.*

I didn't waste time explaining more, but circled a couple of times so all the dragons in the air could catch up a little, and then I led them back to the army the demon had left behind to guard his lair.

They were still in shock from having me spring out from underneath a rocky outcrop right under their noses, but the few handlers left quickly organized their forces. It was a real mix of everything from shadow catchers to humans, and even what appeared to be corrupted dogs.

We all landed, with me a step ahead of everyone else. While the soldiers got down I charged the ground out from us as the animals rushed us, snarling and snapping. Some birds flew in as well, but our second wave of dragons stayed in the air and took them on, rolling and attacking the way Jace had perfected.

There weren't many corrupted humans in front of us, but our soldiers focused on them, shooting them with tranqs for now just to stop them from being a problem.

I tried to be careful what I charged so I didn't hurt any of them, but I took out anything trying to get too close to us at first.

Once the first wave of dragons formed a line with Flick

on one side of me and Alitas on the other, I let the creatures come closer. Plenty of shadow catchers came out of the caves to attack as well.

With surprise on our hands and a fresh, eager-to-fight army, we made short work of a lot of the forces on the ground, and I rushed at the one handler that was showing its face above ground. It had tentacles, but a little magic and some light tricks soon had me past most of its defenses.

I lopped off limbs as I went and watched them fall to the ground where they smoked and became vapor in a matter of seconds. As soon as that demon was dealt with, the forces on the surface faltered—human, demon, and animal alike. The dragons above landed as well, and we made short work of what was left on the surface.

"Hold the area," I told Jace, grateful to see her. "I'm going underground to get the last handler and some shiny treasure."

"Not without me, you're not," Alitas said this time. He sounded cross but there was a slight smirk on his face. Without Neritas and knowing that Flick was tired, I wasn't going to say no to the remaining one of my usual bodyguards and allies insisting on going with me.

"I'd like to join you," Ben added as he rushed up, having only landed in our third wave of dragons. He knew how to fight, but he was still more of a scholar than a swordsman. "I want to see what this lair is like, learn what I can about this demon. After everything I've been studying, I think this might help."

Although I wasn't sure exactly how it would help, I didn't argue with him. I let him fall in. I also let Cios join us and picked out a few other dragons to make sure I had at least one decent-strength dragon of each color. Before I could head off, Douglas appeared and insisted he was coming with me as well. They formed a small but powerful team.

I didn't plan to fight much. Most of the forces had been above ground and were now dead, but I wanted to be careful, just in case. A 'get in, grab the artifacts, and get out' mission. With the demon flying west, we needed to be fast.

Alitas and I led the way, taking different tunnels than the last time I had been down here. We met a little resistance, but mostly in the form of corrupted animals. I kept the ground in front of us charged and it dealt with them before any reached us, making our journey even easier.

A handler still hung back, not far from the artifacts I sought. It had a small army around it, but I knew we could take care of it so I pressed forward anyway. As soon as we were close I gave Alitas a nod and we charged the rest of the way. There were a dozen or so shadow catchers, and they fought hard, but they were soon vaporizing and leaving us with nothing but a handler between us and the artifacts.

I made it simple so no one else would get hurt, and charged the ground up toward it, running close alone and fighting it. The creature looked more like an oversized crab than anything else. It tried to pinch at me with large claws and snip off my limbs, but I kept moving, dodging and using magic to speed my reactions until I could barely keep up with myself.

Instinct and training memory took over as I attacked and sought weak parts of the creature. It wasn't the easiest fight and it took several minutes, but eventually I prevailed. The creature collapsed, and smoke started to come out of the joints in its natural armor. It had taken a lot of different minor cuts, and the charge across the ground under its legs had hit it with painful energy spike after painful energy spike.

As soon as it was out of my way enough, I proceeded.

The creature had been guarding one of the larger caverns, and in it were the artifacts I could feel. I moved toward them before I realized that they weren't the only things in the room. There were other strange objects, a metal treasure trove of relics from different cultures.

I hesitated, wondering what the demon could have wanted with all this, and it made me stop to look around. Ben did the same while Alitas secured the items. Just as I'd done with Griffin's item, he used cloth to pick them up, not touching them himself until we established what they could do and cleaned them up.

Trusting him to handle it, I looked around at the other stuff. Ben fixed on one that looked like some ornamental headdress from some long-forgotten tribe. If we hadn't bumped into a tribe recently, I wouldn't have looked twice at it, but Ben touched it before I could stop him.

He froze as if something had stunned him and then he seemed to collapse.

"Be careful," Douglas called as he came rushing over as well.

"Don't touch him," I yelled, wishing I'd said something sooner. "Don't touch anything in here, anyone."

I could feel what had happened to him, and the corruption beginning to spread through his body.

"That antiserum thing, with the antibodies. Do you have any?" I asked Douglas.

"Yes, but it was meant for humans, I don't know if it will—"

"Give it to him anyway. He needs it. Now!"

Douglas nodded and reached into his trouser pocket before pulling out a small case. It had three needles in it and a large jar, all of them packed in foam so they wouldn't break if battered around. He quickly drew a dose and jabbed it into Ben's arm.

If anything, it seemed to make everything worse, and we all had to back up to avoid being hit or caught by him. I didn't know if the corruption could spread, but I knew that there was nothing else we could do to help him but wait.

Everyone backed up and I watched him writhe, considering reaching for him with my mind and connecting. Maybe I could suck it out of him. Before I could, I felt the speedy approach of another dragon. And this was one I recognized immediately.

Neritas had come back.

CHAPTER TWENTY-SIX

I froze in an entirely different way. If Neritas was coming back here, it could only mean that the demon was on his way too. We couldn't get stuck in a cave when he was out there with an entire army. This was exactly the worst scenario.

Scarlet, get out of there. It's a trap.

Tears welled up as I looked at Ben, seeing him writhe on the floor.

"We've got to go," Alitas added, either getting a mental message from Neritas as well or working it out for himself.

"But Ben." My voice came out as a high-pitched wail. "We can't leave him."

Alitas came up to me and took my arms, making sure he had my attention.

"I know he matters to you, but you've done everything you can for him and it's not working right now. If we stay here we're all dead and so are most of the dragons and friends we have on the surface. We've got some people tranquilized up there, but we can't get anyone to safety if we're down here."

Despite his words, I didn't want to listen. I looked back at Ben lying on the floor. Flick came up to me as well and slapped me, barely doing any harm but making it sting.

"Sorry, Red. But Alitas is right. We need you to keep your head on. You're our queen and we need you to help save the rest of us. I'll stay down here as long as I can with Douglas to try and get Ben out if you want, but—"

I shook my head, liking the idea of him and Douglas risking their lives for Ben even less. He was being infected with corruption and I didn't have time to help him fight it and protect everyone and get them out of here safely. It was yet another moment when I had to choose between winning a war and winning a battle.

"We've got the artifacts and hopefully Ben will follow as soon as his body fights the corruption," I said, not sure I believed what I was saying. "No one is staying behind."

I considered changing my mind and staying as well, but Neritas had landed on the surface and the army was coming back. A group presence was heavy in my mind. At the same time, Ben stopped writhing and got to his feet. He looked at all of us and then lurched forward in a manner very unlike him.

Not missing a beat, Douglas shot him with a tranquilizer and sent him crashing to the ground again.

"He's not in there for now," Douglas reminded me, motioning for all of us to leave.

I still resisted, but only until I felt the demon on the edge of my senses. It was too late, and I had to make sure everyone else was safe. Ben was gone.

The thought filled me with fury and I let out a growl.

"I'm going to end that demon if it's the last thing I do," I said before taking off. I didn't wait for anyone as I sprinted off back up the tunnels toward the surface.

There was no caution this time and no one in my way. I ran toward the surface, wanting to get there before anyone dangerous landed and put pressure on my forces. I was going to give the demon hell and make him pay for everything he had cost me so far. So many had been lost, and now he'd taken yet another dragon from me.

I felt rage fuel me and I ran faster and harder than I ever had before, getting back to the entrance in what felt like seconds. The light barely blinded me as I used the feel of all the different people and creatures to guide me toward the enemy.

Birds came at us first, but I raised my shield and then launched into the air, turning into a dragon as I charged the air around everyone else. Many of the birds dropped from the sky, dead on impact. I carried on, barreling toward the demon and anything else still in the air.

Although I didn't charge the ground, the dragons formed up a line and I heard Douglas call for the soldiers to get behind it and choose human targets.

Red, what are you doing? Neritas asked, coming up on my flank.

I'm going to kill him.

Not like this. Think, Red. Think about what you're doing. We've got the artifacts. We can feel them on Alitas. That means he can too. All the forces are already heading straight for him.

I let out an angry roar, feeling what Neritas was telling me as well. No part of me wanted to admit he was right, but I roared again, letting out some of the fury I felt before circling back around. Flick was standing near Alitas, and they were already fighting hard as shadow catchers and other creatures hammered them.

With no humans close, I charged the ground in front of them to clear the enemy back, and then I landed in front of all of them. Still in dragon form, I let out a third and final roar, charged myself, and swept around in a large circle, hitting anything and everything that got too close with my claws and tail, and snapping at them with my mouth.

As soon as I'd forced the demon's army to keep a wide berth and there was nothing left to attack, I shrank back into human form. Still in front of my own army, I slowly walked forward.

I lifted my sword in one hand and my shield in the other.

"Come on then!" I yelled as loudly as I could. "If you think you are the great evil, come and show me. Throw everything at me and see if you are truly strong enough!"

Despite my calls for attention, the minor demons and others spread out and around me, heading for every opponent. I continued to hold charged ground where I could, but the dragons all rushed toward me, fighting out from the caves and bringing the soldiers toward me.

With the soldiers focusing on hitting humans and most of the dragons focusing on shadow catchers and corrupt creatures, it left handlers to me, and I picked one from the crowd of enemies closest to us. Charging the ground around it quickly isolated it. Again I strode toward it, using my charged armor, shield, and sword to shove and stab enemies out of the way.

The handler eagerly rushed toward me, but I was so focused and angry now that adrenaline filled me and had me moving automatically. I sliced off several appendages as I shoved the handler back and continued my relentless assault. Again Neritas and Flick tried to keep up with me, both of them keeping the area behind me open and safe from enemies.

It helped drive a wedge shape out away from the caves and off to one side. In some ways, it was helpful, as it broke us away from being trapped, but it also meant that those with me could choose to run away instead of fight at any point.

More of the demon's army kept coming and we were still surrounded, however. Many of them went for Alitas, who still had the artifacts in his pocket. Neritas landed finally, becoming human in one of the few spaces there were. I cleared another for Flick, aware he was probably tired, and let him land as well.

Although I had considered falling back into a line, I didn't have to. The soldier with Alitas didn't allow him to do anything but get back to my side and try to protect me.

"Red, you should take the artifacts," Neritas shouted, looking pointedly at the bundle Alitas had sticking out of a very large pocket.

I didn't doubt he was right, and it made me wonder if any of them could be used in this fight to help against the demon. Either way, Alitas shoved the bundle at me and for a couple of seconds I let everyone protect me so I could open my bag and shove them in. The great thing was that I didn't need to be holding them to activate them and find out what they could do.

Despite not knowing what they might do, I tried to work it out and connected to all three anyway. They all tried to suck the energy out of me and feed whatever was inside them, but I held strong, only letting them have so much magic at once. Despite that, I only felt as if I could fight with the sword and shield while I cleaned up the corruption.

I grew weaker as more shadow catchers pressed in and the demon stopped lingering at the edge of the fight to come and attack finally. As my connection to the ancestors waned, I had to fall back even more, no longer able to charge whole chunks of ground without risking running out of my own magic far too soon.

After fighting these forces many times, I knew that they weren't going to stop coming. But we were almost at the edge of the army and clear space was in sight. If we could just take down a bunch of the enemy, I would be happy.

The demon came close and I looked up at him. Our eyes met despite being in different forms. I had what he wanted now and he knew it. More birds came at me, but while wearing the armor, I was impervious. The dragons around me weren't so fortunate. Many took scratches and small hits of decay as so many birds descended on us that I couldn't see the sky for at least a minute.

I wasn't sure where they had come from, but I charged the air again, looking for the demon and wanting to get everything between us out of the way. As my magical energy killed the birds and they started to fall, I had to dodge.

Moving faster than any human body could, I got between the rotting missiles and tried to look for a way through to the demon again. He'd pulled back, and it forced me to weave back and forth and hampered me from getting to him.

The birds eventually all died, however, and I could see the demon again, a dark form in the sky, holding back and hovering above his army. There were a lot of humans who had been sedated, and I saw soldiers working with dragons to give them shots and try to remove the corruption.

I hoped it worked, because I wasn't going to be able to stick around on this battlefield and heal them all. I didn't dare just push out magical energy to any of them either, knowing it would fight the corruption but possibly lead to the death of the person as well.

Anger had fueled me through the first part of this battle, but it was fading from my system and I was left to survey what we had achieved. With the bursts of energy I had used, I had killed a lot of the animals the demon had corrupted, and my dragons were beating back shadow catchers, but I could also feel a lot more forces further back and I was pretty sure several portal-like things were opening up again.

More of the minor demons were coming from somewhere, and I knew we would be overrun. When the demon had added corrupted humans to his forces he had tipped the scales in a way that we couldn't compete with.

Despite knowing this, I wasn't ready to give up. I had gained the artifacts and I would use them against him. Every time I thought of losing Ben, I wanted to take the fight straight to the demon again. I had to make him pay for what he'd cost me. There was no way I was losing someone who meant so much to me and not making him pay.

The demon hovered too far up from me, however, and I knew if I moved to go straight for him I would leave my army vulnerable. One more glance over the battlefield gave me an idea. I looked and felt for every single handler on the battlefield, and then I charged the ground where they all stood, pumping magic into them and everything around them directly.

All of them shuddered, but I didn't stop, pulling magic from all the dragons, what was left of the connection to the ancestors, and my own armor and weapons. I was killing all of them at once and making it look easy, but it was costing me.

As each of them died, one after the other, freeing me up to pump more magic into the remaining ones, the demon's army descended into chaos. With no one controlling the shadow catchers and the corrupted creatures and humans, all of them slowed, and only the few closest to us showed much desire to fight.

By the time the last handler fell, I was dizzy. All of my own magic was drained and a lot had been taken out of the items I carried. One last time I looked up at the demon in the sky and glared defiantly at him.

He might have the larger army, but I was the more powerful one now.

CHAPTER TWENTY-SEVEN

Feeling the pain of using so much magic so fast, I slipped back behind the fighting line and let everyone else kill shadow catchers for a bit. Neritas and Flick were close by and the comfort of knowing they'd got this helped.

Despite everything I had done, we were still surrounded off to one side of the cave entrance. We would need to come up with a strategy to get out of here.

No matter what I tried, nothing seemed to help long-term, and the humans we'd sedated and hit with antibodies were still lying all over the ground. In some cases they were hampering our enemy as much as us, but for the most part it just added to the chaos and carnage.

Overwhelmed, I pulled back even further until I bumped into Douglas. He steadied me and paused beside me, no longer lining up his next shot at a human.

"You look as bad as I feel," he said as he checked his ammo. "And I can only sedate three more humans, assuming I don't miss."

"Better make them count." There were far more of them

ahead of me, and after that there would be little we could do to save them from certain death. I knew none of us were going to want to kill them, and that meant it was time to get out of there.

No sooner had I thought this than there was a ripple from the army ahead. Some of the people started getting up again and the shadow catchers turned and shrieked at them.

It took me a few seconds to realize what was happening, but then it dawned on me. The antibodies were working and the humans were recovering and getting back up.

"Help them," I yelled, making sure as many of the dragons could hear me as possible. It also caught the attention of the humans and they started to fight over to us as well. Some of them had been carrying weapons to hit us with and they picked these up again.

The chaos grew even worse as some of the weapons now hurt them on touch from the corruption held within them. Others were simply inert and decayed away as soon as they were used on a shadow catcher. It made the battle easier on my exhausted dragons, however.

A couple of seconds after that a thought hit me like a bullet. I stopped breathing for a few seconds as I remembered Ben. If this was working for the humans, there was a good chance it would be working for Ben.

I had left him in the cave.

I rushed toward the entrance, readying my shield to push demons out of the way and getting ready to charge the path before me. I felt ahead with my mind as well, trying to feel the magic that would be in him and show me if he was fighting the corruption as well. Would Ben be coming back to us?

I knew he would be vulnerable—the humans were evidence of that—but I couldn't feel him yet.

"Red, what are you doing?" Neritas called, trying to fight after me. Flick wasn't far behind him.

"Getting Ben." I barely stopped as I hacked and slashed at the shadow catchers trying to get in my way. They were still fairly chaotic, but the basic instinct to attack anything moving still stood.

More of the minor demons came our way, getting between me and my friends. I charged the ground behind me a little, making sure nothing dangerous could come at me from behind and making it easier for Neritas and Flick to catch up. For now I was going to trust that everyone else could hold their own.

I lost track of how many of the demons I killed. The magic I used came from what was left in the sword and shield. None of the demons even got close enough for long enough to drain anything from my armor. The last small amount coming from the ancestors was enough to charge the ground.

Long term, I couldn't keep it up, but while I looked for Ben it would be enough. I continued to feel for him with my mind, and a strange individual feeling came from roughly the right spot. It had to be him. It wasn't like the other demons or shadow catchers. He was fighting this. He had to be.

Angry at myself for not sticking with him and protecting the area, I threw myself at any enemy that got in the way, sometimes getting to a human who was coming around. I sent them toward the dragons, trying to help protect them for a while.

Now and then I glanced behind me, making sure that Neritas and Flick were following. Alitas, Jace, Reijo, and several others were trying to follow, and behind them were several soldiers using normal guns, led by Douglas. All of them were fighting toward me and creating a safe corridor for humans to get to the other dragons.

I was stretching it out, however, and able to see the cave entrance again now. Because we had fought out from there in the first place, there weren't many enemies in that direction, but there were enough that I was quickly surrounded as I got close to the entrance. I growled as I started to take hits from behind despite the charged ground.

With my connection to the ancestors so taxed for so long, it couldn't keep up against this many demons getting this close to me. I was no longer keeping them at bay. I stalled out, making no more forward progress.

Each hit I took battered me around, making it harder for me to fight back and protect myself. The shadow catchers slowly died anyway, but they were draining the magic from me and they were coming from almost every direction.

My getting stuck in the circle of demons allowed Flick and Neritas to catch up, and both of them fought hard to get to me. As they added their magic to mine and connected to me, I felt Neritas shove some more magic into me from his weapon, shield, and the armor sets they both now had.

It was a rush to not be so drained, and it helped me fight a little further, but Neritas grabbed my elbow to stop me from striking a shadow catcher. He stabbed it instead, ensuring it didn't hit me, but he didn't let go of me.

"You don't have the strength left to fight back in there. None of us do, and we have an enormous number of humans to protect. We have to go back to the others and get everyone out of here." Neritas spoke as if he wasn't going to be argued with. As if this was information I needed to know and would entirely influence my decision.

Guilt and anger made me want to shrug off his grip and plow ahead anyway, but he let go. I lashed out at the shadow catchers ahead a little longer, cutting them into ribbons and watching them try to pull themselves together. Eventually they all vaporized and an opening appeared before me, with very little between me and the cave entrance.

I took the first of several intended strides toward it, but a cry from behind made me pause. Flick had been hit. A shadow catcher's tail hit him in a gap on the back of his armor as he bent to help a human woman to her feet. It knocked him forward and he almost collapsed on her, putting them both in danger.

Torn, I rushed toward Flick, charging the ground around them both. I slammed my shield down beside us so I could pull out my healing device. Flick tried to stand and pull back, but the rotten flesh and all the oozing that came with the movement made him pause.

Neritas got an arm under him and helped him to the side, freeing the woman underneath.

"Stay close," I told her as I started to heal Flick, working fast and hoping that we could get him back on his feet before his body ran out of everything needed to repair it.

Neritas let him go as my healing took effect and he could at least hold himself on hands and knees. Grabbing his sword again, Neritas took over the job of fighting to defend us and I did what I could to help Flick.

By the time the device had done all it could, Neritas had circled us several times, keeping our enemy back, the woman had bumped into me five times, and Flick was just about able to stand, although he winced with every movement. It would have to be good enough.

With both the woman and Flick needing help, I had no choice but to help Neritas get them back to Alitas.

The captain of my honor guard stopped me. "My queen, I know this battle is hard for you and you want to go rescue Ben, but we need you to think clearly. *We* need you. Your people need you." The concern in his eyes was clear and I halted, gulping as I realized what I had put them all through in dashing off on my own and fighting without thinking about a strategy beyond reaction and my desire to save Ben.

This wasn't how I should fight. This wasn't how anyone in charge should fight.

I took several deep breaths and looked around us once more, taking stock of what I could feel and my magic at the same time.

Humans still fought on ahead of us and in pockets, some of which we could easily rescue if we tried, but there were also a lot behind our lines now, some of whom were wielding guns they had been given and the charged ammo we could provide them.

We couldn't fly this many people out of here, however.

Not without several trips and a safe place to shelter them. We needed reinforcements and an evacuation plan.

Discovering that we couldn't do this and fight the demon alone hurt my pride, but I went to Douglas, letting my dragons hold the line a little longer without me. Flick was almost entirely out of action and he followed me on instinct.

"Can we get any evacuation support for all these people from the US Army?" I asked him, knowing he worked for them still even if he would be on my side at some point.

He frowned but pulled out a phone and tried to get a message sent. It was the crudest way to communicate, but we had people here with us that hadn't been part of our army to start with and they were waking up after the corruption in various states of ability and need.

Some had clearly been corrupted for so long that they were still out for the count on the ground and really needed medical help. I didn't think we were going to get to those, even though the sense I had of the corruption in them was fading. This process was far gentler than the way I had done it. Their own bodies were being boosted to fight it themselves. Many had also only been corrupted recently, because the demon had lost so many to us in the previous battle.

It worried me that he had corrupted so many so fast, but I couldn't change that now. We had to retreat again. I was almost out of magic. I'd almost gotten Flick killed, and even if I wanted to, I couldn't fight back to the cave entrance, let alone deep into it again.

I was going to have to accept it. What energy I had left

was going to have to be used in our battle to hold the line while we retreated.

"Get the humans who are weakest and need the most help to the edge of our group and we'll fight a way through to freedom for them." I knew it wasn't going to be easy to essentially walk an entire group of people away from a battle, but it was the best I could offer.

Until help arrived, we had to work together. I wouldn't abandon my people. Alitas was right—they needed me.

CHAPTER TWENTY-EIGHT

Several minutes later, and it was as if we hadn't moved at all. We were trying to work our way out, but more and more shadow catchers kept coming, and the demon himself was hovering in the air and controlling their movements.

With several portals coming closer to us as well, each one spewing out more of the minor demons, we were slowly getting overwhelmed.

I had thought we could take on the demon and win, take his artifact pieces, and get away again, but the whole plan was proving too much. I'd lost my head and used my magic to fight in the wrong way. Now I didn't have enough left to get us out of here safely.

Still, none of us gave up. We just needed to get a portal or two closed and cut our way out. I had to hope that would be enough.

Flick was barely standing, and it was clear that he wasn't the only dragon who could no longer really fight on.

Although it was going to add exhaustion to their pain, I pulled most of the magic out of them, their weapons, and their shields and armor. Right now I needed it, and they weren't going to use it in combat. Not anymore.

It was almost enough to fill me up again. Fighting more cautiously had also allowed the connection with the ancestors to recover a little, but it still wasn't up to the usual strength. This wasn't going to be easy, but if we stood any chance of holding on until reinforcements arrived, then I had to do something more sensible with what was left of the magic.

The entire group of fighting dragons was hard-pressed, however, and the soldiers were running out of every kind of ammo. No one could help me do this. I had to close the portals on my own.

I did the only thing I could think of to get closer and leaped up into the air, transforming into my dragon form as I did. Within a second, I was flying above the enemy toward the portal and then I dropped down again right in front of it. As soon as I was in human form I charged the ground behind me, fought the shadow catcher right before me, and connected to the portal.

It took all my control and concentration to both fight and pump energy from my connection to the ancestors and the other sources into the portal.

At first, seeing it start to close, I didn't think it was going to be fast enough, but I didn't give up. I fought as if Ben were on the other side of the enemy in front of me and made sure that nothing else got out of the portal.

Somewhere I heard a loud roar, and I was pretty sure I was going to have a demon to face off against in only a few more seconds, but I didn't slow or worry about it yet. I was unable to feel his obvious magical signature in my mind over everything else I was doing.

The portal shrunk faster and faster, getting too small for a shadow catcher to pass through and then closing entirely. I'd been pouring so much magic into it so fast that the pop of losing the connection when it snapped shut almost made me lose my balance.

As soon as I regained my bearings I powered up into the air again and away from that location. I was surprised to find that the demon hadn't been the one to roar. More dragons were coming in from the northeast, the familiar red of Grigick with them.

The group split, and half flew to join me while the other half went to back up Alitas and the rest of the dragons acting as our protective force. Our entire main army was now a circle of dragons around a pressed mass of people either injured or unable to do anything to help anymore. The fresh dragons would help them hold on and spread out a little. For now it was a ray of hope.

Portal closing? Grigick asked.

If possible. I've got one done. I circled and aimed for the next one.

I'd started with the one that was between my army and the north side of the press of demons, the smallest stretch of enemies between them and clear space, hoping that it would make it easier for Alitas to push in that direction, but I aimed for the portal closest to them next.

With any luck I'd be doing them some good, and if nothing else, I was pissing off the demon and making it harder for him to hold ground. There still weren't any more handlers on the battlefield, and I hoped this was a permanent issue for him. After all, it wasn't as if ent-like creatures and tentacled monsters were native to Earth.

As I dropped down in front of the next portal, I was joined by six other dragons, one of each color. I pulled magic from all of them, although at a slower rate, and with seven of us fighting in front of the portal, we didn't need to do this as fast and push ourselves as hard.

Still, I didn't want to take too long. Pushing faster seemed to use less magic, and I used all the magic I could get from the ancestors as soon as I was connected.

Within another minute, the portal was small enough that no more demons were going to come through and bother us. On top of that, Grigick had clearly been practicing how to fight. He skewered the final demon to have come through it, sending yet another puff of smoke and giving us a clear center to fight out from while the portal finished closing.

We collectively took out several more shadow catchers before another portal snapped entirely shut, hopefully never to open again.

I waited for all the dragons with me to get into the air first, holding the fort as Grigick led the way and circled above. The demons pressed in and I was getting low on magic again, but I still wasn't about to give up.

After pushing the enemy back one last time, I also launched into the air. This time the demon was on the move, but he wasn't coming toward me. Instead, his forces appeared to shift. More of them were bunched up around the cave and the final portals moved in that approximate direction.

What was left of his human army started coming toward us, and the demon flew toward the cave entrance and landed somewhere I couldn't see.

All of me wanted to pursue him and take the fight to him, knowing that he was opting to protect the lair and pull back to an easier position to defend. Even after using my magic to an extreme, I was putting him on the defensive. Only a couple of seconds later, shouts, roars, and the feeling of something else approaching let me know the demon had also sensed the tides turning.

Dragons were still arriving, and they had soldiers with them as well. Another handful of dragons arrived, all green, including a particular family from a very small dragon city in the mid-west of the US. They reached our army first as I led Grigick and others back to them.

Army scout vehicles and faster tank-like artillery vehicles came rolling up next. Several dragons helped charge them up so they could barrel through shadow catchers to get to us. Immediately, soldiers and dragons worked together to get the most injured onto the vehicles and get them out of there.

I fought to keep the shadow catchers at bay, but it was as if they were leaderless again and only fighting us because we were nearby and offensive to them. More and more of the demon's forces were retreating, and it soon became clear that we didn't need to retreat but merely hold our ground and let the soldiers get all the people safe and cared for.

By the time we were no longer surrounded by shadow catchers and able to start wading out in a line toward the lair, the demon and the majority of his forces were gone. I could still feel several open portals but I also got the impression that he had found some way to retreat through the cave network and flee.

I considered going after him again, but I couldn't feel anything that could be Ben anymore, and there were still hundreds of enemies in the area, even if some of them were beginning to drift off and the portals appeared to be closing on their own, no longer sustained by the demon's magic.

For a few seconds, I took it all in, trying to feel where the forces were flowing to and where the demon might have gone. Somehow, I would follow him and make him pay. He was fleeing the fight and I needed to go after him to find Ben. But it was already too late. No matter how I searched with my mind, I couldn't feel him, and what was left of his army was scattering, with the exception of the people.

The humans were all coming toward us. So many were still corrupted. But the new wave of soldiers had brought more tranquilizer darts, and they swiftly handed them out. With my magic low and my shield drained entirely, I slung the latter on my back and took a gun. I wasn't the best shot, but I wasn't about to forget the reminder Alitas had given me.

I was the leader of this army and I would lead by example. I wasn't giving up.

We shot and shot, knocking out person after person long before they could get to us, reloading and working as a team with the fresh soldiers. No one stopped if they weren't too injured to hold a weapon, and no one complained. Eventually, there were no humans left shambling toward us and we could return to what was left of the shadow catchers for now.

The battle slowly wound down, but I didn't stop fighting. I kept going and hunting the shadow catchers on the surface until there was nothing standing in front of me, and the soldiers behind me had relaxed.

I looked around to see people moving between the corrupted humans that were sedated on the ground but not cured yet and giving out what antibodies they could to help them. Many of them looked better than the first and second time we had encountered corrupted humans, and I could at least hope no one would need major medical intervention.

Once I made sure that Flick had also been taken care of, I slumped to the ground, exhausted. I put the gun down beside me, my fingers numb from gripping my sword and pulling the trigger so many times. My body was shaking, but I was only vaguely aware of it. Someone was saying something nearby, but it was as if the words were coming from the other side of a thick wall. They were garbled and quiet.

My connection to the ancestors was nothing but a slow trickle of magic now, but I brought it into myself, letting it help me recover. At some point, someone pressed a sandwich into one of my hands and a bottle of water into the other. I consumed them on autopilot, noticing that I wasn't the only Detaris dragon who had sat where I'd last fought and hadn't moved again.

War was ugly, and this battle had been one of the ugliest of them all.

CHAPTER TWENTY-NINE

I lost track of time as I slowly recovered post-battle. Several dragons came to check on me, and at some point Neritas, Reijo, Jace, Alitas, and after a while even Flick came to sit with me. Douglas finally flung himself down near the middle of the group.

"One thing is for sure, life with you dragons is never dull," he said, speaking before any of the rest of us could. He pulled a hip flask from a back pocket, checking it for dents and marks, but seeming satisfied.

Then he opened it and took a swig.

"You look like you need this too, Your Highness." He held it out to me. I took it without thinking and took a gulp as well before passing it back. I felt the alcohol burn before it settled as a warm heat in my stomach. I wasn't a big drinker, but something about it made me feel a little better.

Douglas passed it to each of us in turn. No one refused it, and we practically drank it dry before he got it back at the end. Then Jace produced another. Hers went around as well, starting with me, as Douglas had, after drinking herself.

Once we'd emptied hers as well, I almost expected Alitas or Reijo to pull a third out and keep it going, but it was as if we collectively agreed that we'd had enough. Everyone stood instead.

There were still people being treated around us, and once again the military had erected makeshift shelters to keep the sun off and allow people to work and get everyone on their feet. No one had asked me to heal them yet, but I went over to where it appeared the worst injured were lying and did so anyway.

I couldn't feel any enemies anymore, not even the faint trace of a shadow catcher on the edge of my mind. While we had been busy taking care of our own, the demon had fled with his forces, taking Ben with him, and the rest had run off while I had been too fatigued to think straight.

Although I didn't feel much better and I was so low on magic that I barely had any of my own, I healed a few people. Thankfully, the dragons who could heal spread out to all do the same. There weren't many who needed our help to save their lives, and Alitas stopped me from going to heal someone with what looked like a broken arm who had already been given painkillers and made comfortable.

"Enough. You've done enough. Everyone else will be just fine without your help. We should return to Detaris with the artifacts we've gained."

Although Alitas was right about one part, I still shook my head. "I want to go into the lair. He's abandoned it and I want to see what else he might have left behind."

"That I can understand. But we're all coming with you. No more surprises and no more splitting the party."

"Yes, boss," I replied, smiling a little and trying not to think of Ben. He had been with me and it hadn't done him any good.

Despite that, I led my friends back into the dark again, wondering if I needed to remind them all not to touch anything. I lit objects we all carried this time, trying to create a more ambient, friendly light that didn't drain me too much, and I was equally grateful when Douglas pulled a flashlight out.

Alitas did the same and saved me even more magic. Despite that, I still lit my sword and shield, even though both were almost entirely drained of magic. It was strange to be walking the cavern tunnels again, and for a little while I wasn't sure I was going in the right direction.

The last time I had been down there, I had followed the magic sources, letting them guide me as I made decisions at junctions. Now all I could feel were the artifacts in my bag and us. Nothing else with any trace of magic was within range anymore.

Thankfully, with more dragons on the surface, I knew I'd be able to get us back out again, but the longer we were down in the dark, the more I worried that I had taken a wrong turn and wasn't going to make it back to where I had found the artifacts and lost Ben.

I knew that there wasn't likely to be much else useful in the room, if anything, and I didn't expect to find Ben there , but I had to go and see it again, take in what had happened and at least try to figure out if there was anything I could have done differently.

Eventually we reached the same room. It was almost exactly as we'd left it. Ben wasn't there.

Although I hadn't expected him to be there, my heart still sank at finding him gone. I'd wanted a miracle, something, anything... Even a dead body would have meant I could grieve and move on. Nothing was worse than this emptiness. Now all I had were questions. Was he alive? Was he still a dragon? Was he something else? Had the antibodies helped him? Was the demon taking out his frustration on poor Ben?

And most importantly, was I ever going to see him again?

When Anthony had gone missing, almost the first person I had stumbled into was Ben, and he had held my world together ever since. I didn't know what to do with him gone.

For several seconds I stood in the middle of the room and fought back tears. The room full of strange metals, ornaments, and objects I didn't recognize hazed out as my vision blurred and I tried to hold it together.

No one touched anything. Everyone had been there the very first time and was aware of what could happen. But it didn't stop Alitas from looking around and feeling out with his mind as well.

"There's corruption on everything in this room. It's as if the demon was trying to use it for something, or to make something."

"Or set up a trap," I suggested, my voice cracking on the last word. I closed my mouth with another snap, not sure I could say anything else just yet.

No one else replied, but Neritas slipped his hand in

mine and held it. It brought me some comfort, reminding me that I wasn't alone, as I had been when I lost Anthony. I had a much bigger family now, but Ben was still a big part of it.

"I want to try and take some of this back with us, but I think it needs to be contained properly." Alitas crouched in front of one very ornate piece of metal. It looked as if it had once been a wall decoration or the side of a building or a floor.

"You can probably store it the way I had the artifact pieces," I replied. "Wrap it in something with a very faint charge to protect the wrap from decaying."

That was how I had the three corrupted artifact pieces in my bag without harming everything else in there. Though I'd dimmed their corruption, they had a faint magical layer of protection around them.

Alitas nodded as if I had said something obvious and he should have known it. Ben clearly hadn't. He'd not even spared a thought before touching the corrupted item that hurt him.

I helped Alitas, charging the large t-shirt he pulled from his own pack and helping him lift the small item and wrap it up. I wanted to get this back to Detaris and study it. If it gave us a greater chance to save Ben at some point in the future, I was going to take it. It also might make it easier for me to sense this kind of corruption in the future—me and other dragons.

This kind of incident wasn't something I ever wanted to see repeated. We needed to be wiser, more informed, more aware.

With that collected and no evidence of any other artifacts around, we retreated again. I didn't tell anyone what had happened to Griffin yet, and no one asked. He was dead and he had led us to the demon. In a lot of ways he had served us better as a traitor than he had as an elder.

But he hadn't had any corruption in him, or been a handler. I still had no idea why he had opted to betray us. Had he simply gone crazy? Although I hadn't intended to stop Neritas from killing him, being able to get some more answers out of him first would have been useful. Not that I thought it was likely to have worked. Griffin hadn't been very forthcoming to the elders in Detaris.

Either way, there was nothing left for me where I was and everything to gain by going back to the dragon home city and trying to get answers.

It was only as we came to the surface again and I saw the sheer extent of the military operation that was sprouting up that I took in everything we had achieved here as well. There were a lot of shell-shocked humans being taken care of and it wasn't hard to see that we had saved a lot of lives.

I had come here with the intention of stealing magical relics and finding out where the demon was hiding, maybe get revenge. I had achieved most of that, but we had also succeeded at liberating the enslaved human forces as well. It was a bittersweet victory, but it was a victory, nonetheless.

As soon as I was spotted, many of the people gathered, soldiers and victims alike, started clapping. Before long people were calling my name, cheering, and wanting to come and shake my hand.

I felt numb, but I somehow fixed a smile on my face and

shook hands and accepted the gratitude of everyone who approached me until Alitas saw me sway on my feet and put a stop to it.

"Her Highness is exhausted after the fight and she needs rest." Alitas raised his voice so as many people as possible could hear him. "We also need to strategize our next move. Like all battles, lives were lost today and many were injured. Today, however, we prevailed, and the world shines a little brighter than it did before."

Again there were cheers, many still directing the jubilation at me, even though I hadn't handled the battle well and didn't deserve it. Reporters also came closer, filming everything, and no doubt having caught some of the fighting on air earlier.

Suddenly I didn't want to be there anymore. I just wanted to hide and figure out our next step, clean up the artifact pieces, and find out what they did.

Alitas shut it down pretty swiftly after that and we made our way back to the rest of our army. Many of them had been resting and they also appeared antsy and as if they wanted to leave.

"Want a ride out of here?" Colonel Flint offered before any of us dragons could decide to get in the air. It was the first time I'd seen him there, but he motioned to several large trucks and I nodded.

Although my dragons could all fly, many were tired. Being in the trucks would let us hide from prying eyes for a while, maybe even pass as human. Right now, the last thing I wanted to be was an on-duty dragon queen.

Only once I was inside the truck and all of us were underway on our journey did I let myself think of anything but making sure everyone had a ride home. My mind went back to the artifact pieces and how valuable they could be. I wasn't sure that I had the magical energy to complete cleaning one up, but there was no harm in trying, as long as I didn't drain too much at once from myself again.

I didn't know what any of the artifacts did, but I recognized a couple of them. One looked as if it might be half of a shield. The design was deliberately in two parts. Given I had found the straps to hold a shield onto an arm in the past, I didn't doubt that these two parts went together.

There was also what appeared to be a weapon handle, or at least part of it. One end had a section of metal with thread like a screw and the other had a socket that something else could screw into. If this was part of a larger piece, then there was at least one middle section, and this was it.

I was then thinking about how, now that there wasn't a traitor in our ranks, maybe we would be able to learn where an artifact piece was and go get it before the demon even knew a thing. I remembered that it had been Ben who had found us the locations of all of them so far. He had been the person who had guided me in so many ways.

Of all the dragons who could have touched the objects lying in that room and been taken from me, he was the one whose loss I'd feel the most. I didn't know how I was going to carry on without him, and I didn't know how I was going to explain this to the elders of Detaris.

I'd won a battle and was returning victorious, but at too high a cost.

EPILOGUE

As I moved around the library, I tried to think like Ben. I had no better ideas and I didn't know anyone else who stood a chance of doing so. No one else even came up into this part of the library the way Ben had. Other than the librarian who guarded this small room so passionately, I never saw anyone else in this tower.

Though Ben had been gone for almost a week, I couldn't break out of my habit of coming here almost every evening to talk to him for a bit. Except he wasn't here anymore and there was no one for me to talk to.

I had the books Brenta had been hiding, but they weren't helping much. Some didn't make much sense and the rest were in an old form of the language that was very difficult to read.

The first few times I had come here, I had hidden and cried, pouring out my grief to the books and hoping that Ben would just appear from behind one of the shelves and take all the pain away. After I had cried out all the emotion I felt and was so hoarse from sobbing I could barely speak,

I would go back to my tower, curl up with Neritas and slip into the sleep of the exhausted.

I knew Neritas was worried about me, but his constant presence when I got back was also somehow right. This had never been a place that Neritas had followed me to, and it felt right that he wasn't here whenever I came.

Today I was trying to make my visit useful, but it was proving as fruitless as my other attempts. Ben wasn't coming back, and I had no idea how to find the locations where the artifacts might be. I didn't have a clue what books to study and I had been wandering the library almost aimlessly for what felt like hours.

Sighing, I went back to the table and all the notes Ben had left out the last time he had been here. I'd barely touched any of them and had left his pens and notebooks lying around just as he left them.

To my surprise, I found I wasn't alone any longer. My mother sat at one of the small chairs, careful not to take either of the ones we used to.

"I thought I would find you here again, my child." She got up as I came closer. I had two books under my arm that I had thought might be useful. I put them down on the table and looked at the floor, not sure that I could meet her gaze without crying again. I didn't want to cry anymore. I'd done enough of that lately.

"You really miss him, don't you?" She phrased it as a question although we both knew it wasn't.

"I miss him… I miss him so much it hurts."

I leaned against the edge of the table, putting my back to everything he'd left behind for a moment. My mother slipped an arm around me and let me lean into her.

"He was like a father for so long. He got me through so many things, helped me figure out what was right to do, and made me feel safe here even when it was as if everyone hated me."

"And none of those things are gone just because his physical presence is missing. Ben will remain a father figure to you. And hopefully he's alive out there somewhere. I know this is painful, and I would not deny you the right to grief and everything that goes with it, but hiding away in here won't help anyone get him back."

I opened my mouth to argue with my mother and tell her that I was doing something useful, but I snapped my jaw shut again.

"Alitas tells me that you haven't trained, cleaned the artifact pieces of corruption, or properly done your other duties. While finding where the other pieces are, you shouldn't waste the opportunities you've already got."

"When did you get so wise?" I asked.

"I had over twenty years to regret giving up the only child I had, to hide her in a human life and give her empathy her father thought was essential. I did a lot of thinking."

I swallowed. I hadn't talked to her on that level before. That cluster of thoughts stung at times, as well, and it made this hurt all the more. I'd gone so long with no family at all. I didn't want to lose the people in my family now I finally had one.

Neither of us said anything else for some time as I calmed, and then I looked behind and pointed at all the notes.

"Ben left this here as if he was coming back. It's all only half of anything."

My mother studied it for a moment, and then she took a step back and tilted her head to the side. She let out a small laugh.

"Or is it? It looks to me as if he wanted to leave this for you."

I wasn't sure what she meant at first, but then I realized that everything on the table had been positioned to look a bit like an arrow. At the tip of the arrow, under a lot of scraps of notes and pieces of paper so it was hardly visible, was a book. A book with a plain red cover.

Pushing everything that hid it aside, I hesitantly picked it up. As I did, a letter fell out and slipped to the floor. On the paper, I recognized my name. In Ben's handwriting, much the same way I had once picked up a journal to find a letter from Anthony.

My mother picked it up for me and handed it to me as she kissed me on the forehead.

"I'll leave you to discover his legacy and appreciate how much that is you, exactly as you are." She smiled and left before I could stop her, not that I would have.

Not sure what I'd find, but eager to learn, I sat and opened the letter. I had no doubt that the man I'd come to think of as my father still had plenty to teach me.

THE STORY CONTINUES

The story continues with book nine, *Dragon Transcended*, available at Amazon.

Claim your copy today!

ACKNOWLEDGMENTS

When I write a series, I always begin the series with a rough idea of where I want it to end. I know who the final bad guy is, even if I don't know who else my shero might face on her journey. But this book felt like it surprised me as much as it may well have done all of you.

I didn't plan the last part to this book at all, and therefore where I would normally feel as if I can thank you all for reading this far and coming on this journey with me, I feel I also have to add an apology to that with this book. I'm sorry for Ben and all the worry we probably all feel for him right now. I didn't see that coming either.

With all that said, I also owe a huge thank you to LMBPN. Everyone who works on my books is amazing and I couldn't do any of this without them, especially Robin, Steve, Kelly, Grace, Jacqui, Tracey and a whole bunch more people who I don't talk to with every single book and how often work on my books without me ever even knowing their names. I am blessed to have you all in my lives and will always be grateful for everything you do.

To Bryan for every time you've brought me lunch while writing, drinks because I've forgotten to take them to my nest with me or just taken care of me in some way so I can focus on getting these stories out of my head and onto paper.

To my two tiny humans, for all the ways you challenge me to be a better person, to grow and to see the world in a different way. I'm often exhausted, but full of love when you two are around.

To my friends, for keeping the smiles coming, making me feel accepted with the crazy mind I have and all the strange thoughts that come out of it. You put up with a lot sometimes, but I hope the random fun and crazy adventures more than make up for it.

And to God, who decided that the world needed one of me. Apparently You don't make mistakes and if nothing else, that can be a very comforting thought.

ABOUT THE AUTHOR

Jess is in the process of changing her name. She's been through a difficult year that leaves her wanting a fresh start and a chance to be the person she's always meant to be. Over the next little while all her books will be moving to Talia Beckett and you'll find all future releases under this author name.

Talia was born in the quaint village of Woodbridge in the UK, has spent some of her childhood in the States and now resides near the beautiful Roman city of Bath. She lives with her two tiny humans (one boy and one girl) and near an amazing group of friends who support her career and life choices.

During her still relatively short life Talia has displayed an innate curiosity for learning new things and has therefore studied many subjects, from maths and the sciences, to history and drama. Talia now works full time as a writer and mummy, incorporating many of the subjects she has an interest in within her plots and characters.

When she's not busy with work and keeping her tiny humans alive she can often be found with friends, playing with miniature characters, dice and pieces of paper covered in funny stats and notes about fictional adventures her figures have been on.

You can find out more about the author and her

upcoming projects by joining her on facebook, by watching her live D&D streams, or emailing her via tali-abeckettwriter@gmail.com. Talia loves hearing from a happy fan so please do get in touch!

Talia is also opening up her discord for fans to come chat about what she's up to, and see a few sneak peaks of future work. There's also a chance to become one of her beta readers. If you'd like to check that out you can do so here.

CONNECT WITH THE AUTHOR

Connect with Talia

Mailing list sign up
Facebook group.
Discord group
Actual play D&D stream: Twitch or Youtube
Live writing stream on Twitch.
Email address: contact me here.

BOOKS BY JESS MOUNTIFIELD / TALIA BECKETT

Already published

Urban Fantasy

Dragon of Shadow and Air:

Air Bound

Shadow Sworn

Dragon Souled

Earth Bound

Night Sworn

Dryad Souled

Water Bound

Day Sworn

Pegasus Souled

Fire Bound

Light Sworn

Phoenix Souled

Dragon Apparent:

Dragon Missing

Dragon Seeking

Dragon Revealed

Dragon Rising

Dragon Defying

Dragon Crowned

Dragon Defending

Dragon Unveiling

Time of the Dragon (with Andrew Bellingham):

Dragon's Code

Dragon's Inquisition

Dragon's Redemption

Dragon's Revolt

Dragon's Summit

Dragon's Reckoning

Dragon's Exodus

Fantasy

Tales of Ethanar:

Wandering to Belong (Tale 1)

Innocent Hearts (Tale 2 & 3)

For Such a Time as This (Tale 4)

A Fire's Sacrifice (Tale 5)

Winter Series:

The Hope of Winter (Tale 6.05)

The Fire of Winter (Tale 6.1)

Guild of the Eternal Flame:

Wayfarer's Sanctuary

Protector's Secret

Healer's Oath

Other Fantasy:

The Initiate (under Holly Lujah)

Writing with Dawn Chapman:

Jessica's Challenge (#5 in the Puatera Online series)

Dahlia's Shadow (#6 in the Puatera Online series)

Lila's Revenge (#7 in the Puatera Online series)

Sci-Fi:

Fringe Colonies:

Alliance

Haven

Rebellion

Rebirth

Reclamation

Star Trail:

Hunted

Sherdan series:

Sherdan's Prophecy

Sherdan's Legacy

Sherdan's Country

Sherdan's Road (A short story in the anthology 'The End of the Road')

The Slave Who'd Never Been Kissed (A short in the charity anthology 'Imaginings')

New Beginnings

Santa's Little Space Pirate

In the multi-author Adamanta series:

Episode 1 – Adamanta

Episode 3 – Excelsior

Episode 8 – Phoenix

Episode 13 – New Contacts

Episode 17 – Sacrifice

Other:

Clues, Claws and Christmas

Non-Fic:

How to Write Lots, and Get Sh*t Done: the Art of Not Being a Flake

Find purchase links here

Coming soon:

Urban Fantasy:

Dragon Apparent:

Dragon Transcended

Time of the Dragon (with Andrew Bellingham):

Dragon's Extinction

Dragon's Time

Fantasy:

(Tales of Ethanar):

The Pursuit of Winter (#2 in the Winter series, Tale 6.2)

Books under Amelia Price

Mycroft Holmes Adventures:

The Hundred Year Wait

The Unexpected Coincidence

The Invisible Amateur

The Female Charm

The Reluctant Knight

The Ambitious Orphan

The Unconventional Honeymoon Gift

The Family Reunion

The Immortal Problem

The Unremarkable Assistant

Coming soon:

Mycroft 11

OTHER BOOKS FROM LMBPN PUBLISHING

Sign up for the LMBPN email list to be notified of new releases and special deals!

https://lmbpn.com/email/

For a complete list of books by LMBPN please visit:

https://lmbpn.com/books-by-lmbpn-publishing/

www.ingramcontent.com/pod-product-compliance
Lightning Source LLC
LaVergne TN
LVHW091713070526
838199LV00050B/2373